MEMORIES FOR ETERNITY

NEW YORK TIMES BESTSELLING AUTHOR

BRENDA JACKSON

MEMORIES FOR ETERNITY

A Westmoreland Novel

HARLEQUIN®
entertain, enrich, inspire™

If you purchased this book without a cover you should be aware that this book is stolen property. It was reported as "unsold and destroyed" to the publisher, and neither the author nor the publisher has received any payment for this "stripped book."

MEMORIES FOR ETERNITY

ISBN-13: 978-0-373-53492-0

Copyright © 2013 by Harlequin Books S.A.

This edition published January 2013

Recycling programs
for this product may
not exist in your area.

The publisher acknowledges the copyright holder
of the individual works as follows:

TAMING CLINT WESTMORELAND
Copyright © 2008 by Brenda Streater Jackson

COLE'S RED-HOT PURSUIT
Copyright © 2008 by Brenda Streater Jackson

All rights reserved. The reproduction, transmission or utilization of this work in whole or in part in any form by any electronic, mechanical or other means, now known or hereafter invented, including xerography, photocopying and recording, or in any information storage or retrieval system, is forbidden without written permission. For permission please contact Harlequin Kimani, 225 Duncan Mill Road, Toronto, Ontario M3B 3K9, Canada.

This book is a work of fiction. The names, characters, incidents and places are the products of the author's imagination, and are not to be construed as real. While the author was inspired in part by actual events, none of the characters in the book is based on an actual person. Any resemblance to persons living or dead is entirely coincidental and unintentional.

For questions and comments about the quality of this book, please contact us at CustomerService@Harlequin.com.

® and TM are trademarks of Harlequin Enterprises Limited or its corporate affiliates. Trademarks indicated with ® are registered in the United States Patent and Trademark Office, the Canadian Trade Marks Office and in other countries.

www.Harlequin.com

Printed in U.S.A.

CONTENTS

THE WESTMORELAND FAMILY

Scott and Delane Westmoreland

John (Evelyn) — **James (Sarah)** — **Corey (Abbie)** Madison

John (Evelyn)

- ② Dare (Shelly) — AJ, Allison
- ③ Thorn (Tara) — Trace
- ④ Stone (Madison) — Rock, Regan
- ⑤ Storm (Jayla) — Shanna, Johanna, Slate
- ⑥ Jared (Dana) — Jaren
- ⑧ Durango (Savannah) — Sarah
- ⑨ Ian (Brooke) — Pierce, Price
- ⑪ Spencer (Chardonnay) — Russell
- ⑩ Casey (McKinnon) — Corey Martin
- ⑬ Cole (Patrina) — Emilie, Emery
- ⑫ Clint (Alyssa) — Cain

James (Sarah)

- ① Delaney (Jamal) — Ari, Arielle
- ⑦ Chase (Jessica) — Carlton Scott
- ⑭ Quade (Cheyenne) — Venus, Athena, Troy
- ⑮ Reggie (Olivia) — Ryder

Corey (Abbie)

- Madison

---

① *Delaney's Desert Sheikh*
② *A Little Dare*
③ *Thorn's Challenge*
④ *Stone Cold Surrender*
⑤ *Riding the Storm*
⑥ *Jared's Counterfeit Fiancée*
⑦ *The Chase is On*
⑧ *The Durango Affair*
⑨ *Ian's Ultimate Gamble*
⑩ *Seduction, Westmoreland Style*
⑪ *Spencer's Forbidden Passion*
⑫ *Taming Clint Westmoreland*
⑬ *Cole's Red-Hot Pursuit*
⑭ *Quade's Babies*
⑮ *Tall, Dark...Westmoreland!*
⑯ *Dreams of Forever*

THE DENVER WESTMORELAND FAMILY TREE

Raphel and Gemma Westmoreland

Stern Westmoreland (Paula Bailey)

Thomas (Susan)

Adam (Clarisse) ⑯

Dillon (Pamela)
Denver
Dade ⑰

Micah (Kalina)
Macon ㉑

Jason (Bella)
Clarisse and Caroline ⑳

Riley
(Alpha)

Canyon

Stern

Brisbane

Zane

Derringer (Lucia) ⑲

Megan
(Rico)

Gemma (Callum)
Callum ⑱

Adrian

Aidan

Bailey

Ramsey (Chloe)
Susan and Colton

⑯ *Westmoreland's Way*
⑰ *Hot Westmoreland Nights*
⑱ *What a Westmoreland Wants*

⑲ *A Wife for a Westmoreland*
⑳ *The Proposal*
㉑ *Feeling the Heat*

㉒ *Texas Wild*
㉓ *One Winter's Night*

Dear Reader,

Little did I know that when I first introduced the
Westmoreland family, they would become hugely
popular amongst readers. Originally the Westmoreland
family series was intended to be just six books, Delaney
and her five brothers—Dare, Thorn, Stone, Storm
and Chase. Later I wanted my readers to meet their
cousins—Jared, Spencer, Durango, Ian, Quade and
Reggie. Finally, there were Uncle Corey's triplets—Clint,
Cole and Casey.

What began as a six-book series blossomed into
a thirty-book series when I included The Denver
Westmorelands. I was very happy when Harlequin
Kimani responded to my readers' requests that the
earlier books be reprinted. And I'm even happier that
the reissues are in a great two-in-one format.

Memories for Eternity includes *Taming Clint
Westmoreland* and *Cole's Red-Hot Pursuit.* These
are two Westmoreland classics and are books twelve
and thirteen in The Westmorelands series. Clint and
Cole Westmoreland, part of a set of triplets, are reluctant
bachelors. However, when they meet Alyssa Bartley and
Patrina Foreman, respectively, they take another look
at their single status and decide that handing in their
players' cards may not be a bad thing.

I hope you enjoy reading these special romance stories
as much as I enjoyed writing them.

Happy reading!

Brenda Jackson

To the love of my life, Gerald Jackson, Sr.
Happy 40th Anniversary.
You're still the one!

But you, be strong and do not let your hands be weak,
for your work shall be rewarded!
—*II Chronicles* 15:7

TAMING CLINT WESTMORELAND

Chapter 1

Clint Westmoreland glanced around the airport and silently cursed. It was the middle of the day, he had a ton of work to do back at his ranch and here he stood waiting to meet a wife he hadn't known he'd had until a few days ago.

His chest tightened as he inwardly fumed, recalling the contents of the letter he'd received from the Texas State Bureau of Investigations. He'd learned from the letter that when he'd gotten married while working on an undercover sting operation five years ago as a Texas Ranger, the marriage had never been nullified by the agency. That meant that he and Alyssa Barkley, the woman who had been his female partner, were still legally married.

The thought of being married, legally or otherwise,

sent a chill down his spine, and the sooner he and Alyssa could meet and get the marriage annulled the better. She had received a similar letter and a few days ago they had spoken on the phone. She, too, was upset about the bureau's monumental screwup and had agreed to fly to Austin to get the matter resolved immediately.

He glanced at his watch thinking time was being wasted. It was the first of February and he had a shipment of wild horses due any day and needed to get things ready at the ranch for their arrival.

When he had announced at his cousin Ian's wedding last June that he would be leaving the Rangers after ten years, his cousin Durango and his brother-in-law, McKinnon Quinn, had invited him to join their Montana-based, million-dollar horse-breeding business. They wanted him to expand their company into Texas. Clint would run the Texas operations and become a partner in the business. His main focus would be taming and training wild horses.

He had accepted their offer and hadn't regretted a day of doing so. So to his way of thinking, at this moment he had more important things he should be concentrating on. Like making sure his horse-taming business stayed successful.

He glanced at his watch again and then looked around wondering if he would recognize Alyssa when he saw her. It had been five years and the only thing he could recall about her was that she'd been young, right out of college with a degree in criminal justice. The two of them had been together less than a week. That was all the time it had taken to play the part of a young married couple who desperately wanted to adopt a baby—illegally.

She had played the part of a despairing, wannabe mother pretty convincingly. So much in fact that a sting operation everyone had assumed would take a couple of weeks to pull off had ended after the first week. Afterward, he had been sent on another assignment. From what he'd heard, she had turned in her resignation after deciding being a Texas Ranger wasn't what she wanted to devote her life to doing after all.

He had no idea what she'd done since then, as their phone conversation had been brief and he hadn't been inclined to even ask. He wanted the issue of their being married dealt with so they could both get on with their lives. She should be about twenty-seven now, he thought. On the phone, she'd said she was still single. Actually, he'd been surprised that she hadn't gotten married or something.

The sound of high heels clicking on the ceramic tile floor made him glance at the woman strolling in his direction. He blinked. If the woman was Alyssa, she had certainly gone through one hell of a transformation. Although she'd been far from a plain Jane before, there hadn't been anything about her to make him want to take a second look…until now.

He could definitely see her on the cover of some sexy magazine. And it was apparent that he wasn't the only person who thought so, judging by the blatant male attention she was getting. One man had the nerve to stop walking, stand in the middle of the walkway as if he were glued to the spot and openly stare at her.

Clint cut the spectator a fierce frown, which made the man quickly turn and continue walking. Then Clint felt angry with himself for momentarily losing his senses to play the part of a jealous husband, until he remembered that legally he *was* Alyssa's husband. So he had a right to get jealous if he wanted to…if that rationale at the moment made any damn sense, which it probably didn't.

He shook his head remembering how men used to have the same reaction to his sister, Casey, and he hadn't liked it then, either. For some reason he liked it even less now.

Alyssa was closer and the first thing he thought, besides the fact she was a looker, was that she certainly knew how to wear a pair of jeans. Her hips swayed with each step she took and impossible as it might seem, although he hadn't felt an attraction to her five years ago, he was definitely feeling some strong vibes now.

He was so absorbed in checking her out that it hadn't occurred to him just how close she was until she came to a stop directly in front of him, up close and personal and all in his space. Now he saw everything. The dark eyes, long lashes, high cheekbones, full lips, head of curly copper-colored hair and a gorgeous medium-brown face.

And he heard the sexy voice that went along with those features when she spoke and said, "Hello, Clint. I'm here."

She most certainly was!

He hasn't changed, Alyssa thought as she struggled to keep up with his brisk stride as they walked together out of the airport to the parking lot. At six-four he was a lot taller than her five-eight height, and the black Stetson he wore on his head was still very much a part of his wardrobe.

But she would admit that his face had matured in ways that only a woman who had concentrated on it years before could notice. The first time they'd met she thought he was more handsome than any man had a right to be, and now at thirty-two he was even more so. Even then she had concluded that the perfection of his features was due to the cool, arrogant lines that underscored his eyes and the dimples that set boldly in his cheeks—regardless of whether he smiled or not.

Then there were his chin and jaw that seemed to have been carved flawlessly, not to mention full lips that were, in her opinion, way too perfect to belong to any man. To say he hadn't made quite an impression on a fresh-out-of-college, twenty-two-year-old virgin was an understatement. The one thing she wouldn't forget was that she'd had one hell of a crush on him, just like so many other women who'd worked for the bureau.

"My truck is parked over there," he said.

His words intruded into her thoughts and she glanced up and met his gaze. "Are we going straight to the Rangers' headquarters?" she asked, trying not to make it so obvious that she was studying his lips.

Those lips were what had drawn her to him from the first. He'd been a man of few words, but his lips, whenever they had moved, had always been worth the wait. They demanded attention. And she would even go so far to say, demanded a plan of action that tempted you to taste them. Dreaming of kissing him had been something she'd done often.

Needless to say, she had been the envy of several female Rangers when she'd been the one chosen to work with him on that assignment. He was considered a private person and she seriously doubted that at the time he'd been aware of just how many women had lusted after him, or made him a constant participant in their fantasies.

"Yes, we can go straight there," he answered, breaking into the middle of her thoughts. "I figure it shouldn't take long to do what needs to be done. Hopefully no more than an hour," he said.

She was suddenly tempted to stop walking, place her hand on his arm and lean up on tiptoes and go ahead and boldly steal a kiss. The very thought made her heart rate accelerate.

Inhaling, she tried concentrating on what he'd said. She, too, hoped that what needed to be done wouldn't take more than an hour. If she spent much more time with this man, Alyssa was certain she would lose her mind. Besides, she hadn't brought any luggage, just an overnight bag. After they took care of matters, she would check into a hotel for the night and fly back to Waco in the morning.

"So, how have you been, Alyssa?"

She glanced over at him. She knew he was trying to be cordial so she smiled accordingly, while thinking another thing he'd still retained over the years was that deep, sexy voice. "I've been doing fine, Clint. And you?"

"I can't complain."

She figured he couldn't if what she'd heard from the few friends she still had with the bureau was true. No longer a Ranger, Clint now operated a horse-breeding ranch on the outskirts of Austin on over three hundred acres of land. It was a ranch he had inherited from a close relative. And according to her sources, the horse-breeding business was doing quite well. Although she was curious as to why he had left the force, she really didn't feel comfortable enough with Clint to ask him about it. She would have sworn he'd make a career of it.

Deciding it was none of her business, she thought of something that was and said, "I can't believe the bureau would make such a mistake. The nerve of them sending that letter saying we're married."

They had reached his truck and he shrugged massive shoulders when he opened the truck door for her. "I couldn't believe it at first myself. I guess it's a good thing neither of us ever took a notion to marry."

She decided not to tell him that she *had* taken a notion a couple of years ago, and had come as close as the day of her wedding before finding out what a weasel she'd been engaged to. To this day Kevin Brady hadn't forgiven her for leaving him standing at the altar. But then she hadn't forgiven him for sleeping with her cousin Kim a week before the wedding.

From the corner of her eye she could tell that Clint was looking at her as she slid into the smooth leather seat and couldn't help wondering if he could see the heat that had risen in her cheeks denoting there was something she wasn't telling him.

"You look different than before," he said, as he casually leaned against the truck's open door.

She threw him a sharp glance at his comment and wondered if she should take what he'd said as a compliment or an insult. She decided to probe further and asked, "In what way?"

"Different."

A smile touched her cheeks. He was still a man of few words. "I am different," she admitted.

"In what way?"

She chuckled. Now he was the one asking that question. "I live my life the way I want and not the way others think that I should."

"Is that what you were doing five years ago?"

"Yes." And she figured he didn't need to know any more than that. He must have thought so, as well, because he closed the door and crossed in front of the truck to the driver's side without inquiring further.

"It will be lunchtime in a little while," he said after easing onto the seat and closing the door shut. "Do you want to stop somewhere and grab a bite to eat before we meet with Hightower?"

Lester Hightower had been the senior captain in charge of field operations when they had done that undercover assignment five years ago. "No, I prefer that we meet with Hightower as soon as possible," she said.

He lifted a brow as he glanced over at her. "Maybe I spoke too soon earlier. If you hadn't taken a notion to get married before should I assume you might be considering such a move now?"

She stared over at him and he did something she

hadn't expected. He smiled. And immediately she tried to ignore the heat that touched her body when the corners of his lips curved. "No, you can't assume that. I just don't like surprises and getting that letter was definitely a surprise."

He nodded as he broke eye contact to start the engine. "Yes, but it's one we shouldn't have a problem fixing."

"I hope you're right."

He glanced back over at her as he backed out of the parking space. "Of course I'm right. You'll see."

"What the hell do you mean we can't get the marriage annulled?" Clint all but roared. He could not have been more shocked with what Hightower had just said.

This was the first time, in all his twelve years of knowing the man, that Clint had raised his voice to his former boss. Of course, if he'd done such a thing while still a Ranger, he would have been reprimanded severely. But Hightower was no longer his superior, and Clint felt entitled to a straight answer from the man.

He glanced over at Alyssa. She had gotten out of her chair and was leaning against the closed door. He could tell from her not-too-happy expression that she wanted answers, as well. He frowned thinking he had known the exact moment she had moved from the chair to stand by the door. He had been listening to Hightower, but at the same time he'd been very much aware of her. An uncomfortable sensation slid up his spine. He hadn't been this fully aware of a woman in a long time.

"New procedures are in place, Westmoreland," Clint

heard Hightower say. "I don't like them nor do I understand them. And I agree the one in your particular situation doesn't make sense because proper procedures weren't followed. But there's nothing else I can tell you. We tried rectifying our mistake by immediately filing for an annulment on your and Barkley's behalf, but since so much time has passed and because the two of you no longer work for the agency, the State is dragging their tail in acknowledging that your marriage is not a real one."

"You're right, that doesn't make any sense," Alyssa said sharply. "Clint and I have never lived under the same roof. For heaven's sake, the marriage was never consummated, so that in itself should be grounds to grant an annulment."

"And under normal circumstances, it would be, but the new person in charge of that department, a woman by the name of Margaret Toner, thinks otherwise. From what I understand, Toner has been married for over forty years and takes the institution of marriage seriously. We might not like it or understand her reasoning, but for now we have to abide by it."

"Like hell!" Clint bit out, not believing what he was hearing.

"Like hell or heaven, it doesn't matter," Hightower said, throwing a document on the desk. "Thirty days. Toner has agreed to grant an annulment to your and Barkley's marriage in thirty days."

Neither Clint nor Alyssa said anything for a long moment, both figuring it was best not to, otherwise they would say the wrong thing. Instead they decided to keep the anger they felt inside. But then finally, as if accepting the finality of their situation, Alyssa spoke. "I don't like it, Hightower, but if nothing can be done about it for thirty days, there's little Clint and I can do. It's been five years without me even knowing I was a married woman, so I guess another thirty days won't kill me," she said, glancing over at Clint.

He frowned. Although it wouldn't kill him, either, he didn't like it one damn bit. He enjoyed being a bachelor although unlike his brother, Cole, he'd never earned the reputation of being a ladies' man. But Alyssa was right, they had been married five years without either of them knowing it, so another thirty days would not make or break them. There was nothing in his life that would be changing.

"Fine," he all but snapped. "Like Alyssa, I'll deal with it for thirty more days."

"There's one more thing," Hightower hesitated a few moments before saying.

Clint's frown deepened. He had worked with the man long enough to detect something in his voice, something Clint figured he wouldn't like. Evidently, Alyssa picked up on it, as well, and moved away from the door to come and stand beside him.

"What other thing?" Clint asked.

Hightower shrugged massive shoulders nervously. "Not sure how the two of you are going to feel about it, but Toner wouldn't back down or change her mind about it."

"About what?" Clint asked in an agitated voice.

Hightower looked at him and then at Alyssa. "In

order for the marriage to get annulled after the thirty days, there is something the two of you must do."

Clint felt his heart turn over. He felt another strange sensation slither up his spine. He knew, without a doubt, that he wouldn't like whatever Hightower was about to say. "And just what does Toner want us to do?" he asked, trying to keep his voice calm.

Hightower cleared his throat and then said, "She has mandated that during those thirty days the two of you live under the same roof."

Chapter 2

It didn't take much to figure out that Clint Westmoreland was one angry man, Alyssa thought, glancing over at him. They had left Hightower's office over twenty minutes ago, and now Clint was driving her to a place where she assumed they would grab a bite to eat. But he had yet to say one word to her. Not one. However, that didn't take into consideration the number of times he'd mumbled the word *damn* under his breath.

Sighing deeply, she decided to brave the icy waters and said, "Surely there's something we can do."

He speared her with a look that could probably freeze boiling water and his mouth was set in a grim line. However, to her his lips still looked as delectable as a slice of key lime pie. "You heard what he said, Alyssa. We can try to appeal, but if we're not successful we will still have to do the thirty days, which will only delay things," he said.

Do the thirty days. He'd made it sound like a jail sentence. And since he would have to share the same roof with her, she wasn't sure she particularly liked his attitude. She didn't like what Hightower had said any more than he did, but there was no reason to get rude about it.

"Look," she said. "I don't like this any more than you do, but if we can't change things then we need to do what Toner is requiring and—"

"The hell I will," he said almost in a growl when he looked back at her. He had pulled into the parking lot of a restaurant and had brought his truck to a stop. "I have more to do with my time for the next thirty days than entertain you."

She immediately saw red. "Entertain me? From saying that, I guess you're assuming if we do decide to live together for the next thirty days it will be here at your place."

He shrugged as if to ease the tension in his shoulders and said, "Of course."

She frowned. He sounded so sure and confident. She would take joy in bursting his bubble. "Wrong. I have no intention of staying here in Austin with you."

His eyes narrowed into slits as he continued to glare at her. "And just where do you assume you'll stay?"

She glared back. "It's not where I'll stay but where you'll stay. I'm returning to Waco and if you want to fulfill the terms of Toner's decree you will, too."

If she thought he was mad before then it was quite

obvious he was madder now. "Look, lady. I have a ranch to run and I won't be doing it from Waco."

"You're not the only one who owns a business, Clint. I'm not going to drop everything that's going on in my life just to come out here to live with you."

"And neither will I drop everything I've got going on here to move to Waco, even temporarily. That's as stupid as stupid can get."

She had to agree with him there, but still that didn't solve their problem. According to Hightower, they needed to live under the same roof for thirty days, which meant that one of them had to compromise. But she didn't feel it should be her and evidently he didn't think it should be him, either. "Okay, you don't want to move to Waco and I don't want to move here, so what do you suggest we do to get that annulment?" she asked him.

He pulled his key out of the truck's ignition and said, "I don't know, but what I do know is that I think better on a full stomach." He opened the door to get out. "Right now I suggest that we get something to eat."

By the time the waitress had taken their order, Clint was convinced that somebody up there didn't like him. If they did, they would not have dumped Alyssa Barkley in his lap. The woman was too much of a tempting package and someone he didn't have time to deal with. The thought of her living under his roof, or for that matter, him living under hers, was too much too imagine. But he had been a Ranger long enough to know just how tangled red tape could get. Someone had screwed up. Otherwise they wouldn't still be married—at least on paper. As she'd told Hightower, the marriage hadn't even been consummated. It had been an assignment, nothing more.

"You're a triplet, right?"

He glanced at her over the rim of his glass. "Yes. How do you know that?"

She shrugged. "It was common knowledge among the Rangers. I met your brother, Cole, once. He was nice. I also heard you have a sister."

"I do," he said, thinking about Casey, who had gotten married a few months ago. "If you go by order of birth, then I'm the oldest, then Cole and last Casey."

"Is Cole still a Texas Ranger?"

He figured she must feel a little more relaxed to be asking so many questions. "Yes, he is."

He didn't know her well enough to reveal that Cole's days with the Rangers were numbered. Like him, Cole planned to go out on early retirement; however, Cole hadn't decided what he'd do after leaving the force. Clint wasn't even sure if Cole planned to stay in Texas. His brother might take a notion to move to Montana like Casey had done to be near their father. The father the three of them thought was dead until a few years ago.

He took a sip of his coffee. In a way he knew what Alyssa was doing. She was trying to get his mind off the gigantic problem that was looming over their heads. But the bottom line was that they needed to talk about it and make some decisions. "Okay, Alyssa, getting back to our dilemma. What about you? Do you have any suggestions?"

She took a sip of her coffee and smiled before say-

ing, "I guess I could go back to Waco and you remain
here and forget we ever found out we were married and
leave things as they are. As I said earlier, marriage isn't
in my future anytime soon. What about yours?"

"Not in mine, either, but still, having a wife isn't
something I can forget about," he said. *Several things
could happen later to make him remember he was a
married man.*

For example, what would happen if she decided, as
his wife, that she was entitled to half of everything he
owned? His partnership with his cousin and brother-
in-law was going extremely well. Not saying that she
would, but he couldn't take any chances. He had bought
out Casey's and Cole's shares of the ranch and now it
was totally his. The last thing he would tolerate was a
"wife" staking a claim on anything that had his name
on it.

And then there was the other reason he wouldn't be
able to forget he had a wife. She was too damn pretty.
Her features were too striking and her body was too
well-stacked. Even now sitting across from her at the
table he could feel his temperature rise. Since he figured
she hadn't gotten that way overnight, he wondered how
he had missed noticing how good she looked five years
ago. The only excuse he could come up with was that at
the time he'd been too heavily involved with Chantelle
and only had eyes for one woman. Too bad Chantelle
hadn't had eyes for just one man.

"There has to be a way out of this," she said, interrupting his thoughts with a disgusted look on her face.
Disgusted or otherwise, her frustration didn't downplay

how full and firm her lips were, or how her eyes were
so dark they reminded him of a raven's wing. He wondered if her copper-brown hair was her natural color
and he felt a tug in his gut when he thought of the one
way he could easily find out. He shifted in his seat. His
jeans suddenly felt a little too tight, especially in the
area of his zipper.

Evidently she was waiting for him to respond, because her dark eyes were staring at him. He leaned back
in his chair. "There is a way. We just have to think of it."

Alyssa could feel Clint checking her out the same
way she was checking him out, which only solidified
her belief that living under the same roof with him
wouldn't work. There was a strong sexual attraction
between them, she could feel it. The thought that she
drew his interest was something she couldn't ignore.
Nor was it something for her to lose any sleep over.
Plenty of women probably drew his attention. He was
a man wasn't he? Hadn't Uncle Jessie explained after
finding out what Kim and Kevin had done that when it
came to women all men were weak? They often made
decisions with the "wrong head." Of course, he couldn't
come up with an excuse for Kim's behavior because she
was his daughter.

"What sort of business do you own?"

She glanced up from studying the contents in her
coffee cup to stare into Clint's cool, dark eyes. "I design websites."

"Oh."

She frowned. He'd said it as though he considered

her profession of no importance. Granted it wasn't a mega-million-dollar operation like she'd heard he owned but it was hers; one she'd started a few years ago with all the money she had. She enjoyed her work and was proud of the way she'd built up her company. She had a very nice clientele who depended on her to keep their businesses in the forefront of the cyberspace market. Over the years she had won numerous awards for her website designs.

"For your information I own a very successful business," she said, glaring at him.

He glared back. "I don't recall saying you didn't."

No, he hadn't. But still, she really didn't care much for his attitude. "Look, Clint. You're agitated about this whole thing and so am I. I think the best thing for us to do is sleep on it. Maybe we'll have answers in the morning."

"Fine. I noticed you only brought an overnight bag," he said, leaning back in his chair.

"Yes. I thought that ending our marriage wouldn't take more than a day at the most. I planned to fly home in the morning."

"You're welcome to stay at my place tonight. I have plenty of room."

She appreciated the invitation but didn't think it was a good idea. "Thanks, but I prefer staying at a hotel."

"Suit yourself," he said, easing back up to the table when their waitress placed a plate full of food in front of him. Alyssa watched him dig in. He'd said he could think better on a full stomach, but was he really going to eat all that? She couldn't imagine him eating such hefty meals as the norm, especially since he had such a well-built body that was all muscle and no fat.

"Why are you staring at my plate?"

She shrugged. "That's a lot of food," she said when the waitress placed a sandwich and bowl of soup in front of her.

He laughed. "I'm still growing. Besides, I need all this to keep my strength up. What I do around the ranch is hard work."

"And what exactly do you do?"

He smiled over at her. "I'm a horse tamer. I have some of my men stationed out in Nevada. They capture wild horses then ship them to my ranch for me to tame. Once that's done, I ship them to Montana. My cousin and brother-in-law own a horse-breeding company. My sister works for them as a trainer."

"Sounds like a family affair."

"It is."

Alyssa intentionally kept her head lowered as she ate her sandwich and soup. She didn't want to risk looking head-on into Clint's eyes again. Each time she did so made every cell in her body vibrate.

"I'm thinking of getting one of those."

She raised her head and gazed at him, trying not to zero in on his handsome features, while at the same time ignoring the sensations that flowed through her. "Getting one of what?"

"A website."

She lifted a brow. "You don't have one already?"

"No."

"Why not?"

"Why would I?"

"Mainly to promote your business."

"Don't have to. Durango and McKinnon are in charge of bringing in the customers. We have a private clientele."

"Oh. Who are Durango and McKinnon?"

He wiped his mouth with a napkin before answering. "Durango is my cousin and McKinnon is married to my sister, Casey. They are my partners and the ones who started the horse-breeding company. Now it has grown to include horse training and horse taming," he said.

She nodded. "If you did just fine without a website before, then why are you thinking about getting one now?"

He actually looked like he was tired of answering her questions. His tone indicated that he was only answering her in an attempt to be polite. "Because of the foundation I recently started."

"What foundation?"

"The Sid Roberts Foundation." And as if he was preparing for her next question, he said, "He was my uncle."

Her eyes widened. "Sid Roberts? The Sid Roberts? Was your uncle?" she asked incredulously.

"Yes," he responded, seemingly again with barely tolerant patience. And then as if he'd had enough of her questions he said, "Why don't you finish eating. Your soup is getting cold."

At least he had gotten her to stop talking, Clint thought, taking a sip of his coffee. Although he no-

ticed what she was eating wasn't much. He'd thought
Casey was the only person who considered soup and a
sandwich a full-course meal.

Clint leaned back in his chair. The food was great
and he was full, so now he could think. Yet he was far
from having an answer to their problem. Part of him
wanted to start the appeal process and see what would
happen. But if the appeal failed, they would have to do
the thirty days anyway.

"You didn't say why you are establishing a foundation for your uncle."

He glanced over at her. "Didn't I?" he asked tersely.
He couldn't recall her being this chatty before. In fact,
he remembered her as a mousy young woman who
didn't seem to have the fortitude for her job as a Ranger.
Although truth be told, he would be the first to give
her an A for her acting abilities during their assignment together.

He couldn't help noticing how the sunlight shining
through the window hit her hair at an angle that gave
the copper strands a golden tint. He felt a sudden tingling sensation right smack in his gut. He didn't like
the feeling. Since becoming partners with Durango and
McKinnon nine months ago, he had placed his social
life—and women—on hold.

"No, you didn't," she said, breaking into his thoughts
and seemingly not the least put off by his cool tone.

He didn't say anything for a while and then asked,
"What do you know about Sid Roberts?"

She smiled. "Only what's in the history books, as
well as what my grandfather shared with me."

He lifted a brow. "Your grandfather?"

"Yes, he was a huge Sid Roberts fan and even claimed to being a part of the rodeo circuit with him at one time. I know Mr. Roberts was a legend in his day. First as a rodeo star then as a renowned horse trainer."

"Uncle Sid loved horses and passed that love on to me, my brother and sister. In my uncle's memory, we have dedicated over three thousand acres of land on the south ridge of my property as a reserve. A great number of the wild horses that are being shipped to me are being turned loose to roam free here."

"Why go to the trouble of relocating them here? Why not leave them in Nevada and let them run free there?"

He frowned. "Mainly because wild horses are taking up land that's now needed for public use. Legislation is being considered that will allow for so many of them to be destroyed each year. Many of these wild horses are getting slaughtered for pet food."

"That's awful," she murmured and he knew she was deliberately lowering her voice to keep out the anger she felt. It was the same with him every time he thought about it.

"Yes, it is. So I've established the foundation as a way to save as many of the wild horses as I can by bringing them here."

He felt they had gotten off track, and had put on the back burner the subject they really needed to be discussing. "So what are we going to do, Alyssa, about our marriage?"

She frowned. "You make it sound like a real one when it's not."

"Then tell that to Toner. And maybe it's time to accept that regardless of where we want to place the blame, legally we are man and wife."

Alyssa opened her mouth to deny what he said, but couldn't. He was right. They could sit and blame others but that wouldn't solve their problem. "Okay, you have a full stomach, what do you suggest?"

"You're not going to like it."

"Probably not if it's what I'm thinking."

He sighed deeply. "Do we have a choice?"

She knew they didn't but still… "There has to be another way."

"According to Hightower, there isn't. You heard him for yourself."

"I say let's fight it."

"And I say let's just do what we have to do and get it over with."

She nibbled on her bottom lip. "Fine, but there's still the issue of where we'll stay. Here or Waco." Each knew how the other felt on the subject. Alyssa knew she was being hard-nosed. To handle his business properly, he would have to be on his ranch, whereas she could operate just about anywhere, as long as she had her computer and server.

"Alyssa?"

She glanced up at him. "Yes?"

"I'm sure you prefer handling your business from Waco, but is there any reason you can't do it here if I help get things set up for you?" he asked, evidently thinking along the same lines as she had earlier.

She decided to be honest with him. "No."

"All right. Then will you?" he asked. "My ranch isn't all that bad. It's pretty nice actually. And with the hours I work, I'd barely be home most of the time so it will be as if you have the place to yourself. I won't be underfoot."

She tilted her head to study him. In other words they really wouldn't be under the same roof for thirty days— at least not all the time. In a way, she would prefer it that way. Being around Clint 24/7 would be too hard to handle. But she knew he was right. They had to do something and since it was easier for her to make the change why sweat it. That didn't mean she had to like it. At least the two of them were working together and doing what needed to be done to get their lives back on track and end what had been the agency's screwup and not theirs. But still…

"What about a steady girlfriend?" she decided to ask.

"Don't have one, steady or otherwise. Don't have the time."

She lifted a brow. *When did men stop making the time for women?* She thought they lived for intimacy.

"What about you?" he asked her. "Is there a steady man in your life?"

She thought about the occasional calls she got from Kevin as he tried to make a comeback, as if she didn't know that he and Kim were still messing around with each other. Kim took pleasure in making comments every once in a while to let her know she and Kevin were still seeing each other now and then. "No, like you, I don't have the time."

He nodded. "So, there's really nothing holding us

back to do what we need to do to get the matter resolved," he said.

If only it were that simple, she wanted to say. Instead she said, "I need to sleep on it." She preferred not to make a decision right then.

"Okay. In that case would you mind doing your sleeping at the ranch?" Clint asked. "That way, you can check out the place to see if it will work for you."

She'd rather not stay at his ranch tonight but what he'd said made sense. She was used to living in the city. She wasn't sure how she would handle being out in such a rural setting. "Okay, Clint. I'll spend the night at your ranch and will give you my decision about things in the morning."

He tilted his head and looked at her. "I can't ask for any more than that."

Chapter 3

"Can you ride a horse?"

Alyssa glanced over at Clint. Sunlight streaming in through the windshield seemed to highlight his features. It had been bad enough sitting across from him at the diner trying to eat. Now they were back in the close quarters of his truck and everything male about him was out in the forefront again. She moved her gaze from his face to the strong, sturdy hands that were gripping the steering wheel, and then lower to his lap where the denim of his jeans stretched tight across muscular thighs.

"Alyssa?"

She nearly jumped when he said her name again, reminding her that she hadn't answered his question. "Yes and no."

He glanced over at her and frowned. "You either can or you can't."

"Not necessarily. There's another option—can and don't. Yes, I can ride a horse, but I choose not to."

He gave her a strange look. "Is there a reason why?"

"Yes. What if I say that horses don't like me?"

He gave a half laugh. "Then I'd say that if you feel that way it means you haven't developed your own personal technique of dealing with them. A horse can detect a lot from people. Whether you're too aggressive, too nice, sometimes both. A horse is the most easygoing animal that I know of."

"Yeah, you would say that since you tame them," she said, glancing out the truck window and thinking how beautiful the land was getting the farther they got away from the city.

"I'd say it even if I didn't tame them. If you stay at the ranch I guarantee you will develop a liking for horses."

"I never said I didn't like them, Clint. It's just I've been thrown off one too many times to suit my fancy. I know when to give in and quit."

He chuckled. "I don't. And if I stopped riding based on the number of times I've been thrown, I would have given up riding years ago. That's part of it. Learning to ride with the intent of staying on."

Alyssa heard what he was saying but it wouldn't change her mind. The truck had come to a stop and she glanced over at Clint. He was staring at her in a way that had her pulse racing, was making her feel breathless. A brazen image formed in her mind. "What?" she asked in a low voice.

It was as if that one single word made him realize that he'd been staring and when the truck began moving again, he muttered, "Nothing."

It was there on the tip of Alyssa's tongue to say yes, it had been something and she had felt it, too, in the cozy space surrounding them. As she glanced back out the window, she thought that living on a ranch with him wouldn't be easy. The only good thing was that he'd said he would be gone most of the time. That was good to know for her peace of mind.

"Will your family have a problem with it?"

She glanced back over at him. He was staring straight ahead and she thought that was good. Every time he looked at her, sensations she hadn't felt in a long time, or ever, seemed to unleash inside of her. "A problem with what?" she asked, thinking she liked the sound of his voice a little too much.

"Living with me for a while at the ranch. That is if you decide to do it."

Alyssa sighed. There was no need to go into any details that certain members of her family wouldn't care if she left Waco for good. It was all too complicated to get into and too personal to explain. That was the only good thing about the thirty days. Time away from Waco was probably what she needed. Ruining her wedding day hadn't been enough for Kim. She was determined to sabotage any decent thing that came into Alyssa's life. "No, they wouldn't have a problem with it," she finally answered. "What about your folks?"

He glanced over at her and smiled and that single smile ignited a torch within her. She actually felt heat flowing through her body. "My family is fine with whatever I do. My brother, sister and I are extremely close but we know when to give each other space and when to mind our own business." He then chuckled and the sound raked across her skin in a sensuous sort of way.

"Okay, I admit when it came to Casey, Cole and I never did mind our own business. We felt she was our responsibility, especially during her dating years. But now that she's married to McKinnon all is well," he added.

"Have they been married long?"

He shook his head. "Since the end of November. Cole and I couldn't ask for a better man for our sister."

Alyssa smiled. "That's a nice thing to say."

"It's the truth. Although we do sympathize with him most of the time. Casey can be pretty damn headstrong so McKinnon has his work cut out for him."

"So your immediate family consists of your brother and your sister?"

"We used to think that. My mother was Uncle Sid's sister and she came to live with him at the ranch when her husband was supposedly killed during a rodeo and she was left carrying triplets."

Alyssa slanted him a confused look. "*Supposedly* was killed?"

"Yes, that's the story she and Uncle Sid fabricated for everyone when in fact our father was very much alive. However, she felt she was doing him a favor by not telling him she was pregnant and disappearing. So Cole, Casey and I grew up believing our father was dead."

"When did you find out differently?"

"On Mom's deathbed. She wanted us to know the truth."

Alyssa immediately recalled her grandfather's death-bed confession. He'd revealed that he was her biological father and not her grandfather. It had been a confession that had changed her life forever, one that had caused jealousy within the family—a family that had never been close anyway. "What happened after that?"

He smiled over at her and she knew what he was thinking. She asked a lot of questions. Gramps would always tell her that, too. Thinking of the man whom for years she'd thought of as her grandfather sent a warm feeling through her.

"After that, Cole and I decided to find our father and develop a relationship with him. We knew it wouldn't be easy, considering we would be a surprise to him and the fact that we were grown men in our late twenties."

That hadn't been too long ago, she mused, consider-ing he was thirty-two now. Probably around the same time she had been learning the truth about her own par-entage. "Did you find him?"

He gave another chuckle, this one just as sensitive to her flesh as the other had been. "Yes, we found him, all right. And we found something else right along with him."

"What?"

"A slew of cousins we didn't know we had. West-morelands from just about everywhere. We suddenly found ourselves part of a big family and it was a family that welcomed us with open arms. They've made us feel as if we were a part of them so quickly it was almost overwhelming."

Alyssa studied the sound of his voice and could tell that even now for him it was still overwhelming. He was blessed to be a part of such a loving and giving group. There, however, was one thing she'd noted. He hadn't mentioned how his sister had taken the revelation of the missing father.

"Your sister, how did she handle meeting her father for the first time?" she asked.

A part of her needed to know. She knew how she had handled it when she'd discovered that Isaac Barkley was her father and not her grandfather. A part of her had wished he would have told her sooner. That would have explained a lot of things and then the two of them would have been able to face the jealousy and hatred together. But he had died, leaving her all alone.

"It was harder for Casey to come around and accept things. She'd believed what Mom had told us all those years. She wasn't ready to meet a father who was very much alive. It took her a while to form a relationship with him, but that's all in the past now. In fact she moved to Montana to be close to him. She met McKinnon there and fell in love."

Alyssa sighed. A part of her wished she could find someone and fall in love but she knew that wouldn't be possible as long as Kimberly Barkley still existed on this earth. Kimberly was determined to destroy whatever bit of happiness came Alyssa's way.

"This is the entrance to the ranch, Alyssa."

Alyssa leaned forward and glanced out the windshield and side windows and caught her breath. What she saw all around her was spellbinding. Simply breathtaking. She had lived on a small ranch in Houston for the first thirteen years of her life and had loved it. Then one day, her mother had sent her away to live with her grandfather in the city. That was probably the one most decent thing her mother had ever done in her life.

"It's beautiful, Clint. How big is it?" Everywhere she looked she saw ranges, fields and meadows. She couldn't imagine waking up to this view every morning, every single day.

"If you include the reserve on the south ridge it's over fifty thousand acres. Uncle Sid was a ladies' man who never married and so he left the ranch to me, Cole and Casey."

Alyssa nodded. She didn't want to consider the possibility, didn't want to imagine how it would feel for once to not have to worry about Kim dropping in just make her life a living hell. The truck, she noticed, had stopped, and she lifted a brow as she glanced over at Clint.

He smiled. "I want to show you something."

He got out of the truck and she followed and he led her close to a cliff. "Look down there," he said, pointing.

And she did. It was then that she saw his ranch, sitting down in the valley below. It was huge, a monstrosity of a house that was surrounded by several barns and other buildings. There was a corral full of horses and she could barely see the figures of men below who

were working with the horses. "It's absolutely stunning, Clint," she said, turning to him. It was then that
she became aware of just how close they were standing, of the heat his closeness had generated and how
the darkening of his eyes was beginning to stir a caress
across her flesh.

She moved to take a step back and his hand reached
out to her waist, to assist her, or so it seemed. But his
hand stayed there and his touch burned her skin through
the thin material of her blouse. Her gaze left his eyes
and moved to his lips, the one part of him that had always fascinated her. The fullness of them made her
imagine just how they would feel on hers. She thought
they would be soft to the touch at first, but they would
become demanding and hungry as soon as they connected with hers.

She wasn't a forward person, but one thing Gramps
had always taught her was that sometimes, if it was
something you really wanted, you just had to take the
bull by the horns. Well, she intended to do just that.

He was bending his head toward her, or maybe she
imagined that he was doing so. And just to be sure,
she leaned forward and slid her hands over his chest.
The first touch of his lips on hers sent pleasure points
in her body on high alert and when she parted her lips
on a sigh, he entered her mouth in one delicious sweep.

He tasted hot. He tasted like a man. And she settled into his kiss as if it was her right to do so. With
their mouths locked together, their tongues tangled,
stroked and slid everywhere. And then in a move she
would have thought was impossible, he thrust his tongue

deeper inside her mouth, causing her to instinctively latch on to it, suck it and stroke it some more. This was what you called total mouth concentration, the solicitation of participation and the promise of satisfaction. Everything was there in this kiss. And Clint Westmoreland was delivering in a way that made the quiet existence she had carved out for herself the last two years a waste of good time and energy.

The kiss was incredible, she thought, sinking deeper into it. She might have regrets later but now she needed this. Her entire body felt as if this was what she was supposed to be doing. And considering this was the first day she had seen him in over five years, the very thought of that was crazy and...

Clint abruptly broke off the kiss. He drew much-needed air into his lungs and fought the urgent pull in his loins. *How had he let this happen? Where was that control he was famous for? Where was his will to deny anything he thought might threaten his livelihood?*

He didn't say anything to Alyssa. He just stood there and stared at her while trying to get the rampant beating of his heart under control. Trying to fight the sensations overtaking him. She had been kissing him as passionately as he had been kissing her. At first her lack of kissing experience had surprised him, but she was a quick study. The moment his tongue came into play, she'd allowed hers to do the same, and without any hesitation.

"Okay, Clint, what was all that about?" she asked in a quiet tone.

She was staring at him while licking her lips. The

intimate gesture made his stomach clench. "I think," he murmured, "that I should ask you the same thing. That wasn't a kiss taken, Alyssa, but one that was shared."

He waited for her to deny his words but she didn't. Instead she turned away from him and glanced back down to look at his ranch house. And before she could ask he said, "I'll promise to keep my desire under wraps for the next thirty days."

For a moment she didn't say anything, didn't make a move to even acknowledge that he had spoken. And then she looked back at him and at that moment a wave of desire, more intense than anything he'd ever encountered, raced through him.

"Can you?" she asked softly.

Holding her gaze, he was having a hard time keeping up. "Can I what?"

"Bottle your desire for thirty days." He watched as she inhaled deeply, drew herself up as if she was trying to take back control of the situation and he saw her eyes go from sensuous to serious. "I need to know before I make any decision about staying here with you."

He frowned. Was she afraid of him? He covered the distance separating them and came to a stop in front of her. Forcing her to look up at him, become the main focus of her attention. "Let me explain one thing about me, Alyssa," he said in a voice that he knew had her complete attention. "You don't have anything to fear if you stay here, least of all me. You set the boundaries and I will abide by them. I don't have a woman in my life right now, nor do I need one. What you see down there is my life. You are my wife in name only. I will remember that. I will respect that. But after the thirty days I expect you to go, just like I'm sure you'll want to leave. I don't have time for involvements. The only thing long-term in my life is this ranch and the running of it and the foundation. Those things are all I need. They are all I want."

At his blunt words she asked, "Then why did you kiss me?"

Clint saw her eyes were flashing and knew she was beginning to take what he was saying personally. "The reason *we* kissed each other," he said slowly, "is because of a number of things. Curiosity. Need. Desire. It was best that we took care of all three before we got to the ranch. Trust me, you won't become an itch that I'll be tempted to scratch."

Alyssa frowned, not sure she liked the way he'd said that. Had he found her kiss so lacking that he'd not be tempted to do it again? Kim had always said when it came to men she presented no appeal, or that she wouldn't recognize pleasure if it came up to her and bit her. Clint had certainly made a liar out of her cousin. Under his lips she had definitely recognized pleasure. She had actually drowned in it.

"Now," he said, interrupting her thoughts. "Do you want to go down to the ranch with me or would you prefer that I take you back into town?"

She glared at him. "I haven't made up my mind about anything."

"I didn't say you had. I just want you to have peace of mind in doing so."

Behind Clinton's terse words, she suspected he was

low on tolerance. But then she'd come to that same conclusion earlier at the diner. She glanced down the valley
at the ranch and then she glanced back at Clint. "I'm
still staying at the ranch for the night."

"Then let's go. I've got plenty to do when I get there."

When they got back in the truck and he turned the
ignition, she glanced out the window when the truck
started moving. She had gotten her real taste of passion
from the man who was her husband—at least on paper.
And she had surrendered without thought or hesitation.

For some reason she sensed a wild streak in Clint,
one that he probably didn't even know was there. A
wildness she detected, one that had almost come out
in their kiss. As far as she was concerned the man had
desire bottled and it was fighting to become uncorked.
If it ever broke free she didn't want to think of the consequences, the combustion or the fiery, hot passion.

And if that happened, was there a woman in this
world who would be able to tame Clint Westmoreland?
she wondered.

Chapter 4

Inviting Alyssa to spend the night at the ranch wasn't the smartest thing he'd ever done, Clint decided.

From the cliff the ranch house looked huge. But when you stood directly in front of it and got a close-up view, you got a clear picture of just how spacious it was. He hoped Alyssa would decide that in a house as large as his they could easily avoid each other for four short weeks.

The front door opened and Chester walked out. The man, who for years had been Clint's cook, housekeeper, and if there was need, ranch hand, was big. He stood at least six-four and weighed over two hundred and fifty pounds. At sixty-five he looked intimidating and mean as a bear. Once you got to know him, however, it didn't take long to see he was as soft and easygoing as a teddy bear.

Clint knew that Chester considered himself a surrogate father to the triplets. The old man was quick to brag that he'd helped Doc Shaw deliver the three. For that reason—in Clint's opinion—Chester lived under the false assumption that he knew what was best for them. He had been the one to convince Clint and Cole to find the father they hadn't known they had, and the one to talk Casey into building a relationship with their father.

And now with Casey happily married and living in Montana, Chester was on a bandwagon to get Clint and Cole to follow suit. He felt marriage should be in their future plans, the not-so-distant future. Chester claimed he wanted them to find the bliss he'd found in his own happy marriage of over thirty years. His beloved wife Ada died a few years ago. Even now everyone still missed the presence of the gentle and kind woman who had been the love of Chester's life.

Clint saw the way Chester was sizing Alyssa up. The old man was trying to see if she appeared sturdy enough to handle the roughness of a working ranch, and if she had enough brawn to handle Clint. According to Chester, the Golden Glade Ranch needed a mistress who was strong in both mind and body. Clint knew Chester believed Clint needed a woman who could take him on with fortitude.

He had told Chester that morning about the agency's mistake. Now he dreaded telling the old man he and Alyssa were being forced to live as man and wife for thirty days. Chester would somehow see such a thing as a sign that somebody up there was trying to tell Clint something. Clint easily recognized the calculating look in Chester's eyes and frowned.

"I know I've said it already, Clint, but your home is beautiful," Alyssa said.

Alyssa's words reclaimed Clint's attention. He moved his gaze from Chester and back to her. The side of her face was highlighted by the sun. The soft glow of her features made him remember their kiss and how good she had tasted. Even now he wouldn't mind devouring her mouth again, relishing her taste once more. She glanced over at him and he felt a fierce tug in his stomach. He didn't like the feeling one damn bit.

Knowing she expected a response from him, he said, "Thanks. Let me introduce you to Chester and then I'll show you around."

As if impatient for an introduction, Chester came down the steps and went directly to Alyssa, offered her his hand and gave a half laugh and said, "Welcome to the Golden Glade. So you're Clint's wife. We're mighty glad to have you." Before she could respond he added, "And you're just what Clint needs around here."

And at that moment, Clint actually felt like slugging him.

The man's words drew Alyssa up short. It was true that she and Clint were legally married, but as far as she was concerned it was nothing more than a mistake on paper. A mistake that needed to be rectified. But a comment like that made her aware of the seriousness of their situation and just how quickly they needed to resolve the matter.

Not sure how to respond to Chester, Alyssa decided not to address his statement of their marital status and to accept his comment on the ranch by saying, "It's a beautiful ranch."

Clint had walked around the truck and appeared at her side. She glanced up at him and saw he was frowning at the older man. Evidently he hadn't appreciated the reminder of their situation, either.

"Thanks, and Clint is doing a fine job keeping it that way," Chester said. "But what I've told him numerous times is that what this ranch needs is a—"

"Alyssa, this is Chester. Cook and housekeeper," Clint said, smoothly interrupting whatever it was the older man had been about to say.

Not to be outdone the man merely nodded. "What this ranch needs is a woman's touch," he said as if he had not been interrupted.

Alyssa's thoughts began to whirl. *Why would Chester make such a comment? Didn't he know that her and Clint's marriage wasn't real?* She gave a quick glance at Clint but his features were unreadable. Deciding it wasn't her place to meddle in what was going on between Clint and one of his employees, she turned her attention back to Chester and said, "It's nice meeting you, Chester."

The man gave her a huge smile. "No, Alyssa, it is nice meeting *you*. Come on in and I'll show you around."

"No, I'll be showing Alyssa around," Clint said.

Both Alyssa and Chester turned to Clint. "I thought you had a lot of work to do," Chester said.

Alyssa had thought the very same thing and watched as Clint shrugged massive shoulders before he said, "What I have to do can wait."

Alyssa glanced back at Chester and for a quick second she could have sworn she'd seen a sparkle in the old man's eyes. "Suit yourself, then," Chester said. "I need to start dinner, anyway." And then Alyssa watched as the older man gave her a final smile before going back into the house.

"I'll take you to the guest room you'll be using before giving you a tour," Clint said.

Alyssa turned in time to see Clint walk over to the truck to get her overnight bag. She inclined her head as she continued to watch him. The man had such a sensuous walk, she thought.

As if he'd felt her eyes on him, he turned with a concerned look on his face. "Is everything all right, Alyssa?" he asked quietly.

She suddenly felt the need to hug her arms and protect herself from his intense gaze, but she didn't. Instead she appreciated his thoughtful consideration. No one had asked if everything was all right with her since her grandfather's death. "Yes, I'm fine. Thanks for asking," she said.

He only nodded before opening the truck door to pull out her bag. He then turned and walked back toward her. She knew that he was uncomfortable with the situation they had been placed in and he didn't like it any more than she did. But, they would work things out. She'd discovered five years ago that Clint Westmoreland was a man who could handle just about any-

thing that came his way. She saw that strength in him
and admired him for it.

"Come this way," he said. She noticed he had come
to a stop directly in front of her. His closeness caused
her to breathe unevenly and she swallowed deeply to get
control of her emotions. It wasn't as if they hadn't spent
time together before. While working that assignment
five years ago, for one full week they'd been almost
glued at the hip, trying to make their cover believable.
They'd even shared a hotel room—although at night
she would take the bed and he would crash on the sofa.
But still they had shared close quarters and although
she had been fully aware of him as a man, his presence
hadn't affected her like it did now.

It seemed she was now more aware of the opposite sex. Actually, in this case, she was more aware
of Clint Westmoreland. She had been fascinated with
him when they'd worked together, but now he took her
breath away. And back then she had been so focused on
doing a good job on her first assignment as a Ranger
that everything else, including Clint, had been second-
ary. But that was not the case now. *How on earth would
she survive under the same roof with this man for thirty
days?*

He opened the door for her and then stood back for
her to enter. Her stomach knotted and she felt her senses
tingling. She had a feeling that once she walked over
the threshold her life would never be the same.

Steeling himself, Clint watched as Alyssa entered
his home. He couldn't recall the last time he had been

so fully aware of a woman to the point that every-thing about her—even her scent was registering in his mind—seemed branded onto his brain cells.

If she decided to stay the thirty days, she would only be here for a short while, he reminded himself. He could handle that. His work days at the ranch were long and grueling. If he just kept his mind on the job at hand—running the ranch and keeping his uncle's leg-acy alive—he would be fine.

His thoughts shifted back to Alyssa as he watched her stand in the middle of his living room glancing around. She seemed in awe, incapable of speaking. Had she thought just because he spent most of his time out-doors that he didn't appreciate having nice things in-doors?

"Everything is so beautiful," she said in a low voice when she began to speak.

He wasn't reluctant to agree and said thanks. "I hired an interior decorator to do her thing throughout the house. Especially in the guest rooms."

She glanced over at him. "Do you get a lot of visi-tors?"

He chuckled. "Yes. The Westmoreland family is a rather large one and they love to visit. They like check-ing up on each other. I have a bunch of cousins who were close growing up. Like I said earlier, when they found out about me, Cole and Casey, they didn't hesi-tate in extending that closeness to us."

He glanced at his watch. "Come on and let me show you to your room so you can get settled in. I'll show you the rest of the house later."

* * *

A few moments later Alyssa's fingers trembled as she ran them across the richness of the guest room furniture. There had to be about ten or so guest rooms in this house. Clint had been quick to explain that his uncle loved to entertain and always had friends visiting.

The layout of the house actually suited the magnificent structure. Once you entered the front door you walked into this huge foyer that led into a huge living room. There was also an eat-in kitchen and dining room. The house had four wings that jutted off from the living room. North, south, east and west. Clint's bedroom was huge and was located on the north wing, and although he'd only given her a quick glimpse, she'd liked what she'd seen of it.

The beauty of every room in his home made her speechless. It seemed to be fitting for a king…and his queen, from the expensive furniture to the costly portraits that hung on the walls. He evidently was a man who liked nice things and who didn't mind paying his money for them.

Clint had left her alone to get settled and indicated he would be back in a few minutes. She knew he was trying not to crowd her, give her space and she appreciated that. She wondered at what point her heart would stop beating so wildly in her chest. When would the rapid flutter in her stomach cease?

She glanced over at the overnight bag. It contained her toiletries, fresh underwear, an extra-large T-shirt to sleep in and a pair of jeans and a top. If she decided to stay the thirty days she would have to return to Waco and pack more of her things. She supposed that her friends were wondering where she had gone. She hadn't mentioned her destination or the reason for her trip to anyone except her aunt Claudine. Aunt Claudine wouldn't tell anyone about her trip, Alyssa thought with a chuckle. Her sixty-year-old great-aunt would be tickled that for once she knew something that the other family members didn't.

Alyssa had already put away the few things she'd brought with her and was waiting for Clint when he knocked on the bedroom door. For some reason she felt restless and a call to Aunt Claudine hadn't helped when she was informed that Kim had already begun asking questions about her whereabouts.

When Clint knocked again she quickly crossed the room, not wanting him to think she had taken a nap or something. She opened the door. He stood in the hallway, towering over her. "I told you that I'd be back. Are you ready for me to show you around?"

Looking up at him, his penetrating dark gaze seemed to hold her captive and she became aware of how even more fluttering was going on in her stomach. And it wasn't helping matters that she felt compelled to stare at his lips. Doing so reminded her of the kiss they had shared and how the moment his tongue had wrapped around hers an ache had begun within her. It was an ache that wouldn't go away.

At that moment she wasn't sure if going anywhere with him was a smart move. That and the fact that she seemed to be glued to the spot. But then she quickly decided that she wasn't about to let another man get to her again. Kevin had taught her a lesson she would never forget. She studied Clint's features again. They were still unreadable. "Clint…"

"Yes?"

He took a step closer, stepping into the room, and since she was glued to the spot she couldn't get her legs to move. She inclined her head back and looked up at him, thinking he was so tall, and much too handsome. She then saw the dark frown that creased his forehead. "What's wrong?" she asked. The words had come tumbling out before she could hold them in.

One of his broad shoulders lifted nonchalantly. "You tell me," he said.

She had said his name; however, because of the way he had been looking at her, the way that look had made blood rush through her veins, she had forgotten what she'd been about to say. She then remembered. "I was going to say that if you're busy I can just look around myself."

"I'm not busy, so let's go," he said.

She noticed right before he turned to step back into the hallway that the frown on his face had deepened, and she had a feeling that although he had invited her to stay for the night he still didn't like it one bit that she was there.

After giving Alyssa a tour of his home, he walked by her side down the steps to the outside. Her compliments had again pleased him, although he wasn't quite sure why they had. He'd never been one to place a lot of emphasis on what anyone thought of what he owned. He bought to satisfy his taste and not anyone else's.

"You said your sister moved to Montana. Does she come back to visit often?"

He glanced over at Alyssa as they walked down the stairs. She seemed to have gotten shorter and a quick look at her feet told him why. She had exchanged her three-inch high-heel shoes for a pair of flats. Smart move. A working ranch was no place for high heels. "Casey's been back once since she left and that was to get her wedding dress made. Mrs. Miller, a seamstress in town, always said she wanted to be the one who designed Casey's wedding dress if she ever got married," he said.

Her question quickly reminded him of something. "But she and McKinnon might be visiting within the next couple of weeks. Why?"

She shrugged her shoulders. "I was just wondering." And then she asked, "What about Cole?"

He glanced over at her again. "What about him?"

"Does he live here, too?"

"No, Cole has a place in town but most of the time he's on assignment somewhere." Clint had an idea why Alyssa asked about Casey and Cole and the chances that they would be paying a visit to the ranch anytime soon. "If you're concerned what my siblings will have to say about our situation if they happen to pop in then don't be. They won't ask questions."

At the uncertainty in her eyes, he went on to say, "And no, it's not because I usually let women stay over on occasion. It's just that my family respects my privacy. Besides, it's not like either of us has done anything wrong."

"So you plan to tell them the truth about who I am?"

"The part about you being my wife?"

"Yes."

He met her gaze. "I see no reason not to. Besides, Chester knows and if he knows then they know, or they will soon. He thinks I need a wife."

"Why does he think that?"

"He's afraid that like Uncle Sid, I'll get so involved with my horses that I won't take time out to build a personal life or have a family. He's determined not to let that happen. He would marry me off in a heartbeat if he could."

They said nothing for the next few moments, but as they continued to walk together around the ranch he was fully aware of the admiring glances Alyssa was getting from the men who worked for him. His mouth thinned; for some reason he was bothered by it.

"This is a huge place," she said, as if wanting to change the subject, which was okay with him.

"Yes, it is."

"Do you have a lot of men working for you?"

"Well over a hundred. And as I said earlier, Alyssa, if you decide to stay here, the chances of getting in each other's way are slim to none." As far as he was concerned life would be much easier, less complicated that way. The last thing he needed was for her or any woman to get under his skin.

"Ready to head back?" he asked and watched how she pushed a wayward curl back away from her face.

"Yes…and thanks for the tour."

As they walked back toward the ranch house—strolling quietly side by side—he wished like hell he could dismiss from his mind the memory of her taste that remained on his tongue, and how even now, the memory of his lips locked to hers was uncoiling sensations that were running rampant throughout his body. His loins were on fire just thinking about it. His body, in its own way, was sending a reminder of just how long it had been since he'd slept with a woman. It had been way too long and today he was feeling it right down to the bone.

That wasn't good. He had told her that she wouldn't become an itch that he would be tempted to scratch and he hoped like hell that he didn't live to regret those words. He had to remain calm, in control and more than anything he had to remember that no matter how much desire was eating away at his senses, the last thing he needed in his life was a wife.

Chapter 5

"I tell you, Alyssa, that girl is up to no good."

Alyssa tugged off her earring and switched her cell phone to the other ear. Claudine often said that about Kim, but in this case she was inclined to believe her great-aunt. She hadn't heard from Kim in months, at least not since her cousin's last attempt to sabotage one of the projects she'd been working on for a client.

It had cost Alyssa two weeks of production time and she had had to work every hour nonstop to meet the deadline date she'd been given. Of course, as usual, Kim had denied everything and there hadn't been any way Alyssa could prove her guilt.

"You're probably right, Aunt Claudine, but there's nothing that I can do. You know Kim, she's full of surprises." Usually those surprises cost Alyssa tremendously. Kim's bag of dirty tricks included everything from sabotaging important projects to sleeping with Alyssa's fiancé and then having a courier deliver the damaging photographs just moments before she was to leave her home for the church.

Her troubles with Kim started when Alyssa had arrived in the Barkleys' household to live with her grandfather and great-aunt. Her mother had never given Alyssa a reason for sending her away, but to this day Alyssa believed that Kate Harris had begun to notice her most recent lover's interest in her thirteen-year-old-daughter's developing body.

As Alyssa was growing up, her mother had never told her the identity of her father. In fact, Alyssa was very surprised to learn that she had a paternal grandfather. Right before her mother had put her on the plane for Waco, she had told Alyssa that she was the illegitimate daughter of Isaac Barkley's dead son, Todd. Todd had been killed in the line of duty as a Texas Ranger.

Alyssa had arrived in Waco feeling deserted and alone, but it didn't take long to see that the arrival of Grandpa Isaac and Aunt Claudine in her life was a blessing of the richest kind. They immediately made her feel wanted, loved and protected.

Unfortunately, her new relatives' acts of kindness didn't sit too well with her cousin Kim, who was the same age as Alyssa. Kim was the daughter of Grandpa Isaac's only other son, Jessie. Jessie's wife had died when Kim was six. From what Alyssa had been told, Jessie had felt guilty about driving his wife to commit suicide because of his unfaithful ways and had spoiled

Kim rotten to ease his guilt. Kim was used to getting all the attention and hadn't liked it one bit when that attention shifted with Alyssa's arrival.

Alyssa couldn't remember a single time Kim had not been a thorn in her side. First, there had been all those devious pranks Kim had played so that Alyssa could get blamed. Fortunately, Grandpa Isaac had known what Kim was doing and had come to her defense. But instead of things getting better, the more Grandpa Isaac stood up for her, the worse Kim got.

Alyssa's teen years had been the hardest and if it hadn't been for her grandfather and great-aunt she doubted she would have gotten through them. And it didn't help matters that her mother never came to visit her, never bothered contacting her at all. Kim liked to claim that Alyssa was living off the Barkleys' charity and that there were some in the family who didn't believe that Todd Barkley had been her father anyway. That claim hadn't bothered Alyssa, because she could see that she favored her grandfather too much not to be his grandchild. Before he'd died everyone had found out that she had actually been his child. It had been a revelation that had shocked the entire family, especially when he had left her an equal share of everything. And in Kim's eyes, Alyssa's inheritance had been the ultimate betrayal.

"Alyssa…"

Her aunt pulled her thoughts back to the present. "Yes, Aunt Claudine?"

"Will staying with that man for a month be so bad?

At least the marriage will be dissolved…if that's what you really want."

A smile touched Alyssa's lips. Her aunt was trying to play matchmaker again. "Of course that's what I want. It's what Clint and I both want. We don't know each other and like he said, we are victims of someone's mistake. I really don't think it's fair that we have to suffer because of it," Alyssa explained.

She heard her aunt chuckling. "I can't imagine having to suffer if I was to live under the same roof with a gorgeous man…and you did say he was gorgeous, didn't you?"

Yes, she had said that, and had meant it, as well. Clint's physical features were something she could not lie about. And that in itself was the kicker. Kevin had been a good-looking man but he couldn't hold a candle to Clint. She had never been this aware of a man in her life. "Yes, Auntie, he is a hunk."

"Then I suggest that you stay right there in Austin since your only other option is to bring him here to live. Can you imagine all the commotion that would cause? And it would give Kim another excuse to sharpen her claws and do some damage."

Alyssa had thought of that. She wanted to believe that Clint would not be the weakling that Kevin had been and that he would be able to resist Kim's charms. But usually all it took was for any man to set eyes on Kim and they were done for. Men would actually pause when she walked into a room. Too bad beauty was only skin deep, Alyssa thought.

"I'll ship you some things, Alyssa. Besides, a month

away from this circus of a family will do you some good," Claudine said.

Funny, she had thought the same thing. "I have to think things through tonight and give Clint my decision in the morning. If I decide to stay I'll let you know."

"All right, I won't say anything to the others. Eleanor's daughter swears she saw Kim and Kevin together at some nightclub. Can you imagine the two of them seeing each other again after all they did to you? We heard Kevin got a promotion with that company he works for. That's probably why Kim is back in the picture. She's determined to land a rich husband one way or the other."

In a perverse way Alyssa wished her cousin the best. Even with all the low-down and underhanded things that Kim had done, Alyssa couldn't find it in her heart to hate her. She had tried when she'd gotten those photos of Kim and Kevin in bed together, but now all she could do was feel pity for them both. The thought that he and Kim were seeing each other no longer bothered her. Any love she might have had for him ended the day that should have been her wedding day. If Kim was the type of woman he preferred then more power to him.

She wondered just what type of woman Clint would prefer. She could see a beautiful woman in his arms, in his bed, giving birth to his babies. Alyssa was certain she didn't fit the criteria for Clint's dream woman. She was of average design and she didn't fit the "dream-woman" mold. The only reason they were married now was because of someone's screwup. Even when they'd worked together he hadn't given her a second thought, although they had shared a hotel room for a week. Alyssa could not forget sharing such close quarters with him, inhaling his scent, breathing the same air, or sitting across a table and sharing food with Clint Westmoreland.

That made her think of the meal they had shared less than an hour ago. Chester had prepared a delicious meal, but it had been just the two of them. She couldn't help but notice that the older man, although still extremely friendly, hadn't been as chatty as he'd been when she had first arrived. Clint must have said something to him, probably warning him not to put foolish ideas into her head. Not that he could have. She was a realist, almost too much so at times—at least that's what Aunt Claudine claimed. Alyssa would be the first to admit that her dreams of forever after had gotten destroyed the moment she had seen those pictures on her wedding day. It would be hard, nearly impossible for anyone to make a believer out of her again.

She heard a noise outside her bedroom window and crossed the room to see what had caused it. The sun had set and dusk had settled in. One of the floodlights that were shining from the side of the house provided enough brightness for her to see Clint as he leaned against a post talking with two of his men.

It was hard not to take an assessment of Clint each and every time she saw him. From the window, she couldn't see every single detail, but she had a clear view of his thighs. He was standing with his legs braced apart and the muscles that filled his jeans were taut and firm. Just looking at him standing there in that sexy pose made her pulse race. She was actually feeling breath-less. *This was her reaction to the man whom she was supposed to live with for thirty days?* She doubted she would be able to get through one day living with him let alone thirty. She was well aware from what he'd said earlier that day about his ability to control his desire if they decided to live together. He had basically given his word that he would abide by any boundaries that she set.

While she was thinking about what boundaries she would establish if she decided to stay, he turned toward the window as if somehow he'd felt her presence there. Their gazes locked. Held. And it seemed at that moment something, a tangible connection she could not define, passed between them. It was as if some understanding had been made, but for the life of her she didn't know what it was.

Dazed and more than a little confused, she took a step back on wobbly knees at the same time she dropped the curtain back in place to shield her from his view. She knew she had to rein in her uncontrollable imagi-nation, urges and lust. If he could control his then she most certainly should be able to get a handle on hers. But she had to admit what she was experiencing was not something she encountered every day. She simply had never been the type of woman to get goggle-eyed over a man. But ever since she'd arrived in Austin, she had been doing that very thing.

Sighing deeply, she moved toward the bathroom hop-ing her new state of mind was something she got over real soon.

* * *

Clint frowned as he walked down the long hallway toward his bedroom. It was way past midnight. After taking care of the evening chores, he had hung around the bunkhouse and played a game of cards with some of his men.

He had stayed away from the house as long as he could, and now he was back inside. His mind wandered to what had happened earlier. He'd been standing out in the yard talking to a couple of his men until he happened to notice Alyssa staring at him from her bedroom window. He'd done the only thing he could do at the time, which was to stare back.

It seemed that against his will, his gaze had locked on hers. It was plain to see that Alyssa was getting to him and the brazen images of her that had been forming in his mind all day weren't helping. Hell, he may have bitten off more than he could chew in asking her to stay under his roof. If only there had been another way for them to end their marriage, he mused. Surely there was someone he could talk to about it.

His cousin Jared immediately came to mind. Jared was the attorney in the family. His specialty was the handling of divorce cases. Perhaps his cousin could give him some advice. He checked his watch. Jared was usually up late at night and Clint turned in the direction of his office, deciding to give his cousin a call.

He pushed open his office door and paused. There, sitting at his desk in front of his computer, was Alyssa. She hadn't heard him enter, and so he just stood for a moment and gazed at her. The soft lighting from the lamp, as well as the glow from the computer screen, seemed to beam on her, highlighting her features. Her hair was no longer hanging around her shoulders. She had pulled it up into a knot at the back of her neck.

Her full attention was on the computer screen and he watched her as she sat in front of it. Her head was tilted in such a way that showed off the slimness of her neck and her shoulders. She sat with perfect posture.

She seemed to be wearing an oversize T-shirt. On anyone else there probably would not have been a single provocative thing about her attire, but on Alyssa, just the part he saw was totally alluring. The way she was sitting made the shirt stretch tight across her chest, and he could plainly see the tips of her nipples. She wasn't wearing a bra. His fingers seemed to twitch and he knew he would love the feel of his fingers slowly stroking the budded tips.

His gaze moved to her face at the same time she parted her lips in a smile before she released a satisfied chuckle. Clint shifted his gaze from her lips to the computer screen to see what held her concentration. She was playing one of those games you downloaded off the internet. *Alyssa.* She was busy trying to accomplish some goal and from the look of things, she was succeeding.

Deciding it was time to let her know that he was there, he stepped into the room. "Umm, that looks interesting. Can I play?"

She whirled in her seat and startled dark eyes seemed to clash with his as she stood abruptly. "I'm sorry. I should have asked to use your computer before—"

"You didn't have to ask, Alyssa," he said, interrupting her apology. "You are more than welcome to use it. Please sit back down and continue what you were doing. You seem to be having fun. What is it?"

She hesitated briefly before retaking her seat. Slowly her gaze slid from him to the computer screen. The one thing he had noticed when she stood was that the T-shirt was even more sensually appealing than he'd first thought. It barely covered her thighs and if that wasn't bad enough, it outlined her curves in a way that had blood racing through his veins.

"It's a game called 'Playing with Fire,'" she said softly and he had a feeling he was making her nervous. She glanced back over at him. "Have you ever played Atomic Bomberman before?"

He smiled, inwardly fighting the acute desire he felt at that moment. "No, I don't believe that I have," he said.

"Oh. 'Playing with Fire' is sort of a flashy remake of 'Atomic Bomberman.' The object of the game is to blow up your opponent before they blow you up," she explained.

Clint chuckled. "That sounds rather interesting. I take it you like playing games on the computer."

She shrugged. "Yes, it's a way for me to unwind. Whenever I can't sleep I usually get up and play a game or two," she said.

He leaned against the closed door. "I see. Is there a reason you can't sleep?" Already his mind was thinking of his own version of "Playing with Fire" and the various ways it could be played. "Is the bed not comfortable?" Although he wished it wouldn't go there, his mind quickly thought of her in that huge bed alone.

"No, the bed is fine, really comfortable," she responded with what he denoted as a soft chuckle before adding, "It's just that I'm not used to sleeping in any bed but my own."

"I see."

She cleared her throat before standing again. "Well, I don't want to keep you out of your office," she uttered as she prepared to leave.

"You're not. I had come in to use the phone, but I can make the call from my bedroom just as easily. I'll leave you to your game." He paused a second then asked, "By the way, who's winning?"

He saw the smile that touched her lips, the sparkle that lit her eyes and the proud lifting of her chin. "I am, of course," she answered.

"Now why doesn't that surprise me? Good night, Alyssa," he said, returning her smile.

"Good night, Clint."

Clint turned and moved toward the door. When he felt the sudden rush of blood to his loins he muttered a curse under his breath and turned back around. Before Alyssa could blink he crossed the room and pulled her from the chair. The moment her body was pressed against his and her lips parted in a startled gasp, his mouth swept down on hers at an angle that called for deep penetration. He took hold of her tongue, wanting the taste of her again with a need that was hitting him all at once, and when she returned the kiss—their tongues participated in one hell of a heated duel—a disturbing acceptance entered his mind. He was not prone to giving in to sexual desires like this, he thought. He could get turned on just like the next guy, but never to this magnitude. His response to any woman had never been this strong, this intense, this mind-bogglingly obsessive. The more he tasted her, the more he wanted, and it wasn't helping matters that she felt perfectly right in his arms. Her softness felt so good against his hardness. *What the hell was wrong with him?*

He quickly decided he would have to figure out this change in him later, but not right now. Not when she'd wrapped her arms around his neck and pressed her body closer to his, and not when he could feel the tips of her breasts through the cotton of his shirt. His mind began imagining all sorts of things. He imagined how it would feel to have the tips of those breasts in his mouth, to toy with them using his tongue, or how he would love to spread her on his desk and take her there. Then there was the idea of him sitting in the chair and tugging her down in his lap and...

She suddenly broke the kiss and he watched as she backed away while forcing air into her lungs. He was doing likewise. He was breathing like he had just run a marathon, but each time he inhaled, her scent filled his nostrils. It was a scent that was getting him aroused all over again.

She lifted her head to look at him and that's when he noticed the knot in her hair had come undone and it was flowing wildly around her shoulders, making her look even sexier than before.

"Was that supposed to be a good-night kiss?" Her voice was soft and breathy.

That hadn't been what he'd expected her to say. Actually, he had expected her to dress him down in the worse possible way. *Was it possible that she was admitting that she had wanted the kiss as much as he had?* She didn't seem to be placing the blame entirely on him, although he had been the one to make the first move.

He leaned back against the door as his gaze went to her mouth. "Yes, it was a good-night kiss," he said. "Want another one?"

"No. I doubt if I could handle it," she responded, shaking her head.

A smile touched his lips. Again her comment had surprised him. "Sure you can. Do you want me to prove it to you?"

"No, thank you."

He chuckled softly. "In that case, I'll let you get back to your game." Without giving her a chance to say anything else, he opened the door and quickly walked out of the room, closing the door behind him.

He paused for a second thinking it was obvious that they had the hots for each other. If she remained under his roof there was no way he would be able to keep his hands off her. He wondered if the kisses they'd shared would be a determining factor in whether she stayed or went back to Waco. Would living together be too much of a temptation? Thirty days was a long time.

She'd said she wasn't used to sleeping in any bed other than her own. In a way he had been glad to hear that. On the other hand, he figured she had to know that if she remained at the Golden Glade, at the rate they were going, she would eventually share his.

As he made his way toward his bedroom, thinking

about the explosive chemistry between them began to annoy the hell out of him. He was a man known to have a multitude of control. In the past when lust consumed his body he had a way of dealing with it. Any available and willing woman would do. But he had a feeling that his usual solution would not work this time. His body wanted only one woman and that wasn't good.

Alyssa released a deep breath the moment Clint closed the door behind him. It was simply amazing that one man could have that kind of effect on her. Every single time she saw him, every time he kissed her the result was the same—passion. *When would the attraction she had for him wear off? What if it never did?*

Maybe she needed to rethink her decision to remain at Clint's ranch for the thirty days. It was a decision she hadn't yet told him she'd made, only because she had mentioned that she would need to sleep on it. And she had, which was the main reason she was up now. Once the decision had been made she couldn't get her body to go back to sleep. It had become restless and for the first time ever, fiercely aroused.

And for him to find her in his office wearing only a large T-shirt was embarrassing. But the house had been quiet for a long while and she figured everyone had gone to bed for the night. His bedroom was in a different wing and so she had assumed the coast was clear. She thought that she could sneak into his office for a while and not be noticed. But he had noticed. And so she made a new promise—no more late-night game-playing on the computer for her.

She inhaled deeply. In the morning she would tell him of her decision to stay. She would also tell him that her decision came with stipulations. He'd said earlier that day, after their first kiss, that he was able to control his desire for her. If kissing her the way he did was his desire under control, she didn't want to think how the kiss would be with those same desires unleashed.

Chapter 6

Alyssa's heart immediately began beating harder when she walked into the kitchen the next morning to find Clint seated at the table. Although it appeared he was just starting in on breakfast, she knew he was there waiting on her. His expression indicated that he wanted to know her decision.

She glanced around the large kitchen, trying to ignore the pulse that was erratically thumping in her throat. It was a sin and shame that Clint looked so good this early in the morning. He was staring at her with those dark, piercing eyes of his, and the way the sunlight captured the well-defined planes of his face made him appear hauntingly handsome. Alyssa found his good looks quite disturbing, given the fact she was trying to resist her attraction to him.

Seeing him only reminded her of her behavior with him last night in his office. He had once again kissed her mindless, engulfing her with a degree of passion she thought was possible only in those romance novels Aunt Claudine read. Alyssa had gone to bed dreaming about him, their kiss and the things she wanted to do with him beyond a kiss. She had awakened mortified that such thoughts had entered her mind. She would need to take steps to make sure her dreams never became a reality.

For her own sake and well-being, she had reached the conclusion that setting ground rules with Clint would be the only way they would survive living under the same roof. Otherwise, she was setting herself up for many tiring days and disturbing nights, Alyssa realized.

"Where's Chester?" she asked.

Clint leaned back in his chair. "He's off on Wednesdays. At least, he takes off after breakfast and then returns at dinnertime. It's the day he's at the children's hospital being Snuggles the Clown."

Alyssa lifted a brow. "Snuggles the Clown?"

"He spends his day in the children's ward making the kids laugh. He's been doing it for over twenty years now and he's a big hit. That's how he and Uncle Sid met. Chester used to be a rodeo clown," Clint said.

At first Alyssa couldn't picture Chester as a clown, but then as she thought about it, she changed her mind. He had a friendly air about him and would probably be someone who loved kids. She didn't know any clowns and found the thought of him being one fascinating. "You have to love kids to do something like that," she said.

"He does. It was unfortunate that he and Ada never had any of their own."

"Was Ada his wife?"

"Yes. They were married over thirty years. She died six years ago from an acute case of pneumonia," Clint explained.

"That's sad," she said quietly.

"It was. He took her death pretty hard. They had a very strong marriage."

A very strong marriage. Alyssa wondered if that meant the same thing as the two of them were deeply in love. "So he's been working at the ranch a long time?"

"Yes, Chester's been working here since before I was born," Clint said.

Alyssa could hear something in Clint's voice that went beyond a mere liking for Chester. It was easy to tell that Clint considered Chester more than just a housekeeper and a cook. He considered the man an intricate part of his family. While giving her a tour of the outside of the house, he had introduced her to several of the men who worked for him. Some of them were older and full of experience in the taming of the horses. The younger ones were learning the ropes, but everyone, as Clint had been quick to point out, played an important part in the running of his operation. The men had been friendly and respectful and when he had introduced her as nothing more than a good friend, it was apparent they had accepted his word.

"You'd better dig in while the food is warm," Clint said.

Taking his statement to mean he was tired of answering her questions, she walked over to the stove to fix her plate and pour a cup of coffee, feeling Clint's gaze on her with every move she made.

"I'm glad you know to do that," he said.

She turned and looked at him, bewildered. "Do what?"

"Fix your own food."

At her confused look he said, "A lot of women wouldn't. They would expect to be waited on hand and foot."

Alyssa turned back around to scoop eggs onto her plate wondering if he'd ever met Kim. Her cousin would definitely be one of those type of women. Uncle Jessie still called Kim his princess and she took it literally. "Well, I'm not one of them," she said when she came to the table to sit down. "I'm used to fending for myself."

She had barely taken her seat when Clinton folded his arms across his chest and asked, "Okay, what have you decided?"

Instead of answering him, she stared down into the dark liquid of her coffee for a moment before glancing up at him. "Do you have to know this minute?"

"Any reason you can't tell me this minute?" he countered, with a little irritation in his voice.

She set her cup down knowing the last thing they needed was to get agitated with each other. Besides, he was right. There wasn't a reason she couldn't tell him now. "No, I guess not."

She didn't say anything for a few moments and then

met his gaze. "Before I commit to anything, I want you to agree to something," she said.

He lifted a dark brow. "Agree to what?"

"Agree that you won't try to get me into your bed."

He smiled. "My bed?"

"Or any bed in this house." She thought it best to clarify. "And to be more specific, I want your word that you won't try to seduce me into bed with you."

He laughed softly and held her gaze for a long moment. "Define *seduce*," he said.

Alyssa was aware that he was toying with her, but she was more determined than ever to make sure he understood her position. "You're a man, Clint. You know very well what seduction entails," she said.

His smile deepened. "And you think I'd do something like that?"

She didn't hesitate in answering. "Yes. I'm certain of it. In less than twenty-four hours we've kissed twice, which leads me to believe you would try seducing me."

He stared at her for a moment, eyed her reflectively and then said, "You're right. I would in a heartbeat." And then he asked, "And we've kissed twice, you say?"

Like he didn't know it. "Yes," she said, now very annoyed.

"Want to go for three?" he murmured in a voice that was so husky that it sent shivers through her body.

She eyed him sternly. "I'm serious, Clint."

"So am I."

She stared into his deep, penetrating gaze. Yes, he was serious. He was dead serious. The very thought that he wanted to kiss her again, tangle his tongue with hers and taste her, made the breath she was breathing get caught in her throat. *Had he just admitted that he enjoyed kissing her?* Well, she could admit that she enjoyed kissing him, as well. There was something devastatingly mind-blowing about the feel of him thrusting his tongue deep into her mouth, moving it around, latching on to hers and...

"Anything else you want from me?"

She shot him a cool look. "Maybe I'd better add kissing to the mix. I think it's a good idea if we refrain from doing it," she said.

"That can't happen," he said. She noticed that his lips curved into an easy smile.

His response had been quick and decisive. Alyssa tried remaining calm. She felt a rush of blood that gushed through her veins. "Why can't it happen?"

"Because we enjoy kissing too much. The best thing to do is to stay in control when we do kiss. Personally, I don't see anything wrong with us kissing. It's merely a friendly form of greeting," he said.

Yeah. Right. It was a form of greeting that she could do without. Especially because kissing Clint Westmoreland made her want to indulge in other things. Things that were better left alone.

"Like I said, Alyssa," he said, interrupting her thoughts. "The key is self-control. As much as I want you and as much as kissing you places temptation in my path, I promise I won't take our attraction to the next level. I have too much work to do around here to get involved with a woman—in any way," he said.

She admired his iron-clad control...if he really had it.

He sounded so confident, so sure of himself, she would love to test his endurance level to see what it could or could not withstand.

"But I have to admit you bring something to the table a lot of women haven't," he said.

She glanced over at him and her pulse jumped at the way he was looking at her.

"And what might that be?" she asked softly.

"Although it's only on paper, you're my wife. Perhaps it is because I've seen things from a male perspective, but it's as if knowing you're bound to me is opening up desires and urges that I usually don't have. The fact that we are married makes me crave things."

She frowned. *In other words, having a woman under his roof was making him horny,* Alyssa quickly surmised. "Then I need to add another condition to my visit. That from a female perspective, whatever desires are opening up for you, I suggest that you take your time and close them. I may not have all the self-control you claim to have, but I have no interest in getting involved with a man—in any way. Besides, if I were to get involved with a man it would have to be serious. I'm not into casual relationships where the only goal is relieving sexual frustrations," she said.

He was silent for a moment as he stared at her, and for a fraction of a second she thought she saw a challenging glint in his gaze. And then he said, "I won't try getting you into my bed…or yours…but I won't promise to keep my mouth to myself. I can't see us denying ourselves that one bit of indulgence."

"Why? When it won't lead anywhere?"

He inclined his head. His gaze locked with hers. "I desire you. Kissing you is a way to work you out of my system. I believe the same could be said for you, as well. At the end of the thirty days I suspect you will be ready to leave as much as I'll be ready for you to leave," he said.

Alyssa held his gaze and read what she saw in his eyes. He really believed that and she would go even further to say he was counting on it.

"Because we would have kissed each other out of our systems by then?" she asked, needing to be sure she understood his logic in all of this.

"Yes," he replied evenly.

"And you think you're that elusive and wild at heart."

He lifted a brow. "Wild at heart?"

"Yes. You don't think there's a woman who exists who's capable of capturing your heart," she said.

"I know there's not."

He had said the words with such venom that she was forced to ask. "Have you ever been in love, Clint?"

She could tell by the look that appeared in his eyes that her question surprised him. She saw the way his shoulders tightened, the firm grip he held on his coffee cup and knew she had waded into turbulent waters.

For a while she thought he wasn't going to respond, but then he did.

"No," he said.

For some reason she didn't believe him. Not that she thought he was lying to her, but she figured that the love he might have had for someone had been so effectively destroyed that it was hard to recall when that emotion had ever gripped his heart. It had been that way for her after she'd discovered what Kevin had done. It was as if her love had gotten obliterated with that one single act of unfaithfulness. She couldn't help wondering about the woman who had crushed Clint's heart.

"Are you satisfied with our agreement?"

Alyssa dragged in a deep breath. The issue of them kissing hadn't been fully resolved to her liking, but the way she saw it, he was not a man to force himself on anyone. If she resisted his kisses enough times, he would find some other game to amuse himself. "Yes, I'm satisfied," she said.

"So, are you agreeing to remain here for thirty days, live under the same roof with me?"

Intimate images flooded her mind. She forced them out. His home was humongous. His bedroom was on one side of the house and hers on the other. Chances were there would be days when their paths wouldn't even cross. "Yes, I'm agreeing to do just that," she said.

He nodded. "I'll call Hightower and let him know. By the way, what about more clothes for you? You only brought an overnight bag," Clint said.

"I spoke with my aunt yesterday and she told me if I decided to stay she would send me some things."

"Your aunt is the only family you have?"

She might as well be, she wanted to say.

"No, I have an uncle and several cousins," she said instead. "My mother sent me to live with my grandfather and Aunt Claudine when I was thirteen. Over the years Aunt Claudine has become a surrogate mother to me," she added.

"And your grandfather?"

A pain settled in her heart. She wanted to correct him so badly.

"My grandfather died four years ago," she said softly.

"That was about the same time I lost my mother," he said, looking down at the coffee in his cup. She could hear the sadness in his voice. He glanced up and at that moment an emotion passed between them—a deep understanding of how it felt to lose someone you truly cared about.

"Were you close to her?" she asked.

"Yes. Casey, Cole and I were her world and she was ours. She and Uncle Sid, along with Chester and the other old-timers on the ranch were our family. What about your mother? You said she sent you to live with your grandfather and aunt when you were thirteen. Do the two of you still keep in touch?"

In a way Alyssa wished he would have asked her anything but that. That her mother could so easily send her away and not stay in touch was still a pain that would occasionally slither through her heart.

"No. I haven't seen or heard from my mother since the day she sent me away," she said.

Deciding she didn't want to subject herself to any more of his inquiries about her family, she stood. "I need to make a few calls. In addition to contacting my aunt, I need to make sure I have everything I need to continue my business while I'm here. That means I will need to use your computer a lot," she said.

"I don't have a problem with that."

Alyssa nodded. "Okay. I'm sure you have a lot to do

today, as well," she said, picking up her plate and cup and carrying both over to the sink. "And since today is Chester's day off, I'll take care of the dishes as soon as I've made those calls."

With nothing else to say, Alyssa walked out of the kitchen.

Clint continued to sit at the table. From the moment he had gotten the letter from the bureau advising him of his marriage to Alyssa, he had simply assumed that getting out of the marriage would be easy—a piece of cake. He had miscalculated on a number of things. First, the bureau being so hard-nosed over such a blatant mistake and second, his attraction to the woman who was legally his wife. Now, he was fully committed to go to extraordinary restrictions to keep his hands off of her. In other words, to stay out of her bed and to make sure she stayed out of his.

Neither would be easy.

That was what made the thought of the next thirty days so disconcerting. A part of him wanted to rebel. *Why not have sex with her?* After all it was just sex, no big deal. They were mature adults who evidently had healthy appetites with no desire to get caught up in anything other than the moment. Right? Wrong.

He couldn't help but recall her words about not being one to indulge in casual affairs, which gave him a glimpse into her character. While engaging her in conversation, he had taken in everything she'd said—even some things she hadn't said, especially about her family.

The Texas Ranger in him could detect when someone was withholding information. He hadn't wanted to pry, but she'd deliberately omitted mentioning a few things. Such as why her mother had given her up at thirteen and had never once come back to see her. And when she had mentioned her cousins he hadn't heard that deep sense of love and warmth he'd felt whenever he spoke of his. Granted, he didn't expect every family to be like the Westmorelands, but still he would think there was a closeness there. He had heard the deep love and affection in her voice when she had spoken of her grandfather and aunt.

And then he could very well be reading more into it than was there. It could be that she was a private person and hadn't felt the need or wasn't stirred by any desire to tell him any more than she had. Wife or no wife, it wasn't "expose your soul to Clint" day.

He rubbed his hand down his face. Why did he even care? he wondered. What was there about Alyssa that made him want to dig deeper and unravel her inner being, layer by layer? With that thought in mind, he was about to get up from the table when his cell phone went off. He stood to pull it off the attachment on his belt. "Hello," he said.

"So what's this I hear about you having a wife?"

He couldn't help but smile when he sat back down. He could envision his sister with her long black lashes lifting in a way that said she had every right to know everything she asked him.

"I see Chester's loose lips have been flapping again," he muttered, thinking he needed to have a talk with the old man. Of course, Clint knew that all the talk in the world wouldn't do any good with Chester.

"He knew I had a right to know," Casey Westmoreland Quinn said in a serious tone. "So tell me about her."

He sighed. Since she hadn't asked what happened to make him have a wife in the first place, he could only assume that Chester had covered that information with her already. "What do you want to know?"

"Everything. What's her name? Where is she from? How old is she? Is she someone that you used to work with who I've met already? And so on and so forth."

Clint frowned. Alyssa reminded him of Casey with her endless questions.

"Her name is Alyssa Barkley. She's from Waco and she's twenty-seven. And no, you've never met her. She became a Ranger right out of college and then left not long after that assignment we did together. She was only with the Rangers for a year," he said.

"So you didn't make a good impression on her then, did you?"

"I wasn't trying to. I was all into Chantelle at the time," he said.

"Please don't mention her name," Casey said in feigned terror.

Clint chuckled. Casey and Chantelle had never gotten along from day one. His sister had warned him about her but he wouldn't listen. Now he wished he had. But at the time he had been thinking with the lower part of his body and not his brain. Chantelle caught the attention of any man within one hundred feet. But then so did Alyssa. However, it had taken only a few moments spent with Alyssa to know she and Chantelle were very different.

Alyssa wasn't all into herself. She didn't think she was responsible for the sun rising and setting each day. Chantelle had thought she was all that, and like a testosterone-packed fool, he had played right into her hands without considering the consequences.

"So what have the two of you decided to do since the bureau won't annul your marriage?"

Casey's question reeled his thoughts back in. "Do what they want and live together for thirty days," he said.

"That's asking a lot of the two of you. Maybe you ought to seek out the advice of an attorney," Casey said.

"We thought of that, but in the end it might only delay things," he said, and his conversation with Jared last night had only confirmed his suspicions. "Alyssa thinks it will work since she's able to do her job from anywhere. She's a website designer."

"Um, maybe you can get her to design the website for Uncle Sid's foundation that we're setting up," Casey suggested.

"I mentioned it to her briefly, and you're right. It might be something she can do while she's here if she has the time."

"She'll be at the ranch when McKinnon and I visit in a few weeks," Casey said as if thinking out loud. "I'm looking forward to meeting her."

Casey's intonation immediately sent up red flags. He knew his sister. After that Chantelle fiasco she had gotten a little overprotective where he was concerned.

He found it rather amusing although not necessary. "Don't forget who's the oldest, Casey," he decided to remind her.

Over the phone line he heard her unladylike snort. "But only by a mere fourteen minutes. I would have been the oldest if it wasn't for Cole holding me back."

Clint laughed. That's the reason Casey liked telling everyone for her being the last born. She had gotten that tale from Chester, who had convinced her she was in position to be born first. "Whatever. Look, Case, I have a lot of work to do around here today. I'm expecting another shipment of horses," he said.

"Wonderful. McKinnon and I will talk with you later to let you know the exact day we'll be arriving."

Moments later Clint ended the call with Casey thinking that she was usually a good judge of character. He wondered what she would think of Alyssa.

Chapter 7

Alyssa glanced around Clint's office thinking how the one in her home was a lot smaller. She loved her small apartment. It was just the right size for her. All she needed was a kitchen, bedroom, bath and working space. She had considered the living and dining rooms as a bonus.

She studied the different pictures on the wall and recognized the one of Sid Roberts. Another showed a woman with three little ones—about the age of five or six—at her side. She knew that it was a picture of Clint, his mother and two siblings. There was another framed photograph of his mother alone. She was beautiful and Alyssa could easily see Clint's resemblance to her; the likeness seemed very strong. She thought that Clint favored his mother until she saw yet another photograph of a man she immediately decided had to be Clint's father. Any resemblance she'd attributed to his mother dimmed when she compared the image of Clint she had in her mind to the picture of his father. Clint had his father's domineering features. Both Clint and Cole, whose looks were nearly identical, had inherited their father's forehead, chiseled jaw and matching dark eyes. They had also inherited their dad's sexy lips, the lips that she loved to look at on Clint. The father, whom Clint said he'd only met a few years ago, definitely was a good-looking man. Alyssa quickly formed the opinion that Casey, although she had her father's eyes, had inherited more of her mother's features.

Alyssa tensed when she heard her cell phone ring. She had recently gotten a new number and hoped that Kim hadn't gotten hold of it. Flipping the phone open, she smiled when she saw it was her aunt calling. "Yes, Aunt Claudine?"

"Just wanted you to know that I got those boxes shipped off like I said I would. You should get them in a few days."

"Thank you. I appreciate your going to the trouble," Alyssa said.

"No trouble. Kim dropped by this morning trying to sweet-talk me into telling where you were. I didn't tell her a thing. Actually, I told her you were off seeing a client."

"Thanks, I appreciate it," Alyssa said.

"Jessie also called asking about you, but I figured Kim put him up to it."

Alyssa had to assume the same thing. Her uncle rarely sought her out these days.

"And how are things with you and your cowboy?"

Alyssa chuckled. "He isn't my cowboy, but things are going just fine." At least she hoped they were. She hadn't seen him since breakfast that morning. She knew he had returned for lunch because she had heard him when he'd ridden up on his horse. She had glanced out the window—being careful not to been seen this time—and watched as Clint dismounted and walked with his horse toward the stables. The way the jeans hugged his body nearly took her breath away.

"I'm glad to hear it. Well, I've got to go. Eleanor is dropping by later and we're going to attend a church function together."

"Okay, Aunt Claudine, and thanks for everything," Alyssa said.

"You're welcome."

Alyssa hung up the phone thinking how appreciative she was of her aunt.

"How are things going?"

She turned to see Clint standing in the doorway.

"They're going fine. My aunt is shipping some boxes to me and I'm hoping to get them in a few days," Alyssa said.

Opening her mouth and getting words out had been a real challenge, especially with the way he was looking at her. Heat was beginning to slither through her body from the intensity of his gaze. He stood leaning in the doorway and she could feel her control begin to unravel. Whether she liked it or not, desire seemed to grip her each and every time she saw him.

"In the meantime," he said, interrupting her thoughts, "I figured you might need some additional clothing so I placed a few items of clothes on your bed."

She lifted a brow. "Clothes?"

"Yes."

"Women's clothes?" There was a suspicious note in her voice which she wished wasn't there. She further wished he wouldn't pick up on it.

"Yes, women's clothes. You and Casey are about the same size so I took the liberty of borrowing some of her things for you. When she left for Montana she wasn't certain she would be staying so she left some of her things here," Clint said.

Alyssa felt relief that the clothes belonged to his sister and not some other woman. She was mature enough to know that Clint had probably dated a slew of women over the years. Some had probably stayed at the ranch. That was his business. And what he did after the thirty days were up and their marriage was annulled was also his business. *So why did the thought that his business could include other women bother her?*

And then there was the thought that he had been in her bedroom. Granted, this was his house, the one he'd grown up in as a child, which meant that he probably knew the location of every room blindfolded. But the idea that he had been in the room where she'd slept last night, had gotten close to the bed, made every nerve in her body tingle.

"Thanks for being so thoughtful," she managed to say as she stood.

"No problem."

When it became obvious that he had no intention of leaving—he just stood in that same spot staring at her—she raised a brow.

"Is there something else?"

"Yes, there is," he said.

She felt the lump in her throat. She didn't want to ask but felt compelled to do so anyway.

"And what is that?"

"Chester wanted to know if you would be joining us for dinner," Clint said, clearly uncomfortable with extending the invitation to her.

Alyssa released another deep sigh as she studied his expression. That hadn't been what she expected him to say and she felt a touch of unwanted disappointment. It had been her idea that they agree on how far they would take their attraction, so why was she feeling so edgy?

"Alyssa?"

"Yes?"

"Will you be joining us?"

She wondered if he really wanted her to.

"And how do you feel about me joining you for dinner, Clint?" she asked quietly.

He rubbed his chin as he continued to look at her. She watched as his gaze slowly scanned her body from head to toe. He smiled slightly and then said, "We're having meat loaf. I'd much rather look at you across the table than down at a plate of meat loaf." He added,

"Chester usually burns it. He says it's supposed to taste better that way."

She couldn't help her smile. "Does it? Taste better that way?"

"Not really," he said, looking thoughtful. "But then the only taste I seem to enjoy lately is yours."

His words singed fire through her body with the force of a blowtorch. A woman could only take so much flirting with a man like Clint. She watched as he slowly moved away from the door to walk toward her. And as if her feet had a mind of their own, they moved, and she found herself coming from around the desk to meet him. He came to a stop right in front of her and his eyes stared into hers.

"This is crazy. You know that, don't you?" As he asked her that question, he leaned forward and circled her waist with his arm. The heat of his words warmed her lips.

"Yes. Real crazy," she heard herself mumbling in response.

"I'm going to be real pissed about it later," he said, catching her bottom lip between his teeth for a gentle nip. "But right now, at this minute, I have to taste you again."

And then as if to prove his point, when she tilted her head up to him he reached out and gently took hold of a section of her hair and tenderly pulled her mouth closer to his, locking it in place. He was determined to take the kiss deeper. Make it even more intimate.

She didn't think that was possible until she felt the tip of his tongue coaxing hers to participate. Hers gave in and together they explored every sensitive area of her mouth. Her senses went on full alert and she became a turbulent mass of longing. In all her twenty-seven years, it had taken a trip to Austin to discover what it meant to be kissed senseless.

The kiss seemed to go on nonstop and Alyssa felt herself being passionately consumed with a need that was making her feel weak. It just didn't seem possible that within days of seeing Clint again after five years, she could be this attracted to him.

He pulled back and ended the kiss, but not before gently nipping at her bottom lip as if she was a tasty morsel he just had to have. And then he took his fingertip and traced it across her wet and swollen lips. "You did want my kiss, didn't you?"

She didn't answer immediately, and then she decided to be totally honest with him. "Yes, I wanted it. But—"

He quickly swooped down and captured her mouth with his again, and she hungrily opened her mouth beneath his. Yes, she had wanted it and he was making sure she was getting it.

This time when he pulled back he placed a finger against her lips to make sure she didn't utter a single word.

"No buts, Alyssa. I know my limitations. I'm aware of the terms that I agreed to. The only person who can renege on them is you," he said.

Arousal was shining in his eyes and she could feel his erection pressed hard against her stomach. "And if you ever decide to do so," he added in a husky tone, "you're fully aware of where my bedroom is located. You are more than welcome to join me there at any time."

"Are you sure Alyssa will be joining you for dinner?"

Clint first glanced at the clock on the stove before meeting Chester's gaze. "That's what she said, but who knows, she might have changed her mind."

Chester stood leaning against the counter and held a spatula in his hand. He narrowed his eyes at Clint as he placed his arms across his chest. "What did you do to her?"

Clint rolled his eyes. "I didn't do anything to her. I merely told her that—"

"Sorry I'm late," Alyssa said as she rushed into the kitchen.

Both men's gazes shifted to Alyssa. Clint's gaze went from her to Chester's accusing glare. *If you didn't do anything to her then why are her lips all swollen?* the old man's expression seemed to say.

Instead of cowering under Chester's glare, Clint stood and returned his gaze to Alyssa. "No harm done. Besides, you are worth the wait," Clint said.

And he meant it. She was wearing one of Casey's outfits that he'd placed on the bed for her. Funny thing was, he never remembered Casey looking that good in the sundress.

"Thank you," Alyssa said.

She crossed the room to take her place at the dining room table—space usually reserved for the lady of the house. Clint wondered if she knew that. He sat down as she began easily conversing with Chester, asking how his day had been at the hospital. While setting everything on the table, Chester told her of how one of the kids had been afraid of him and how he had finally won the child over by doing magic tricks.

"Will the two of you need anything else before I go?"

"Where are you going?"

"I'm going to the bunkhouse to feed the ranch hands," the older man said and smiled.

"Oh," Alyssa said. "No, I won't need anything else."

"Neither will I," Clint tacked on, more than ready for Chester to leave the two of them alone. He had heard the catch in her voice letting him know that the thought of being alone with him made her nervous. She should be nervous, Clint thought. Whether she knew it or not, she was driving him crazy. If the outfit she was wearing wasn't bad enough, her scent was definitely getting to him, almost drugging his senses, eating away at his control. The sundress had spaghetti straps and revealed soft, creamy flesh on her arms and shoulders. It was skin he ached to feel, touch and taste. He would love to trace his tongue along her arm and work his way up to her shoulders and—

"Clint, Chester is saying something to you," Alyssa was saying.

He blinked at her words and then sent a sharp glance in Chester's direction. The old geezer had the nerve to smile as if he knew where Clint's thoughts had been.

"What?" Clint probably asked the question more roughly than he should have, but at that moment, he really felt like he was losing it.

The older man's smile widened when he said, "I was trying to get your attention to remind you that I won't be here in the morning. Snuggles the Clown is doing another performance at the hospital."

"I remember," Clint said shortly.

"Oh, by the way, Alyssa offered to do breakfast for the men in the morning," Chester said, undeterred by Clint's sour expression or gruff tone.

Clint shifted his gaze from Chester to Alyssa. "You did?"

"Yes. It's the least I can do around here," Alyssa said.

Clint frowned. "That's a lot of food to prepare. Nobody said you had to do anything around here," he said.

"I know, but everyone around here has chores. Fixing breakfast tomorrow will help me to feel useful," she replied.

"What about the work you were doing on the computer for that client?" Clint was not sure he liked the idea of her in his kitchen performing domestic tasks. There hadn't been a woman in his kitchen since Ada died.

"I'm almost done and on deadline," Alyssa said, smiling proudly.

Clint leaned back in his chair. "Well, let me know when you're ready to take on another customer. I was serious when I mentioned I needed a website for the Sid Roberts Foundation."

She lifted a brow. "And you want me to do it?"

"Only if you have the time. The next time you're in my office take a look in the side drawer on your right. There's a folder with information about the foundation

in there. If you decide to do it, we can sit down and discuss it when I get back," he said.

"Get back? Are you going someplace?"

He heard the catch in her voice again. "I'm not going
off the property so I'll still be safe in saying we were
together for the thirty days, but I'll be spending a couple
of nights under the stars on the south ridge. The horses
arrived today and the ones I've decided not to train I'll
be setting free on that designated land that's governed
by the foundation," Clint said.

"And how long will you be away from the ranch?"

He shrugged. "It usually takes a couple of days."

"Oh," Alyssa said.

"Well, folks, I'll be leaving," Chester said. Clint shot
the older man a glance. He'd forgotten he was still in
the room. He had been too focused on Alyssa and that
wasn't good.

"So, did you get a lot accomplished today?" Clint
asked as he loaded his plate with food.

Alyssa watched him and was again amazed at the
amount of food he consumed. "Yes, I put in a lot of
time doing that website. It's for a teachers' union in
Alabama."

He nodded. "How do you get your clients?"

"Word of mouth mostly. One satisfied client will tell
another. But I'm also listed in all the search engines and
that helps," she said.

"I take it that you're good at what you do," Clint said.

She glanced up and met his gaze. She hoped they
were still talking about the same thing. "Yes, I'm good.

I believe in satisfying my customers and I rarely get complaints. If you need references then I can—"

"No, I don't need references."

Conversation between them ceased again, which was fine with her since he seemed keen on eating his meal. She wondered if he still thought the taste of the meat loaf had nothing on her. It was hard to tell since he seemed to be enjoying every bite of it. But then whenever he kissed her it appeared that he tried to gobble her up, as well.

"Is something wrong?"

She blinked. "No. Why?"

"You're staring. You have a tendency to do that a lot when we eat together. Is there a reason why?"

Alyssa shifted in her seat. There was no way she could tell him that she found watching him eat fascinating… and a total turn on. He seemed to appreciate every piece he put into his mouth. And the way he would take his time to chew it, methodically getting all he could from each bite, let her know he would make love to her the same way. Given the chance, Clint would savor her in the same way that he ate. Goose bumps formed on her arms at the thought of it.

"No reason," she said after pausing for a moment to gather her thoughts. "It's just that I'm totally in awe of how much you eat."

He lifted a brow. "And I'm in awe as to how little you eat. You remind me of Casey. She eats like a bird, as well," he said.

She heard the fondness in his voice for his sibling.

"I appreciate your sharing her clothes with me. I hope she won't mind," she said.

"She won't," he said, effectively closing discussion on the subject. "Will you be using the computer later?"

"No," she said, shaking her head. "I'm through for the day. I thought I might look through that folder you were telling me about on your uncle's foundation. Why?"

"Because I need to use it to log in the information on the horses we got in today," he said. He glanced at his watch as he pushed his plate aside. It was clean. "I play cards with the men on Wednesday night so I'll be leaving the house again after logging in that information. And I won't be back until way after midnight," he said with a smile. "I'm telling you this just in case you want to play another game on the computer later. I promise not to interrupt you this time."

"This is your house, Clint. You have free rein of any place in it."

He cocked his head and looked at her. "Even your bedroom?"

The glint in his eyes indicated that he was teasing her. At least she hoped he was.

"No. According to our agreement bedrooms are off-limits," she said.

"Um, that really doesn't bother me. The bedroom is one of the places I least like for making love," he said slyly.

She suddenly felt like she was under the influence of some sort of drug. Sensations were surging through her, touching all parts of her body, but especially the area between her thighs.

"What is your favorite place?" she couldn't help asking.

Alyssa stared as he put his glass of lemonade down. His gaze was intent on holding hers. She tried fighting it but she was being pulled into his sensuous web.

He smiled and that smile, like his words, touched her all over. It added kerosene to her already blazing fire. "Before the thirty days are up," he said in a deep, throaty voice, as his gaze held hers, "I intend to show you."

An hour or so later Alyssa stood at her bedroom window and watched as Clint walked across the yard to the bunkhouse, which meant his office was empty again. She needed to think and wanted a quiet place to do so. His office was the perfect place.

The man was getting to her in a big way and he was doing so with a degree of confident arrogance that astounded her. He wasn't pushy or demanding. He wasn't even using manipulating tactics. He was merely being his own sexy self.

Before the thirty days are up, I intend to show you.

Those words were still ringing in her ears, still causing an ache in parts of her body that aches had never invaded before. The area between her thighs was actually throbbing. Clint had basically assured her that he would make love to her at some point before she left his ranch. Such a statement was bold, bigheaded…and heaven help her, probably true.

She inhaled sharply. *How could she of all people,*

someone who rebuffed men's sexual advances with mediocre kindness, even contemplate such a thing happening? She was not only contemplating it, Alyssa was actually anticipating it.

She shook her head to clear it, needing to focus mainly on the facts. Clint Westmoreland was the sexiest man she had ever seen in clothes, so naturally a part of her—the feminine part—couldn't help wondering what he looked like without clothes. That kind of curiosity was new for her.

Then there was the way Clint carried himself. He had a self-assured nature that was very attractive. And lastly, she couldn't downplay the fact that since meeting him, she experienced an all-consuming desire that had invaded her entire body. It wasn't in her normal routine to lust after a man but she was definitely lusting after Clint Westmoreland.

She turned away from the window, her mind stricken by what she was thinking, her body shaken by what it needed. The couple of times she had made love with Kevin, it hadn't done anything for her. She hadn't felt the earth shake and she hadn't experienced the feeling of coming out of her skin. In fact, she had been inwardly counting the minutes when it would be over. Was it possible an experience with Clint would be just the opposite? Would it be one she wouldn't want to end? Such thoughts made her draw in a shaky breath.

As she crossed the room and slipped between the cool covers of the bed, she had a feeling that sleep wouldn't come easily for her tonight, especially since the aches in her body wouldn't go away.

By the time she finally closed her eyes, she was convinced that dreaming about all the things Clint could do to her wasn't sufficient. She wanted to experience the real thing.

Chapter 8

The next morning Alyssa entered the kitchen to find Clint already sitting at the table drinking coffee. She frowned. She had hoped to get up before him and have breakfast started.

"Chester said he usually doesn't start cooking until around five o'clock. You're up early," she said, glancing at him while going straight to the sink to wash her hands.

A smile touched the corners of his lips as he shrugged one broad shoulder. "I thought I'd have a cup of coffee while watching you work," he said.

She raised her chin defiantly. "You don't think I can handle things?" Alyssa asked in an accusing tone.

"Oh, trust me. I believe you can handle things. Chester wouldn't let you in his kitchen if he thought otherwise. I just wanted to watch you do it and offer my help if you need it," he said.

"Thanks."

"Don't mention it."

A short while later Alyssa wondered if she'd been too quick to give Clint her thanks. Each time she moved around the kitchen she felt his eyes on her and had a feeling his intense stares had nothing to do with her culinary skills. She was dressed in another of the outfits belonging to his sister. This one was a pair of jeans and a top. He'd been right. She and Casey were about the same size and so far everything she'd tried on fit perfectly.

She turned around from the stove to tell him that everything was ready and her gaze collided with his. She saw something flicker in the dark depths of his eyes and that fiery light sent a burning sensation through her middle. She swallowed the lump in her throat. "Everything is ready."

Then, following Chester's instructions, she called the foreman at the bunkhouse to let him know the meal was ready to be picked up. She had prepared enough food to feed at least fifty people and was grateful for all those times she had helped Aunt Claudine and the other older ladies at church prepare meals for the homeless.

She hung up the phone only to find Clint standing only inches away from her and her pulse rate escalated. He was the epitome of handsome and radiated a sex appeal she couldn't deal with this early in the morning.

"You did an outstanding job," he said, and the sound

of his voice only added to her discomfort. Alyssa began to feel a tingling sensation all over.

She tried playing off the feeling. "Save your compliment until after you've tasted it," she tried saying lightly.

He smiled. "Don't have to. I watched you. You definitely know your way around the kitchen."

She chuckled. "Thanks to Aunt Claudine, I would have to agree. I helped her out with feeding the homeless at least once a week. I never thought doing so would come in handy one day," she said heartily. "It felt good doing it. Chester has everything so well organized. This kitchen is a cook's dream."

"And you, Alyssa Barkley, are a man's dream," he said in a low voice.

He leaned forward and she knew he was going to kiss her. Just then she heard the sound of footsteps on the back porch. She took a step back.

"The guys are coming for the food," she said softly.

"So I hear," he said silkily and took a step back, as well. He glanced at his watch. "It's time for me to go, anyway."

"You're not going to stay and eat breakfast?" she asked quickly, before she could stop herself. Alyssa prayed he hadn't heard the disappointment in her voice.

"I'm going to eat with the men in the bunkhouse before leaving." And then before she could blink, he had recovered the steps and placed a tender kiss on her lips. "I'll see you in a couple of days."

Alyssa nodded, thinking she could definitely use two

days without him hovering about. She would have two full days to get her head screwed back on right.

That first day Alyssa was still convinced that distance was just what she needed from Clint. She was glad he would be away from the ranch. Once her boxes had arrived, she'd taken the time to unpack. Her aunt had sent her everything she needed, from an adequate supply of clothes for the chilly days of February yet to come, to a sufficient supply of underwear.

By the second day Alyssa found herself glancing out the window wondering if perhaps Clint would return a day early—even though she tried to convince herself that she really didn't want him to. She enjoyed her talks with Chester and a few of the ranch hands who had remained behind.

On the third day, Alyssa paced the floor in his office when she couldn't sit still long enough to work at the computer. And every time she heard a commotion outside the window she found herself racing toward it to see if it was Clint returning. By late evening after sharing dinner with Chester, she found herself standing on the front porch staring out into the distance. She was reminded of a woman standing on the shore waiting for her man to return from the sea. The comparison struck her. For the first time since coming to Austin, she began to realize that her emotions were getting too deep. It was becoming obvious to Alyssa that she was developing feelings for Clint.

She sighed deeply, knowing it didn't make sense. They had been reunited just days ago. The only excuse

she could come up with was that Clint Westmoreland—
with his arrogant confidence and untamed sensuality—
was more virile than Kevin could ever hope to be. She
hadn't been involved with a man since that fateful
day—her wedding day.

Finding out Kevin had been unfaithful had been a
blow, but what had been even more of a shocker was
the very idea that he felt they should forget what he'd
done and move on. She couldn't move on. Instead she
had sought to protect her heart from further damage
the only way she knew how—avoid any personal deal-
ings with men. She had responded in just the way Kim
had counted on.

Alyssa had long ago accepted that her cousin didn't
want her to be happy and didn't want Alyssa to have
a man in her life. The thought of Alyssa having a man
who loved her, who wanted to give her his world and his
babies was something Kim was determined to prevent.

She knew Aunt Claudine was right when she would
say that she needed to move on and not give Kim the
victory. But she hadn't met a man worthy of such a
task…until now.

Clint Westmoreland made her want to take a chance
on living again in a way she had denied herself for almost two years. And even if it was only for the time she
stayed on his ranch, she knew that she wouldn't have to
worry about Kim being around to sabotage her relationship with Clint. Alyssa was smart enough to know that
any relationship that she developed with him wouldn't
last. At the end of the thirty days he would want her
gone, off his ranch and out of his life.

In the past, Alyssa had avoided casual relationships, but for some reason she didn't see the time that she would spend with Clint as a casual fling. It would be more than that. Indulging in pleasure seemed a fitting term for their relationship. She considered her feelings for Clint a reawakening. If she had an affair with him, it would be a way to rebuild her self-esteem and regain her confidence as a woman. It would also be a way to enjoy life before returning to the mundane existence she'd carved out for herself in Waco.

"Nice night, isn't it?"

Alyssa was pulled out of her reverie when Chester walked out onto the porch. She was discovering each and every day just how much she liked the older man. He was loyal to Clint and his siblings to a fault and she liked that. It reminded her so much of how her relationship with her grandfather had been and the relationship she shared with her aunt now.

"It is a nice night," she said simply. She knew he was perceptive enough to figure out why she was outside standing on the porch in the dark and his next statement proved it.

"Sometimes it takes longer than the two days to set free the horses. Some of them can get real frisky when they are taken out of their element. I bet the reason Clint hasn't returned yet is because he'd had his hands full."

Alyssa sensed that Chester was telling her that Clint hadn't been staying away from the ranch just to avoid her. *How had Chester known that was exactly what she had been thinking?*

Alyssa smiled as she pulled the jacket she was wearing more tightly around her shoulders. February was proving to be a colder month than January.

"Clint said that your grandfather used to be a bronco rider," Chester said.

"Yes, he was. In fact that's how he met Sid Roberts. It was an experience he took pride in telling me about while growing up."

"You were close to him," Chester said.

"Yes, he was the most special person in my life."

Less than an hour later when getting ready for bed, Alyssa remembered those words and knew in her heart that Clint was becoming a special person to her, as well.

Clint almost weakened as he gazed down at a sleeping Alyssa. A stream of light from a lamppost poured into her window and illuminated her features. He wasn't sure what she was wearing under the bedspread because her body was completely covered, but she looked incredibly sexy.

Okay, he had broken their agreement and had come into her bedroom. He'd done so because Chester had told him that she had stood outside on the porch that night waiting for him to return.

At first Clint hadn't wanted to believe it, but then a part of him realized that the possibility existed that she had indeed missed him…like he had missed her. Clint stiffened at the thought that he could miss any woman, but whether he liked it or not, he had. And she had constantly invaded his dreams since she'd come to the ranch. He didn't like that, either.

How could she get to him so deep and so quickly?

He'd had other women since Chantelle, but none of them had made a lasting impression. None of them had even come close. But Alyssa was making more than a lasting impression. She was carving a niche right under his skin and it got deeper and deeper each and every time he saw her.

He studied Alyssa when she made a sound in her sleep. A lock of her hair had fallen onto her face. He leaned down and brushed the tendril back, careful not to wake her. He sighed knowing he had no right to be there, but also knowing that he would not have been able to sleep a wink if he had not looked in on her. He also knew his presence in her bedroom was about more than that. It was about wanting to be close to Alyssa.

He hated knowing how much he had wanted to see her and be with her. Clint fervently hoped that by the morning he would have regained control of the situation. He had to get whatever emotions he was battling in check and start putting her at a distance.

He frowned as he turned to leave the room and contemplated his plan of action with difficulty. It would mean more days spent away from the ranch. That had been his plan in the beginning. *Then why did the thought of following through with his original strategy leave such a bitter taste in his mouth?*

Upon awaking the next morning, Alyssa heard a group of men talking not far from her bedroom window. She got out of her bed and slipped into her robe before crossing the floor to the window and glancing out. Her heart nearly stopped beating. The three men she saw were among those who had left the ranch with Clint, which could only mean he had returned, as well. She couldn't help the smile that covered her lips as she headed for the bathroom.

Less than thirty minutes later she was dressed and eager to get down to breakfast before Clint left for the day. She felt a burning desire to see him, come face-to-face with him and get all into his space. She looked at herself one last time in the mirror before she left the room. She didn't look bad in her jeans and shirt, she thought with a smile. She also wore the new boots she had purchased the day before yesterday when she'd caught a ride into town with Chester. Alyssa felt like a bona fide cowgirl.

She breathed in deeply and with shaking hands she reached to open her bedroom door. Alyssa hoped that by the time she made it to the kitchen her heart would no longer be beating so wildly in her chest. It would be a struggle to keep it together knowing Clint was back and they would be once again breathing the same air.

She opened the door to step out into the hallway and her heart caught. Standing there, leaning against the opposite wall as if he'd been waiting for her, was Clint. Alyssa was speechless. And before she could open her mouth to utter a single word, he moved from the spot, pulled her into his arms and kissed her, devouring her mouth with an urgency that astounded her.

Alyssa sagged against him and wrapped her arms around his neck as his mouth and tongue continued plundering hers. She didn't think about struggling to keep herself together or trying to gain any semblance of control of the situation. The only thing she could think about was that he was back. He was here. And he was taking her mouth with a hunger that meant he had missed her to the same degree she had missed him. That thought made her giddy.

Everything was forgotten. How she had intended to protect her heart from further damage, and how she had decided at some point during the night to retreat back into her hands-off strategy. All her concentration was on the intense arousal overtaking her belly as she kissed Clint with the same fervor and passion that he was kissing her.

And then when he finally released her mouth, he didn't let go of her lips. He took the tip of his tongue and outlined a sensuous path from one corner to the other, over and over again. Alyssa heard herself groan. She actually felt her panties get wet. Clint had the ability to reach down, deep inside of her, to a place no man had gone for two years. He was stirring up a need, one as intense as anything she had ever encountered.

"I've got to go," Clint whispered against her moist lips. The deep, raspy tone of his voice knocked down the last reserve of strength she was trying to hold on to.

"Breakfast?" she asked. The only word she could get her lips to form.

"I've already eaten. I need to be on that back pasture. I'll be gone all day and wanted to see you before I left. I wanted to taste you."

His words made every single cell in her body multiply with excitement. Then, as if the kiss they'd just shared would not be enough to sustain him through the day, he took hold of her mouth with lightning speed once more. She returned the kiss. She hadn't been aware that she was so starved for such male interaction until now, but not interaction from just any male. She wanted it only from Clint.

When he finally released her mouth she knew her lips would be swollen again. Anyone seeing her would know why, but at the moment she didn't care.

"I have to go," he said again, and as if fighting the urge to take her into his arms yet again, he stepped back. He stared at her for a long moment before reaching out and gently touching her swollen lips with his fingertips. "I promised myself last night that I wouldn't do this," he said in a low, throaty voice. "But I can't seem to help it. You, Alyssa Barkley, are more of a temptation than I counted on you being."

Without giving her a chance to say anything he turned and she watched him walk away.

"Hey, boss, are you okay?" one of Clint's men inquired some hours later as he was saddling one of the horses.

Clint glanced up at Walter Pockets, frowned and said gruffly, "I'm fine. Why do you ask?"

The man, who had only been working for him a couple of years, hesitated. "Well, because you're putting the saddle on backward," he said.

"Damn," Clint said and quickly removed the saddle. He placed it on the horse's back correctly, grateful that only Pockets had seen him make such a blunder. "My mind was elsewhere," he said. He knew that was a lame excuse. He would be the first to get on his men if they were to let their minds wander while performing even a menial task. Working on a ranch required focus. And yet, he was not focused at all today.

"I can ride out and check on things if you want me to," Pockets said.

Clint thought about the man's offer. It was almost lunchtime already. He had pretty much decided to stay out on the range and eat with his men, but now he was thinking differently. Kissing Alyssa had not gotten her out of his system. Instead it seemed that each time their lips connected she was getting even more embedded under his skin. Yet he could no more seize an opportunity to kiss her than he could stop breathing.

"Thanks, Pockets," he finally heard himself say. "I'd appreciate it if you would. I've got a matter up at the house I need to take care of." That was saying it as honestly as he could.

Less than thirty minutes later he was walking into the kitchen. Chester glanced up from stirring a pot with a surprised look on his face. "I didn't expect you back until late tonight."

Clint shrugged. "I finished early. Where's Alyssa? Is she in my office?"

"No, she asked if she could borrow the truck to go into town. She said she was going to take a shower, so I guess she's in her bedroom getting dressed."

The thought of a naked Alyssa standing under a spray of water got him even more unfocused and aroused and he was grateful to be standing behind the kitchen table.

Wondering why Alyssa needed to go into town, Clint headed toward his office.

"Maybe you ought to think about going with her," he heard Chester say. Clint drew up short and turned around.

"Why should I think about doing something like that?"

Chester smiled. "Because you could help her with all those bags and boxes she plans to bring back."

Clint frowned. "What bags and boxes?"

"From shopping. I figure she's going into town to do some shopping," Chester said.

Clint folded his arms over his chest. "Why in the hell would I want to accompany any woman shopping?"

Chester chuckled. "That would give you a chance to spend time with her under the pretense of being helpful. And don't insult my intelligence by asking why I think you'd want to spend time with her, Clint. I saw her lips at breakfast."

Clint's frown deepened. "And?"

"And I think you need to go easy on them," the older man said with a sly chuckle.

Clint honestly didn't think he could. Instead of telling that to Chester he turned and walked out of the kitchen.

"Where are the keys to the truck, Chester?" Alyssa asked, glancing around. She could have sworn when Chester had given them to her earlier she had placed them on the top of the breakfast bar.

"Clint has them," Chester said.

She whirled around with a surprised look on her face. "Clint?"

"Yep," Chester answered without looking up from stirring the pot on the stove.

"Oh. I thought he was going to be gone all day," Alyssa said.

The older man did manage to smile. "Yeah, I thought so, too, but I guess he had a change in plans."

"Does that mean he needs to use the truck?"

"No," Chester said, chuckling. "I think it means that he's going into town with you."

Alyssa swallowed the lump in her throat. "Are you sure?"

"Positive. In fact he's waiting outside for you," Chester said.

Alyssa knew she looked startled, but Chester wouldn't know because he didn't seem to be paying attention to her. He was focused on his cooking.

"Well, I guess I'll see you in an hour or so," she said, glancing at her watch.

"Don't count on it," Chester said.

"Excuse me?" she responded, not sure she had heard Chester correctly.

"Nothing," the older man said.

Alyssa eyed Chester in confusion, certain that he had said something. However, instead of questioning him further, on wobbly legs she headed toward the living room to leave. *Why would Clint want to accompany her into town? Had he gotten a call from Hightower? Surely he would have told her if he had.*

She stopped short of opening the door, needing to

pull herself together. This would be the first time she saw him since their morning kiss. It was a kiss from which she still hadn't fully recovered. And she had assumed that since he would be away from the ranch all day and she wouldn't see him again until tomorrow at the earliest, that she would have time to compose her senses.

Taking a deep breath, she opened the door and saw Clint standing in the yard. He was leaning against his truck and her stomach became filled with butterflies when she realized that he was waiting for her.

She was careful walking down the steps, trying not to trip. She was amazingly aware of the appraisal he was giving her with his dark, intense eyes. He was looking her up and down, from the top of her head to the toes of her booted feet.

She decided to return the favor and check him out, as well. She saw that he'd taken the time to shower and change, too. He looked good enough to eat leaning against the truck in a pair of jeans and a blue chambray shirt. His legs were crossed at his booted ankles and he wore a black cowboy hat on his head. He was the epitome of sexy, the essence of what she definitely considered a fine man and the personification of everything male.

As she walked up to him she saw desire in his eyes and she took a misstep. He reached out and caught her arm and brought her closer to him. The front of their bodies touched and his lips were mere inches from hers.

"Are you okay?" he asked in a low, husky tone.

She wanted to tell him that no, she wasn't okay, and

she wouldn't fully recuperate until she left his ranch for good. In the meantime, for the first time in her life she was beginning to think about all the things she could get into while she was there. And when she left, she would have solid, red-hot memories to hold on to during the night while lying in her bed alone. "Yes, I'm fine," she finally managed to say.

In response, as quick as a cricket, he swiped his tongue across her lips just seconds before releasing her. She blinked, not sure he'd done it until she felt the wetness he had left behind.

"Ready to go?" he asked in a husky voice, transferring his hold from her arm to her hand. The feel of his touch had her heart thudding in her chest.

"Yes, I am," she said.

He opened the truck door for her and she slid inside. He stood there a moment and she wondered if he was going to kiss her again. He leaned closer but instead of kissing her he snapped the seat belt into place around her hips.

"Thanks," she barely managed to get out.

He smiled. "No problem." And then he straightened and closed the door.

With almost stiff fingers she clutched her purse as she watched him walk around the front of the truck to get inside while whistling a tune she wasn't familiar with. Then he was buckling up his own seat belt and starting the engine. "Where to?" he looked over and asked her.

Her eyebrow arched. He definitely seemed to be in a good mood. "You're taking time away from your busy schedule to be my personal chauffeur," she said as a grin touched lips that were still warm and wet from his kiss.

He grinned back. "I guess you could say that. When I heard you were going to do some shopping in town I decided that now was a good time to get that new belt that I need."

"Oh." But that didn't explain why he was back at the ranch when he had mentioned that morning he would be gone all day. Alyssa decided it really didn't matter why he had altered his plans. He had and she was glad about it.

"So where to first?" he asked her again.

"What about the Highland Mall?" she asked. That particular mall had been her favorite when she lived in Austin as a Ranger.

"The Highland Mall it is."

She settled back in her seat, anticipating how the rest of the day would pan out.

Chapter 9

It was late afternoon before Clint and Alyssa returned to the ranch. In addition to shopping, Clint had suggested they see a movie. He could tell that Alyssa had been surprised by his suggestion. There were ten movies showing and they had narrowed their selections down to two. They couldn't decide which of the two to see, so they ended up viewing both.

Clint had enjoyed Alyssa's company immensely. He'd discovered several new facets of her character. For instance, Alyssa loved Mexican food and she was thrilled about her work as a web designer. During the course of the day, she'd explained the process of setting up a website and how each design was tailored to the individual needs of each client. She'd also gone into detail about search engines and how invaluable they were to anyone who frequented the internet.

They ate lunch at the mall food court and he had enjoyed watching her eat every single bite of her meal. In fact, he had gotten turned on just from watching her eat. *Was that crazy or what?*

And another thing that was crazy was that he had enjoyed being with her while she shopped. In his opinion, she was a smart shopper. He had definitely learned a lot today about working a clearance rack.

"So where do you want these bags and boxes?" he asked as he followed her into the house.

"You can carry them into my bedroom."

He glanced over at her and grinned. "Is that an invitation?"

She shook her head and grinned back. "You may enter my bedroom this time, but only to deliver my packages, Clint."

As they walked together down the wide hallway that turned off into the wing where she was staying, a part of him regretted his decision to make sure the guest room she used was so far from his bedroom.

"Did I tell you how nice you look today?" he asked softly as they neared her bedroom.

She glanced over at him. "Thank you."

He could tell his compliment had caught her off guard. When they reached the bedroom, he stood back while she led him in. "You can place everything on the bed."

"Sure," he said. He had come into the bedroom last night while she had slept and the memory of seeing her so relaxed and at peace sent sensations of desire spiraling through him now.

After placing the items on the bed, he turned and saw her watching him. And there it was again. He had felt it all day around her—the spark, sizzle and steam that seemed to emanate between them. He knew she was aware of it, too.

"I believe this one is yours," she said, retrieving a single bag from the bed and offering it to him.

"My belt," he said and chuckled.

He took the bag and then gently pulled her to him. He saw the flicker of passion in the depths of her eyes. "I always say I'm not going to kiss you and end up doing it anyway," he said.

"Why?"

A smile touched his expression. "I've told you why. Do you want me to remind you?"

"Yes, why not?" she teased.

He leaned into her, let her feel the evidence of his desire that was pressed hard against her. He spread the palms of his hands at the center of her back, bringing her closer to the fit of him. "Should I say more?" he asked in a voice that sounded deeper to his own ears.

She held his gaze. "Yes, say more," she said daringly.

He leaned over and licked her cheek with the tip of his tongue. "I like tasting you and one of these days, Alyssa, I plan on tasting you all over."

He heard her sharp intake of breath. He was being blunt, but he was also being truthful. Things couldn't continue between them at the rate they were going. They hadn't made it to their second week together and already things were almost sizzling out of control. Hadn't Chester just today hinted that he should go easy on her lips? As if he ever really could.

"Remember our agreement," she said in a quiet voice.

"I remember it," he said, still holding her close. "Do you?"

She tilted her head up and looked at him. "Yes, I do."

"You're the one who initiated this, Alyssa, and you're the only one who can finish it. I will adhere to our agreement as long as you want me to," he said.

"B-but what about all these insinuations you're making?" she whispered accusingly.

He smiled, thinking about all he had said. "What about them?"

She studied his features and then evidently decided he wasn't serious. "You're teasing me," she said.

"No," he said. "I'm not teasing. I'm dead serious."

As if tired of what she perceived as his game-playing, she lifted her chin and said, "You can't have it both ways, Clint."

He laughed although his features were without humor. "Sweetheart, when I finally have you, I plan on having it in ways I've only recently dreamed of." And as if to prove his point, his thighs moved at the same time he pressed gently in the curve of her back to bring her closer to him.

He then leaned down and placed a gentle kiss on her lips and felt himself harden even more. "I'll see you at dinner."

"I'm skipping dinner tonight," Alyssa replied.

"Not because of me, I hope," he said in a low tone.

"No," she said tightly. "Because of me."

* * *

Alyssa stretched out on the bed. It was nearly midnight. She had taken a shower and changed into one of many oversize T-shirts she enjoyed sleeping in.

Good to her word, she had skipped dinner because she needed to be away from Clint. She had called her aunt earlier and they had chatted awhile. Luckily, Aunt Claudine hadn't asked her anything about Clint and Alyssa had had no reason to bring him up.

Chester had knocked on her door earlier to make sure she really didn't want anything to eat and had even offered to serve dinner to her in her room if she preferred. She had assured him she was fine and she wasn't hungry. She figured Chester thought the reason she was missing dinner was because of a tiff she'd had with Clint, which wasn't the truth. She just needed distance from him right now. He had the tendency to prevent her from thinking straight. He would say things with such conceit that he rattled her confidence. He seemed so sure of her when she wasn't sure of herself, she thought.

Her cell phone rang and she frowned wondering who would be calling her at this hour. Aunt Claudine was usually in bed by nine. She sat up and reached for the phone. Her frown deepened when she saw the caller indicated Kim was on the line. She wondered how Kim had gotten her number. There was no way Aunt Claudine would have given it to her.

"Yes?" She decided it was time to stop avoiding her cousin.

"Well, well, for a moment I thought you had dropped off the face of the earth," Kim said.

Alyssa rolled her eyes. "What do you want, Kim?"

"Where are you?"

"It doesn't matter to you. What do you want?"

"Everyone is wondering where you are. You just took off without telling anyone," Kim said smartly.

"I did tell someone," Alyssa replied.

"Yeah, we figured Aunt Claudine knew where you are but she isn't talking. All she's saying is that you left town to go visit a client."

"Whatever," Alyssa said, sidestepping Kim's attempts to get more information.

"Really, Alyssa, don't you think it's time for me and you to sit down and have a little chat? I'm sick and tired of you blaming me because you can't keep a man. It's not my fault that they end up finding you inadequate and prefer me to you," Kim said.

"Look, Kim, I have to go."

"And you're not going to tell me where you are?"

"No."

"Suit yourself."

"I will. Goodbye and please don't call back." Alyssa then hung up the phone.

Inhaling deeply, she swung her legs off the bed as she fought back the anger she felt. Overconfident people were wearing on her nerves, although she had to admit that Kim was very different from Clint. She couldn't imagine Clint ever deliberately hurting anyone. Deciding she needed to work off some of her negative energy, she decided to slip into Clint's office to play a game on his computer.

It was late and chances were he was in bed asleep by now. At least she hoped so. She opened her bedroom door and, as expected, the entire house was quiet. She appreciated the night-lights that lined the hallway as she made her way from her wing toward the one where Clint's office was located. As far as she knew, they were the only ones living in the main house. Chester lived a few miles away in a house on land Sid Roberts had willed to him.

Alyssa slowly opened the office door and found the room empty. She quickly moved across the room to Clint's desk. Kim's words had put her on edge. She was still fuming while waiting for the computer to boot up.

She turned when a knock sounded on the door. She went still when Clint walked in. Closing the door behind him, he leaned against it.

Alyssa tried not to let her focus linger on his dark eyes, but when she moved her gaze to his strong jawline and kissable lips she realized she was in trouble looking there, too. She returned her gaze to his.

"I thought you were asleep," she said when she finally found her voice.

A smile touched the corners of his lips. "As you can see I'm very much awake."

Yes, she could definitely see that. She could also see in his nonchalant stance against the door just how perfectly his jeans fit his body, and with his chambray shirt open past the throat, she got a glimpse of his hairy, muscular chest. But what really caught her attention was the area below the belt. Not only was Clint very much awake, he was very much aroused, as well.

The thought that he wanted her was enough of a reason for her heart to pound and her pulse to drum. If that wasn't bad enough, her lips began tingling from remembered kisses. She already had a number of them tucked away in her memory bank.

She swallowed deeply as desire began to thrum through her and felt her body automatically respond to his. "Is there a reason why you're here?" she asked, hearing the slight quiver in her voice.

"Yes," he said in an arrogant tone as he moved away from the door and slowly strolled toward her.

From the glow of light off the computer screen she was conscious of every single thing about him, including the dark pupils in his eyes and the faint growth of stubble on his chin.

When he reached the edge of the desk he placed his hands palms down as he leaned closer and brought his face mere inches from hers.

"Tonight," he whispered against her lips, "I want to teach you another version of 'Playing with Fire.'"

Alyssa slowly backed away. She then tilted her head and looked up at him. "You agreed," she reminded him in an accusing voice, one she could barely force past her lips.

"I agreed not to seduce you into my bed, Alyssa," he said. He momentarily released her gaze to glance around the room. "There's not one bed in here," he said.

She tilted her head a half inch higher. "You don't need a bed to do what you want to do. You've said so yourself," she said defiantly.

He smiled. "Yes, I did say that and it's true," he said in a husky voice. "To make love to you I don't need a bed. But you'll have to be willing, Alyssa. I would never force myself on you."

She believed him. But she also knew it wouldn't take much coercing on his part right now. He had become her weakness.

"I won't do anything you don't want me to do. Come play with me," he said throatily. "Trust me," he added as he offered her his hand.

The look in his eyes stirred her in a way she would not have thought possible and without realizing she was doing so, she began leaning toward him. And when she reached out and placed her hand in his, she knew she had literally sealed her fate.

Clint Westmoreland was demanding more of her than she had ever shared with any man. She was taking a risk, opening her heart up in a way she had never done with Kevin. And as she continued to gaze into the turbulent darkness of his eyes she suddenly knew why. Not only did she trust him, she had fallen in love with him, as well.

She was not going to waste her time wondering how it happened, or why it had happened. She was willing to accept that it had happened…just as she was willing to accept it would be a one-sided love affair that would lead nowhere. At the end of the thirty days she would be leaving. But at this very moment, she had tonight and wanted to take full advantage of it.

"I do trust you, Clint," she finally said softly. "Teach me how to play your game."

Chapter 10

Still holding her hand in his, Clint moved around the desk to gently pull her up from her seat and into his arms. He knew she had to see the desire flaring in his eyes, had to know from his aroused state just how much he wanted her. And he did want her and had from the first, when he'd seen her at the airport.

Leaning slightly, he took the liberty to place his open hands over her bottom, bringing her closer to him, and groaned through clenched teeth when he felt her softness come to rest against his hardness. Desire ripped into him, adding to the heat that was already there.

"Alyssa." He moaned her name just moments before covering her mouth with his, devouring with an intensity that shook him to the core. He'd become familiar with her taste, the very essence of her flavor, and each time his mouth was reacquainted with it, one part of him wanted to savor it slowly, while the other part wanted to devour her whole.

He was too far gone to savor yet he refused to be rushed. He wanted to make their passion something she would enjoy. That way she would let him make love to her again…and again…and again.

In his mind, nothing about their relationship had changed. They were just taking things to the next level. They were adults and they would be able to handle it. They would make no promises, just pleasure. In thirty days, their marriage would be annulled and Alyssa would leave. His life would continue just the way it had before getting that fateful letter from the bureau. For some reason the thought of Alyssa leaving made him feel uneasy.

She pushed against his chest so he could release her mouth and when he saw her lips he understood why. Already they looked thoroughly kissed. "Don't know just how much of that I can handle," she whispered, trying to catch her breath.

He knew he could kiss her in other ways and was anxious to explore those options with her. In his mind, the game of playing with fire was basically doing just that, and he was curious to see just how much heat she could handle.

"Come with me," he said as he led her over to the sofa. He sat down and then pulled her down in his lap. Immediately, he brushed a feathery kiss on the top of her head. When he saw her trying to pull the T-shirt she was wearing down to cover her exposed thighs, he stilled her hands.

"Don't," he whispered.

He reached out his hand to stroke her flesh there, liking the feel of her soft skin. From that first day he had enjoyed looking at her legs. But lately she had covered them up with jeans. The jeans she wore always emphasized her womanly curves, so he'd had no reason to complain, until now.

In fact, when it came to Alyssa, he was unable to find fault with anything. The only thing that gave him reason to pause was her unwillingness to discuss her family at any great length. He had tried getting her to talk about them while they were at the mall, but she hadn't had a lot to say. He couldn't help but wonder what they thought of her living with him for thirty days. Had she told them the full story like he had told his siblings? he wondered.

Cole had called earlier tonight from Mexico where he'd been for the past month on assignment. Like with Casey, Chester hadn't wasted any time sharing the news. It didn't come as a surprise that Cole had thought the situation rather amusing. Cole said he was glad it was Clint caught in that predicament and not him. Cole had claimed that he was too much of a ladies' man to be tied down to just one woman. The first question his brother had asked was if Alyssa was pretty. Clint had assured him that she was.

"Are you sure you don't want to keep her around?" Cole had asked.

Clint's response had been quick and resounding. "I'm positive. At the end of the thirty days she's out of here."

"Clint?"

The sound of Alyssa's voice pulled him from his reverie. He realized his hand had moved higher on her thigh. He smiled when he answered her. "Yes?"

"What are you going to do to me?" she whispered, tilting her head back to look at him.

In an amazingly calm voice, he said, "I'm going to introduce you to another version of 'Playing with Fire,' but the object of the game will remain the same. My goal is to blow you up and, baby, I'm about to make you explode all over the place."

He murmured the words against her lips and felt them quiver beneath his. He then shifted her position in his lap to remove her T-shirt and wasn't surprised to find her completely naked underneath her nightclothes. She said she trusted him; now he would see just how much.

He stood with her in his arms and then laid her back on the sofa, fully open to his view. His gaze slid over her, lingering on her breasts, the gold ring in her navel, her womanly core and her long, beautiful legs.

"You are beautiful," he whispered, barely able to get the words out. Entranced, fascinated and totally captivated, he slowly dropped down to his knees in front of her, needing to touch her, taste her all over.

He reached out and his fingers immediately went to her breasts, cupping them in his hands before leaning closer to let the tip of his tongue taste the curve of her throat. Then he pulled back and watched his fingertips swirl around a budded nipple, feeling it pucker beneath his touch.

A soft moan escaped her lips and he saw she had closed her eyes, was biting on her lower lip. Little did she know he hadn't even gotten started.

"How does my touch feel, Alyssa?" he asked in a low voice as he continued drawing circles around her nipples with his fingertips.

"Good," she murmured in a voice so low he could barely hear her.

"Do you like it?"

"Yes," she responded and it seemed her words had been an effort. She refused to open her eyes to look at him.

He then slowly moved his hands, lowering them to her stomach, skimming the taut skin there. She felt soft to the touch and he smiled at the ring in her navel.

He eased his hand between her open thighs and heard her sharp intake of breath when he nudged her thighs even farther apart, wanting to touch and explore her everywhere. His fingers dipped inside of her. She was wet, drenched, and her scent consumed him totally.

Fighting the urge to taste her, he removed his hand from her and let his fingers travel downward past her knees and then to her beautiful feet. There wasn't a part of her he wanted left untouched.

"Now for the taste test," he whispered, determined to taste Alyssa's first orgasm on his lips.

She opened her eyes and stared at him. "I don't think I can handle much more."

He smiled. "You can. Trust me."

She nodded and he leaned forward and captured her nipples in his mouth. And things started from there. Never had he wanted to taste a woman so badly, and he went about showing her how much. She looked so sensual and sexy that intense emotions tore into him as he moved his mouth lower to the area he craved.

She let out another deep groan the moment he lowered his head between her legs, and when the tip of his tongue touched her she nearly came off the sofa. But he had no intentions of letting her go. He pulled back only long enough to shift her body to place her legs over his shoulders. He was filled with a primitive sexual energy that was consuming him. He intended to transfer that energy to her in this very intimate way.

He tightened his hold on her hips and lowered his mouth to her and immediately found his mark, capturing her womanly core, locking his mouth to it. She tasted sweet. She released a litany of moans and arched her back and he greedily began tormenting her with his tongue.

Her body was on fire, he could feel it. She was on the verge of exploding. He could feel that, as well. His grip tightened on her hips when she let out a scream and he continued to hungrily stroke her with his tongue, enjoying the way she was pushing her body against his mouth.

God, she was responsive, completely filled with passion, a fantasy come true. And when she couldn't take any more and blew up, when an explosion racked her body, he continued to give her a hard kiss. He felt his own loins about to burst and fought back for control. This was her time. His time would come later.

Tonight was for her.

When the last quake left her body, he pulled her into his arms and kissed her. He would give her time to recover and then he intended to perform the process all over again.

Sitting across the room at his desk, Clint's gaze encompassed Alyssa, who was knocked out on his sofa. He smiled, thinking that too much passion could definitely do that to a person. Deciding he wanted to let her sleep but didn't want to leave her alone, he decided to pass the time browsing the internet.

First he checked out the website that advertised her company and was impressed with what he saw and the listing of references. Her clients consisted of both corporations and a mom who was using the site to organize a carpooling network.

Deciding to use one of those search engines she had told him about at lunch, he was able to locate several foundations that had a similar goal as the Sid Roberts Foundation—saving wild horses. One such organization was located in Arizona. Reaching for a pen, he jotted the information down. He would contact the organization the next day.

Then with nothing else to do, he decided to search Alyssa's name. Perhaps such a search would list other websites that she'd done or was associated with.

In addition to bringing up several sites that her name was linked to, he was also given a list of news articles in which her name appeared. One was an article about an award she had received for web design. A semblance of pride touched him at her accomplishment.

Then his gaze sharpened when it came across another article. It was one that announced her marriage engagement. Clint instantly felt a sharp pain that was similar to a swift kick in his abdomen. Alyssa hadn't told him she'd been engaged.

He flipped to another article and his breath caught at the headlines that read Attorney Kevin Brady Weds Alyssa Barkley.

Clint's shoulders stiffened but he managed to force them to lean forward in his chair as he read the article that was dated two years ago. "In the presence of over five hundred guests, prominent Waco attorney Kevin Brady wed local web designer Alyssa Barkley." There was also a picture of a beautiful Alyssa in a wedding gown.

Clint flipped off that particular screen, angered beyond belief at the thought that there was a possibility he had just made love to someone else's wife. During their very first conversations the day she'd arrived in Austin, Alyssa had told him she was not married. Yet the article indicated that she had been married. Even if she had gotten a divorce, she should have told him about it. This changed everything, Clint thought angrily.

Stunned, he stood and moved away from the computer, feeling let down and used. Taking the chair on the other side of the sofa, he decided not to wake her. So he waited until she finally awakened a half hour later. He watched as she slowly opened her eyes, saw him sitting in the chair and smiled at him. He could tell by her expression that she was confused by his refusal to return her smile.

"Clint?" she asked, pulling her naked body up into a sitting position. "What's wrong?"

He didn't say anything as he tried to ignore her nudity before she reached for her T-shirt and pulled it over her head. Then in a voice tinged with the anger he was trying to hold in check, he asked, "Why didn't you tell me you had gotten married, Alyssa?"

Chapter 11

Alyssa went stiff. From Clint's expression she knew he mistook the gesture for guilt. A part of her immediately wondered if it mattered what he thought since he had been quick to think the worst of her, to believe she could be married to someone and willingly participate in what they had shared tonight. Her anger flared. *Just what type of woman did he think she was?*

But then she knew what he thought did matter. What he had done tonight, not once but twice, had been intense, passionate and an unselfish giving of himself. "I asked you a question, Alyssa," Clint said in the same hard voice.

Reining her anger back in and holding his gaze, she shook her head. "I'm not married, Clint."

"But you were," he said.

It wasn't a question, it was an accusation. She wondered where he had gotten his information. It would seem like the handiwork of Kim, but she knew that couldn't be the case.

"Alyssa," he said.

Apparently she wasn't answering quickly enough to suit him. The details of the humiliating day of her wedding were something she didn't like remembering, much less talking about. Having all those people at the church know the reason she hadn't gone through with the wedding—that she had been unable to satisfy her future husband to the point where already he'd gone out seeking the attentions of others—had been a degrading experience for her.

Knowing Clint was waiting for a response, she lifted her chin and tilted her head and slanted him a look.

"I've never been married, Clint," she said.

She saw his anger die down somewhat, but she also saw the confused look in the depths of his dark eyes.

"Then explain that picture and this article on the internet," he said.

So that was where he'd gotten his misinformation, she thought. With as much dignity as she could muster, Alyssa sat up straight on the sofa.

"The wedding was supposed to take place, but it didn't and it was too late to pull the article scheduled to run in the newspaper. To be honest, I didn't even think about calling the papers to stop the announcement from printing the next day. I had other things on my mind," Alyssa said.

Like how my cousin could hate me so much to do

such a thing, and how my fiancé, the man I thought I loved, could allow her to use him to accomplish such a hateful act, she thought.

"You're saying that you called things off on your wedding day?"

She heard the incredulous tone of his voice as if such a thing was paramount to the burning of the flag. "Yes, that's what I'm saying," she said.

She knew that statement wouldn't suffice. He needed to know more. So she began talking and remembering that dreadful day. Her feelings of shame and embarrassment hadn't lessened with time.

"I was home that day getting ready to leave for the church when a courier delivered a package for me. It contained pictures of my soon-to-be husband in bed with someone I knew. The pictures arrived just in time to ruin what should have been the happiest day of my life," Alyssa said.

She watched Clinton's fury return, but this time it wasn't directed at her.

"Are you saying that while engaged to you your fiancé was sleeping around? And with someone you knew and that the person deliberately wanted to hurt you?"

She nodded. "Yes, and the pictures were very explicit. Kevin didn't even really apologize. He said he felt his behavior was something I should be able to forgive him for. He said I should get over it because it just happened that one time and meant nothing."

"Bullshit," Clint said.

Alyssa tried not to smile. "Yes, that's what I said."

"And the woman involved?"

"She accomplished her goal, which was to hurt me and embarrass me. She wanted to prove that there was nothing that I considered mine that she couldn't have," Alyssa said.

He frowned. "She doesn't sound like a very nice person."

She thought that over for a moment. "In my opinion, she's not."

The room got quiet and Alyssa was very much aware of him staring at her, so she tried looking at everything else in the room but him. She wondered what he was thinking. Did he agree with some of the others who'd pitied her because they felt she hadn't been able to hold on to her man, keep him from wandering?

She heard Clint move and when she glanced over in his direction she was startled to find him standing in front of her. She lifted confused eyes to his. When he reached out his hand to her, she took it and he gently pulled her to her feet and off the sofa. Instantly, his arms went around her waist and he pulled her tighter to him.

"I just made a mistake in accusing you of something when I should have checked out the facts first," he said, in a low, husky tone. "I'm sorry and I can assure you that it won't happen again," he said, holding her gaze with his.

"And I'm glad you didn't marry that guy because if you would have married him, you wouldn't be here with me now." A few moments later he added while placing his palm against her cheek, "Besides, he didn't deserve you."

That's the same thing her aunt had said that day. Over

the years, Claudine had just about convinced Alyssa that it was true. Touched by what he'd said, Alyssa tilted her head back and slanted a small smile at him. "Thank you for saying that," she said.

"Don't thank me, sweetheart, because it's true. Any man who screws around on a woman like you can't be operating with a full deck."

Alyssa shrugged. "You haven't seen the other woman," she said.

"Don't have to. Beauty is only skin deep and a real man knows that. I'm not the kind to get taken in by just a pretty face," Clint said and he smiled down at her. "Although I would be the first to admit that you do have a pretty face," he added in a husky voice. "Come on. Let me walk you to your room."

She drew in a deep breath thinking how quick and easy it had been to fall in love with Clint. Even now, when she knew he didn't feel the same way, she loved him so deeply it made her ache. It also made her want to express her love in the only way she knew how, and with the time limit they had, the only way she could.

"We didn't finish the game," she said softly, remembering the two orgasms he had given her and how she had passed out before returning the favor.

He reached out and gently caressed her bottom lip. "No, we didn't, but you've had enough for one night. We'll play again at another time. Trust me."

She did and it suddenly occurred to her at that moment just how much.

Alyssa woke up the next morning overwhelmed that in just one night things had changed between her and

Clint. There was no doubt in her mind that he still expected them to annul the marriage and for her to return to Waco at the end of the thirty days. But then, she thought, smiling, there was also no doubt in her mind that he wanted her the way a man wanted a woman. He had proven as much last night.

She glanced over at the clock and quickly sat up as her heart jumped in her chest. It was just before eight in the morning. Clint was an early riser. On most mornings he was up and out before six. She wondered if she had already missed him.

She slid out of bed and moved quickly to the bathroom to take a shower, remembering his hands and mouth on every part of her body. Moments later in the shower and under the spray of warm water, she glanced down and saw the marks of passion his mouth had made on her skin. Most of them, like the ones on her stomach and thighs, could be easily covered by her clothes, but the ones on her neck were blatantly visible. They would be hard to hide. At the moment she didn't care.

A short while later she'd finished dressing. She'd decided to wear a new pair of jeans she had purchased the day before and a top she had picked up while at the mall. Sighing deeply, she left the bedroom, hoping Clint was still around and hadn't left the ranch for the day.

"Is there any reason your eyes are glued to that door?" Chester asked, chuckling. Clint didn't answer. "Hey, give her a while. She'll be coming through that door at any minute. Unless your wife has a reason to sleep late this morning," Chester teased.

Your wife.

Clint felt his stomach roll into a knot. It was only when he was conversing with Chester that Clint remembered that legally Alyssa was his wife. As his spouse, she was as deeply embedded as any woman could get in his life.

"*Does* she have a reason to sleep late, Clint?"

Chester's question broke into his thoughts. He didn't bother glancing over in Chester's direction because he had no intention of answering the old man. Yes, Alyssa had plenty of reasons to sleep late this morning and all of them involved what they had done in his office last night. He got hard just thinking about their "game" and was grateful he was sitting down and away from Chester's prying eyes. The old man saw way too much to suit Clint.

"Clint, you're not answering my question."

Clint's gaze remained glued to the door that separated the kitchen from the dining room. "And I don't intend to, Chester. Don't you have work around here to do?"

"Don't you?"

Clint frowned. He did have plenty of work to do and he was getting behind in it if the truth was known. But he needed to see Alyssa. All through the night he thought about what she had shared with him about her unfaithful fiancé and her horrible wedding day. Her revelations had nagged at him to the point where he'd been unable to sleep.

He then recalled how he had found out about Chantelle's infidelity. When she believed his future aspirations did not include anything else other than being a Texas Ranger, Chantelle had sought out greener pastures and had married a banker.

Clint knew all about betrayals. He knew how it felt to believe you were in love with someone and believe that person loved you back only to have that love tarnished with treachery.

Somewhere in the house he heard a door close and the sound snapped him out of his thoughts. He glanced over at Chester. "Don't you have the men to feed?"

Chester chuckled. "I've fed them already, but if that's a way of asking me to get lost, then I'll take the hint," he said, wiping off his hands with a kitchen towel. "Lucky for you I can come back and clean this stove later." The older man smiled over at Clint before grabbing his hat off the rack and turning toward the back door.

Before reaching it Chester turned around. "Have you given any thought to attending the annual benefit for the children's hospital I was telling you about? This year it will be held at the governor's mansion. Important people from all over Texas will be there. I reminded Casey about it. The function will happen during her visit, and she and McKinnon have agreed to go.

"And I even took the liberty to contact some of your cousins. Most of them said they would fly in to attend. Wasn't that real nice of them?"

Chester paused only long enough to add, "I haven't gotten a firm commitment from Cole or you, though." He chuckled. "At least this year you won't have a problem getting a date since you have a wife."

Clint shot Chester a glare before the man turned

around to open the back door. Chester was barely out of the door when Clint stood up, immediately dismissing what Chester had said from his mind. The man was becoming a smart-ass in his old age.

Clint heard steps and felt his stomach clench in anticipation. He was eager to see Alyssa. Ready. Eager. Waiting. The kitchen door swung open and then she was there. Smiling at him. And she looked so damn good in a pair of jeans, shirt and cowboy boots. Her thick, copper-brown hair flowed around her shoulders, framing her gorgeous face. She looked prettier than anything or anyone he had seen in a long time.

"Good morning, Clint," she said.

Without responding, he walked around the table and pulled her into his arms and whispered, "Good morning, Alyssa." He leaned down and captured her lips, needing to taste her again, to have her in his arms, to be consumed by her very essence. He didn't understand what was happening to him and at the moment, he didn't want to analyze his feelings or scrutinize his actions. The only thing he wanted to do was what he was now doing, exploring Alyssa's mouth with a hunger that astounded him.

He finally raised his head and gazed down at her moist lips, and when she whispered his name he leaned down again for another taste as pleasure tore through him. It was the kind of pleasure that licked at his heels, filled him with a warm rush and had certain parts of his body aching for relief.

This time when he pulled back again he placed a finger against her lips. "I love kissing you," he whispered.

She smiled sweetly. "I figured as much, especially after last night."

He smiled. "Come on, let's feed you. Chester kept your breakfast warm."

"And yours?"

"I've already eaten, but I'll join you at the table and drink another cup of coffee while you eat."

"All right," Alyssa said.

He took her hand and led her to the table thinking that he could definitely get used to her presence in his home.

She melted a little bit inside each and every time Clint glanced her way. A couple of times he had looked at his watch. She knew he had work around the ranch to do, but he was putting his work aside for her. But she didn't want to keep him from doing his job.

"I got a chance to read all that information about the foundation and the reason for it," she said, to break the comfortable silence between them.

He took a sip of his coffee as his intense gaze still held hers. "Did you?"

"Yes. And I got some wonderful ideas for the site that I would like to share with you. That is if you were really serious about my doing a web design for it," she said.

"Yes, I'm serious. I've even spoken to Casey about it," Clint assured her.

She raised a brow. "You have?"

He chuckled. "Yes. I'm president and executive director of the board that consists of my brother and sister. We've hired several others to work with us who are just as determined as we are to relocate as many horses as we can. We also want to educate the public to the plight of the wild horses," Clint said.

She nodded. "I guess all three of you love horses."

He grinned. "With a passion, and speaking of horses, I want you to have all your work done by three o'clock today."

She lifted a brow. "Why?"

"Because you and I are going riding," he said.

She frowned. "If you recall, I told you I'd rather not get on a horse," Alyssa said.

"I recall, but riding a horse is just like riding a bike. If you take a fall you get back on and try again."

"Even if you break your arm in the fall?"

"Yes, even if you broke your arm. How old were you when it happened?"

"Ten," she said.

"Ten? Then it's definitely about time we do something about conquering your fear about riding. So, do we have a date at three?"

"Yes, we have a date," she said with a smile.

Chapter 12

Alyssa took a deep breath as she stepped out on the front porch. Like the day before, Clint was in the yard waiting for her. This time he wasn't leaning against his truck. Today he was sitting on the back of what Alyssa perceived as the largest horse she'd ever seen. The big black stallion was beautiful, although he looked very mean.

"He won't bite," Clint said.

She glanced up at Clint, not at all certain. "Are you sure about that?"

"Positive. I wouldn't let anything harm a hair on your head. I thought I'd start you off easy. Today you'll ride with me. Royal can handle the both of us."

"Royal?"

"Yes. He was the first stallion we brought from Nevada last year. He was very wild and unruly," he explained.

She grinned. "And of course you tamed him."

"I did. And he's been my horse ever since," Clint added with pride.

She looked at the fierce-looking animal and then back at Clint. "Evidently you're good at what you do."

"I'm not perfect. I make my share of mistakes, but thanks," he said. "Now come closer so I can lift you up."

Ignoring the way the horse was looking at her, she went closer so that Clint could hoist her up onto the horse's back. He effortlessly pulled her up to sit behind him. She gripped her arms tightly around his waist.

He glanced over his shoulder at her. "Ready?"

"As much as I'll ever be. And you promise I won't fall off?"

He smiled. "I promise," he said.

Satisfied with his answer, she rested her chest against his back. "Then, yes, I'm ready," she said, trying to sound brave.

And she held on as Clint trotted for a few moments around the yard. And then when they reached the wide, open plain, he took off and she held on to him for dear life.

Clint liked the feel of Alyssa holding on to him as they continued their ride. He knew where he was taking her. Clint had a special spot on his ranch and he wanted to share it with Alyssa.

"You okay back there?" he asked her. She hadn't said much since they had left the ranch.

Instead of answering right away, she tightened her arms around him and snuggled even closer. He could feel the hardened tips of her breasts against his back. He could tell she wasn't wearing a bra and it felt good. And the way her thighs were squeezing him as she tried to grip the horse's sides turned him on.

"Yes, I'm fine," she finally said. "Where are we going?"

"You'll see," he said over his shoulder. "We'll be there in a minute."

As if satisfied with his response, she continued to hold on and together they rode against the wind.

It didn't take them long to get to the south-ridge pasture and he brought Royal to a stop near a thicket of oak trees. Dismounting, he took the horse's reins and securely tied them to a tree. He then glanced up at Alyssa, who was sitting demurely on the animal's back, and thought she looked totally incredible. Thick desire flowed through his bloodstream as he looked at her.

He walked back over to the horse and lifted his arms to help her dismount. The moment their bodies touched, fire blazed his loins and more than anything, he wanted to kiss her right there, under the beautiful blue sky.

And so he did.

He took her mouth with a hunger that always astounded him, and when she offered him her tongue, he greedily devoured her. The sounds of her moans ignited his cells. She continued to kiss him back and every stroke of her tongue was sure, refined and totally into what she was doing.

He pulled back. It was either that or else be tempted to take the kiss all the way. He hadn't brought her here for that. He had wanted to show her something, share something with her. "Come here," he said, grabbing hold of her hand and leading her toward the edge that looked down into a valley.

She followed his gaze and he knew she saw what he was seeing. Down in the valley there were thousands of wild horses running free. "Clint, this is truly magnificent," she said.

He glanced over at her, continued to hold her hand. "That night while you slept and I was on the computer, I looked up several other foundations that are similar to the one we started for Uncle Sid. Others have made it their business to save the horses, too."

A sound below caught their attention and they glanced down to see two horses that seemed to be at war with each other. "Stallions constantly struggle for dominance of their herd," Clint explained as they watched what was happening below. Two stallions were fighting it out, rearing up, biting and kicking each other. "Stallions go about gathering breeding mares into a band that they consider theirs," Clint said.

He chuckled. "Sort of like a harem, so to speak. And then they have the job of defending their band from other stallions who try to steal their mares. That's when there's fighting. The stallions are merely trying to hold on to what they consider theirs."

"So a herd only consists of a stallion and their mares?" Alyssa asked, seemingly fascinated by the information he was sharing.

"Eventually," Clint responded. "Once the mares give birth then the young foals stay with the band. However, once those young foals grow up and become young stallions they are chased away from the herd by the leader of the pack."

"What happens to them? The young stallions?"

"Usually young stallions gather together in their own herd—a bachelor band," he said and smiled. "They are fine until horniness sets in and then they go out looking for an available mare—which usually is in a band belonging to another stallion, and that's when more fighting takes place," he said.

"I understand horniness can be just plain awful," Alyssa said, smiling up at Clint.

"Yes," he agreed, returning her smile, knowing she was trying to tempt him. It was working. He pulled her to him, wanting her to feel just how much he desired her. "How about another game of Playing with Fire in my office later tonight?" he asked throatily.

She smiled up at him. "I wouldn't miss it."

When they returned to the ranch they were met by one of Clint's men, who said one of the wranglers had been thrown and was being rushed to the emergency room. Clint immediately went into action. Telling Alyssa that he would call her later, he got into his truck and took off.

While waiting for him to return, Alyssa tried to do some work. She made notes on the proposal she would present to Clint and his siblings on the website design for the foundation.

Hours later, she stood and stretched her body. It was almost nine in the evening and Clint still hadn't returned. Nor had he called. Chester had assured her the young man had only broken a few bones and should be okay. Alyssa truly hoped he would be.

She almost jumped when she heard the sound of her cell phone ringing. Picking it up, she smiled when she saw it was her aunt Claudine. She was glad it wasn't Kim calling to harass her again. Her cousin hadn't bothered calling her back after that night.

"Aunt Claudine? How are you?"

She hadn't spoken to her aunt in a couple days so they spent the next hour or so catching up. When they finally ended their call, Alyssa decided to take a long and leisurely bubble bath.

A short while later after slipping into a T-shirt, she couldn't help but recall the words Clint had spoken to her a week or so before.

I know the terms of the agreement and the only person who can renege on them is you. And if you ever decide to do so, you're fully aware of where my bedroom is located. You are more than welcome to join me there at any time.

He had issued the invitation and now she intended to accept it. Walking out of her bedroom, she headed down the long hallway that led to the wing where Clint's personal domain was located.

When he came home tonight she would be there, waiting for him.

Clint entered his house thinking hospital chairs were murder on a person's body. But at least Frankie would be okay. The kid was tough. He had a broken rib and collarbone to prove it. While at the hospital when he'd been trying so hard not to worry about Frankie, he allowed his mind to think about Alyssa. Clint hoped she hadn't been waiting for him in his office as he had asked her. He glanced at the large shopping bag that he was carrying. A display at one of the hospital's gift shops had reminded him that tomorrow was Valentine's Day. It seemed like years since he had purchased a card or candy for a woman, but tonight he had bought something for Alyssa.

Deciding the first thing he needed to do was take a shower, he entered his bedroom. The moment he opened the door, he picked up Alyssa's scent. A small table lamp provided a faint glow in the room and he quickly scanned the area. His breath caught in his chest when he saw Alyssa curled up in his bed.

He placed the gift bag in a chair and then went into the bathroom and closed the door to take a shower. She needed as much sleep as she could get now, because he fully intended to keep her awake for the rest of the night.

Alyssa was dreaming. Clint was in bed with her, caressing her stomach with his fingertips at the same time he was kissing her awake. But she refused to wake up for fear her fantasy dream would end.

"Alyssa."

She heard his voice and smiled dreamily at the way he said her name. Dreams could seem so real at times, she thought....

"Wake up, sweetheart. I want you."

And then she realized it wasn't a dream. Alyssa felt Clint's very real, hot breath caress the words against her lips. She forced her eyes open and found his eyes holding hers. She was immediately pulled into their dark depths.

"You're home," she whispered sleepily.

"Yes, I'm home," he said.

And then he was kissing her with an intensity that shook her to the core, made her wet between her legs, filling her with a physical hunger that was just as intense as it had been the previous night. She became warm and tingly all over and she felt she was under some sort of sensual torture.

And then he pulled back from her lips and began using his tongue like he had last night—causing tiny little quivers to invade her body every place it traveled. First, he caressed her in the hollow of her collarbone, and then lower to her breasts. When he moved his mouth even lower, she gritted her teeth, refusing to scream out like she had last night. The effort was useless. When the tip of his tongue began greedily lapping the essence of her femininity, she lifted her hips off the mattress at the same time his name was ripped from her throat.

"Clint!"

And then she felt her thighs being nudged farther apart as he settled the weight of his body between them, and just seconds before her body exploded into a shattering climax, he entered her in one deep thrust.

She screamed again and arched her body as he continued to thrust powerfully into her, without any signs of letting up. Each stroke was with relentless precision that suddenly brought her to another climax. It was as if he couldn't get enough of her and the greedier he became, the more shamelessly she welcomed him, encouraging him to penetrate deeper.

Her nails raked his back and she bit him several times on the shoulder, but he refused to let up. A primitive need was driving him. The same need that was taking over her.

And then he shouted her name at the same time she felt the sensational buildup of his body coming apart on top of her. Together they shuddered as pleasure ripped through her in a way she felt all the way to her bones.

And while the last of the tremors vibrated through their bodies, he pulled her closer into his arms and kissed her tenderly. She knew how it felt to be consumed in passion, gripped in the clutches of desire and then to glory in the aftermath of fulfillment. The experience was simply priceless and she knew in her heart she would only be able to reach that level of satisfaction with him.

It was close to nine the next morning before Alyssa came awake to find she had spent the night in Clint's bed. A smile touched her lips when she remembered their night together. It was as if a searing need had taken over them and they had filled that need the only way they knew how. Sensations flooded her just thinking about it. Luckily for her, he'd been prepared and had used a condom. Birth control had been the last thing on her mind. They had made love several times, all through the night, and each time she reached an orgasm, he had been right there with her.

She lay on her back a moment thinking Clint would have had breakfast already and left the ranch, which meant she wouldn't get the chance to see him until later. She had a number of things to do today to stay busy. She slid out of bed thinking it was time to return to her own room when she noticed the huge red gift bag sitting on Clint's dresser with her name on it. She quickly crossed the room and pulled off the card.

Her heart caught at the single question on the card.

Will you be my Valentine?
—Clint

It then occurred to her that today was Valentine's Day. It had been years since she'd had a reason to remember it or for someone to give her a gift. Even while she'd been dating Kevin he hadn't bothered to acknowledge the day. His excuse was that he didn't need a designated day to give her something. Kevin had claimed the day was nothing more than a day for businesses to make money off gullible consumers.

She smiled. If Clint was a gullible consumer then she appreciated it because it really made her day knowing he had thought of her. She then looked into the bag and her smile widened when she saw among the tissue paper a box of chocolate candy and an oversize T-shirt. She chuckled when she read the wording on the shirt— I Like Playing with Fire.

She knew the shirt was a private joke between them.

She turned her attention back to her Valentine's Day card and smiled. She would definitely be Clint's Valentine, she thought. And set her mind to work on ways to make him hers.

It was almost ten that night before Clint returned to the ranch. He and his men had spent the majority of the day away from the ranch and he was glad to be back. He figured Alyssa would be asleep now and wondered if like last night she would be in his bed.

He also wondered if she had liked the gift he had left her. Conflicting emotions were running through him. She had been an itch he thought he would never be tempted to scratch. Now he was tempted beyond reason.

He opened the door to his bedroom and his gaze went to the empty bed. Immediately, he felt a sense of disappointment. Then his heart skipped a beat when he saw the note on his pillow. He quickly crossed the room. He picked it up and read the words Alyssa had scrawled on the paper.

Yes, I will be your Valentine.
Come to me. I am waiting.
—Alyssa

Clint had no idea how long he stood there, glued to the spot, rereading her message. And then with an insatiable thirst he knew that only she could quench, he quickly headed for the bathroom, already tugging his shirt out of his jeans. He would take a shower and then he would go to Alyssa, determined not to keep her waiting any longer than he had to.

Alyssa heard the soft knock on her bedroom door and her pulse began to race. She glanced around the room, hoping the lit candles weren't overkill, but she liked candles. She thought the lush vanilla fragrance that filled the air was nice. She hoped Clint thought so, as well.

She then glanced down at herself. Clint had seen her in enough T-shirts so she decided tonight would be different. She had borrowed the truck and gone into town and purchased this particular outfit to stir things up a bit. Not that she thought it took much to arouse Clint. He seemed capable of that feat just from looking at her at times, she thought with a smile. Alyssa wanted this night to be special.

She made it to the door on shaky legs and inhaled deeply before turning the handle. There he stood in the doorway and when desire flared in his eyes when he looked at her, she smiled knowing her outfit would be a big hit. They would definitely be playing with fire tonight.

My God, Clint thought as he stood there staring at Alyssa. She was wrapped up like a gift, in bright red wrapping paper with a huge white bow. How in the hell had she managed it?

As if reading his thoughts she said, "It wasn't all that difficult getting into it. But the only way it comes off is for you to *unwrap* me. Now that might be the hard part."

Not in his book, he quickly thought. *Unwrapping* her

would be easy, especially taking off the big white bow which covered the essence of her femininity. Now that would definitely be a treat and not a challenge.

He swiftly entered the room, closing the door behind him. It was then and only then that he allowed his gaze to shift from her just long enough to glance around. He saw the lit candles and heard the soft music playing in the background. His gaze then returned to her.

He reached out, closed his hands around her waist, found the start of the ribbon and began pulling, watching before his eyes as she unwrapped. By the time he was able to pull off the bow, his body was hard and thick. He parted her thighs the minute the last piece of wrapping dropped to the floor.

The bed was not far away, but he doubted he would make it that far. Instead he went to the zipper of his jeans and took out his aroused member. Like last night he was prepared and had already put on a condom, not willing to take any chances. He knew to what degree he wanted her.

He lifted her onto him and entered her in one smooth thrust. It had been years since he'd made love to a woman in a standing position, but tonight he had no choice. He wanted Alyssa now.

He backed her against the wall as she wrapped her legs around him and tilted her hips for deeper penetration. And with another deep thrust he planted himself inside her to the hilt.

"You're some gift, sweetheart," he whispered as he began moving in and out of her. And moments later when he felt her come apart in his arms he followed her over the edge and they clung together, drowning in the waves of ecstasy as he murmured her name breathlessly. She clung to him and it took all he could do to continue to stand upright.

"Now for the bed," he said a moment later when he felt himself getting hard all over again. Every nerve in his body, every cell, seemed branded by her touch, the essence of her being. His senses suddenly became filled with an emotion he refused to accept. And as he crossed the room to the bed, he knew they were counting down the days together. These precious moments were meant to be savored.

Chapter 13

The days passed so quickly that a part of Alyssa wished there was some way she could slow things down. But then she looked forward to each night that she spent in Clint's arms. Neither of them spoke about the short time they had left, although they were both aware that in less than a week their days together would end.

Everyone was looking forward to Clint's sister and her husband's visit. Chester was already preparing what he knew to be Casey's favorite foods.

"You're going to like Casey," Chester had said to Alyssa one day while she helped him prepare lunch for the men. "I'm glad she has McKinnon. He has definitely made her happy."

Chester seemed so sure of what he said that Alyssa couldn't help but be happy for Casey. She would be able to spend the rest of her life with the man she loved. Alyssa knew that she wasn't to be so lucky. But at least she would have plenty of memories to sustain her.

She smiled. Clint had already warned her not to even think about not sharing his bed during his sister's visit. She knew Cole and some of Clint's cousins and their wives would also be visiting. Even Clint's father and stepmother were coming. They all were coming to attend the charity ball that would be held in the governor's mansion that weekend. To say the house would be filled to capacity was an understatement.

She knew that Cole and Casey already knew why she was there, but she couldn't help wondering how many of Clint's other relatives knew the reason for her presence. *Had he talked to them about it? Did his father know she and Clint were married?* She tried not to consider their circumstances as an embarrassing situation any longer. Besides, a part of her didn't want to worry about what other people thought about her relationship with Clint. Why should they hide their love affair? she wondered. They were lovers. She couldn't help but shake her head at the absurdity of it all. They were a married couple who were also lovers.

And on top of everything else, they were becoming close friends. Good to his word, Clint took her riding every day and now she no longer feared riding on a horse alone…as long as Clint was close by.

She glanced at the folder on the desk as she sat in Clint's office. The proposal she had worked up for the foundation was complete and ready to present to Clint and his siblings when they arrived.

If they liked her proposal and accepted it, she and Clint would still be in contact with each other, at least until she had the site up and running. After the site was operational, she would be available to maintain it. It was a service she offered to all her clients. She didn't relish the thought of having a continuing business relationship with Clint after their marriage was annulled. It would open her up for heartbreak if Clint decided to begin to date again.

She closed her eyes, not wanting to think of such a thing happening, although she knew that eventually it would. Clint was too good-looking a man not to have a permanent lady in his life. But then, according to Clint, his uncle Sid had died a carefree bachelor, although Chester was convinced Sid had an offspring out there somewhere. He recalled a woman once writing Sid telling him she had given birth to his son, but stating she didn't want or need anything from him. She'd merely felt it was the right thing to do to let him know. However, she hadn't provided a return address, which eliminated the chance of Sid finding out if the claim was true, or establishing a relationship with his child.

"Alyssa?"

At the sound of her name she immediately came out of her reverie and discovered the sound was coming from the intercom system. It was Clint. She stood and quickly crossed the room to the box on the wall and pressed a button. "Yes?"

"Where are you?"

She smiled. "In your office. Why?"

"I'm in the living room. I want you to come out and meet my sister and brother-in-law," Clint said.

A lump suddenly formed in Alyssa's throat. She was definitely nervous about meeting Clint's family, but knew she couldn't hide out forever.

"I'm on my way."

In less than a day Alyssa was convinced she totally liked Casey Westmoreland Quinn. And her husband, McKinnon, in addition to being knockout gorgeous, was a very kind person. Alyssa thought the two made a beautiful couple and it was very easy to see they were very much in love.

"You and I need to go shopping," Casey exclaimed to her the following morning at breakfast.

Alyssa's lips spread into a smile as she took a sip of her coffee. "We do?"

"Yes. You mentioned you don't have anything to wear to the charity ball this weekend and neither do I. Besides," Casey added as a grin spread across her lips, "that way I get to spend time with you without Clint hovering about. He seems to think I'm going to reveal some deep, dark, embarrassing secret about him from our childhood. He's really overprotective where you're concerned. I guess I should thank my lucky stars that the two of you are already married."

Alyssa frowned. Surely Casey knew her and Clint's marriage wasn't going to last forever. In fact they were merely biding time waiting until the day came where they could end it. Alyssa's thoughts were interrupted when Casey's cell phone went off.

"Excuse me, Alyssa, while I get this."

Alyssa stood from the table to refill her coffee while Casey answered the phone. Clint and McKinnon had left the ranch early that morning and weren't expected to return until dinnertime. Clint was eager to show McKinnon the most recent pack of wild horses that had been shipped from Nevada.

"Great! That was Spencer," Casey informed her, after she had finished the call. "He and Chardonnay just arrived and are at the airport. They should be arriving at the ranch within the hour."

Alyssa raised a brow. "Chardonnay?"

Casey smiled. "Yes, that's her name. Her family owned a winery in California and she was named after her grandfather's favorite wine."

"Oh."

"So we might as well wait and take Chardonnay with us," Casey said.

Alyssa then decided to ask, "Do you know who else is coming?"

"Shopping with us?"

Alyssa shook her head, grinning. "No, coming to the ranch to attend the charity ball this weekend," she said.

Casey looked confused. "Didn't Clint tell you?"

"Not really. He mentioned some of his family was coming, but he didn't say exactly who. I'm sure he mentioned it to Chester for him to get the guest rooms prepared, though," Alyssa said.

Casey frowned. "Never mind if he did mention it to Chester. You're the mistress of the ranch and he should have specifically told you. You shouldn't be hearing it secondhand. Men can be so fruity at times," Casey said.

From what Casey had just said, it was apparent she wasn't aware of the circumstances surrounding her and Clint's marriage. "It's not that Clint's fruity," Alyssa said, coming to his defense. "It's just that he doesn't consider me as the mistress of this ranch."

Casey raised a brow. "And why not?"

Alyssa sighed. If Clint hadn't informed his sister of anything, she wasn't sure it was her place to do so. She hesitated to find the proper words, couldn't find them, shrugged and then said, "Because he just doesn't."

Casey stared at her as if trying to figure out what she meant and then a smile touched her lips. "Oh, you're talking about that business with the thirty days and how the two of you have to live under the same roof and all of that?"

Alyssa nodded. *So Clint had told her.* "Yes."

Casey chuckled before taking a sip of her coffee. "I wouldn't worry about that if I were you. Trust me, Clint plans to keep you," Casey said.

Alyssa shook her head. "No, he doesn't," Alyssa argued.

Casey laughed. "Yes, he does and what's so sad is that besides being fruity, some men are also slow. Clint is one of the slow ones. Chances are he hasn't even realized what he plans to do with you yet, poor thing."

Alyssa stared at Casey, wondering how she could make such an assumption. The only excuse she could come up with was that since Casey was happily married and in love she thought everyone should be the same way. Alyssa decided not to argue, and to let Casey continue to think whatever she wanted to believe. But Alyssa was fully aware of the real deal surrounding her marriage to Clint and that at the end of thirty days he expected her packed and ready to leave.

Two nights later Alyssa lay in Clint's arms after thoroughly being made love to. The sound of his even breathing let her know he had gone to sleep, but she was wide-awake...and thinking.

All of Clint's relatives who were attending tomorrow night's ball had arrived and she found all of them to be extremely nice and friendly. The house was full and without it being verbally expressed, Clint looked to her to be his hostess and instinctively she had taken on the role. When he introduced her, he simply said she was Alyssa. He didn't give her last name or what role she played in his life. She could only assume the masses thought she was his live-in lover since she wasn't wearing a wedding ring and it was obvious they shared the same bed. But what was confusing was that when the relatives talked among each other in her presence and his, she was referred to as Clint's wife and he did nothing to correct them.

She guessed in a way it didn't matter what they thought since all of them would be leaving on Monday. And then she would leave less than a week later.

Less than a week.

Boy, how time flies when you're having fun, she thought. And she was having fun. Returning to Waco didn't have the appeal it once did. She had bonded with

Chester and the men who worked for Clint, and she thought he had a very special family. They were so different from hers. Even his father, Corey, and step-mother, Abby, were absolutely wonderful. She could feel the closeness and the love among everyone. Those were two things that her family lacked.

"Alyssa."

Clint had whispered her name in his sleep and she snuggled closer to him. She would miss this. Going to bed with him every night and waking up to his love-making each and every morning. But as someone once said, all good things must one day come to an end. Over the week she would prepare for the heartbreak she would encounter the moment Clint drove her away from the ranch to the airport. To prepare for that day she needed to start distancing herself from him and she would do so once his family left and it was just the two of them again. It would be for the best.

Alyssa glanced around the huge ballroom filled with people. Chester had been right. Everyone important from all over Texas was attending the charity benefit to give their financial support to the children's hospital. It was even rumored that the President and First Lady would be making an appearance.

She had to admit that she was rendered speechless when they arrived and Clint introduced her to the host and hostess as his wife. Alyssa figured the reason he had done so was to not cause her any embarrassment later. So far no one had questioned his sudden acquisi-tion of a wife. And a few times when one or two people referred to her as Mrs. Westmoreland, she had to stop from stating that wasn't her name.

Another thing she noticed was that the Westmorelands seemed to run in a pack. All of them were standing together in one spot and it was obvious they were a family. All the men in the family resembled one another in their facial features, height and sex appeal. And the Westmoreland women—sisters, cousins and wives—were all beautiful. They made stunning couples. There were Clint's cousin Jared with his wife, Dana; his cousin Storm with his wife, Jayla; his cousin Spencer and his wife, Chardonnay; his cousin Dare and his wife, Shelly; his cousin Thorn and his wife, Tara; and his cousin Ian and his wife, Brooke.

The group also included Clint's brother Cole, who didn't bother to bring a date; his cousin Reggie, who hadn't brought a date, either; Casey and McKinnon; and Clint's father and stepmother, Corey and Abby Westmoreland. Such an imposing group, she thought, and several times Thorn, who was nationally known for the motorcycles he built and raced, was approached by several people wanting his autograph.

"Did I tell you how beautiful you look tonight?"

Alyssa glanced up at the tall, handsome man who hadn't left her side all evening. She smiled up at him. "Yes, you told me. Thank you," she said.

And if he hadn't, his gaze had said it all when she had walked out of the bathroom after getting dressed. Casey, who had once owned a clothing store, had been instrumental in helping her select a dress, a short, black, clingy number that Casey claimed would hit her brother between the eyes when he saw it. Alyssa wasn't sure whether Clint had gotten hit between the eyes, but it was evident he liked seeing her in the dress. And if she was reading his mind correctly, he was counting the hours until he would get the chance to take it off of her.

"Well, well, look who's here. I can't believe my eyes. What are you doing here, Alyssa?"

Dread settled in the pit of Alyssa's stomach at the sound of that voice. She turned and tried to retain her composure when she not only saw Kim but also Kevin. She shook her head, shocked, not believing they were here tonight, of all places, and together. Kim was plastered to Kevin's side as if she wanted to make it obvious that tonight they were a couple.

Alyssa found her voice to speak. "Kim, Kevin, how are you? It's nice seeing the both of you and I'm here for the same reason you are, to support the children's hospital."

"Like you can afford to do that," Kim said with an obvious sneer, not caring who standing around her was listening. "Aunt Claudine claims you left Waco to go work for a client, but I figure you're still licking your wounds because I took Kevin away from you."

Alyssa knew Kim was deliberately trying to embarrass her in front of everyone and a part of Alyssa wished at that moment she was anywhere but there. Having all her personal business exposed to everyone, especially the Westmorelands, was humiliating.

But then she happened to notice that Clint had moved closer to her side, had placed a protective arm around her waist. And out of the corner of her eye she saw the other Westmorelands closing ranks around her, as well.

"Please introduce me to your friends, Alyssa," Clint said.

Only someone as up close, intimate and personal to Clint as she was would detect the edgy steel in his voice. She glanced up at him. He hadn't taken his gaze off Kim and Kevin, and the look in his eyes matched the tone she had heard in his voice.

She cleared her throat. "Clint, this is Kevin and Kim. Kim and I are cousins. Kevin and Kim, this is Clint Westmoreland," Alyssa said.

It was only then that Clint shifted his gaze back to her and she was aware that already he had figured things out. Kevin was her former fiancé and Kim was the woman who had deliberately slept with him to ruin her wedding day. Kim was also Alyssa's cousin.

Kim, who appreciated a good-looking man when she saw one, smiled sweetly at Clint. "So, you're that client she ran off to work for," she said in a smooth, silky voice as her flirty gaze rake him from head to toe.

Clint smiled at Kim, although anyone knowing him could see the smile didn't quite reach his eyes. "No, I'm not Alyssa's client," he said in a clear and firm voice. "I'm Alyssa's husband."

Chapter 14

Alyssa thought for as long as she lived she would never forget the shocked look that appeared on Kim's face with Clint's statement. Kim was dumbstruck. Kevin had also seemed to lose his voice, but had quickly regained it. While Kevin stood there babbling, trying to apologize for Kim's rudeness, Clint had taken Alyssa's hand in his, and he, as well as the other Westmorelands, had walked away leaving Kim and Kevin looking like fools. In the end, the embarrassment had been theirs.

They had returned home a few hours ago. Neither Clint nor any of the other Westmorelands had brought up the incident with Kim and Kevin. Alyssa guessed that before the night was over Clint would talk to her about the ugly scene and the party.

She was already in bed, but Clint, his brother and

cousins were engaged in a card game. Although she was tired and sleepy, she was determined to stay awake and talk to him. He deserved to know the entire story as to why Kim disliked her so.… Not that it was an excuse for her cousin's behavior.

Later, Alyssa glanced toward the bedroom door. It opened and Clint walked in. He had removed his jacket and tie, and the two top buttons of his shirt were open. He closed the door behind him and stood leaning against it and stared at her. She knew she owed him an apology. In trying to embarrass her, Kim and Kevin had probably embarrassed him, as well. He hadn't deserved it, just like he didn't deserve the predicament that had placed her here, messing up his life as he knew it.

He didn't say anything. He just continued to stare at her. He hadn't seemed upset with her during the course of the evening but she couldn't help wondering if he'd only held his temper in check around his family, and if now, since they were alone, he would let her know how he really felt.

"Why didn't you tell me the full story?" he finally asked.

Alyssa sighed. There was no need to pretend she didn't understand what he was asking. "At the time I didn't think there was a need, Clint," she said, hoping he understood. "Besides, whenever you spoke of your relatives I could feel the love and warmth all of you shared. It's not that way in my family."

He then moved and came closer to the bed and sat on the edge. "Kim really has issues, doesn't she?"

Alyssa thought that was a nice way of putting it.

"Yes. She'd always been the center of attention and when I arrived on the scene it didn't sit well with her. And later when I found out my grandfather was actually my father, then she—"

"Whoa. Back up," he said, interrupting. "What do you mean your grandfather was actually your father?"

Alyssa knew that he deserved to know everything. "On his deathbed, the man who I thought was my grandfather confessed to being my father. Before then I'd always thought I was the illegitimate daughter of his dead son, the one who had been a Texas Ranger and had died in the line of duty."

She paused before continuing. "From what I understand, my grandmother died years ago and my grandfather was a widower who had raised two sons, Todd and Kim's father, Jessie. When Todd was killed, Grandpa was really torn up about it and went out drinking to drown in his sorrows. That's the night he had an affair with my mother. She was working as a waitress at the bar. She told him she had gotten pregnant and he provided for my care. When she sent me to live with him, a decision was made to let everyone think I was Todd's illegitimate daughter. The only person who knew the truth other than Grandpa was Aunt Claudine."

Clint nodded. "What was the reason that your mother gave you up?"

Alyssa sighed again before answering. "Because she found out that her new boyfriend was trying to come on to me."

She saw Clint's face harden at that statement. "And you haven't seen or heard from her since?" he asked.

"No. And according to Aunt Claudine, she never wrote or asked how I was doing. She no longer cared," Alyssa said sadly.

The pain she felt whenever she remembered her mother's denial came back, and she didn't realize tears were in her eyes until Clint reached out and took his fingertip and wiped one away. "This has been one heck of a night for you," he said softly. "Go on and get some rest."

She nodded, still unable to decipher his mood or feelings on what she had told him. Without removing his clothes he stretched out on the bed beside her and held her in his arms. And he stayed there with her until she went to sleep.

Alyssa woke the next morning in bed alone. She couldn't help wondering what the Westmorelands thought of her. Nor could she help wondering what Clint thought of her, as well. This was the first morning, since they'd begun sleeping together, that he hadn't woken her with lovemaking.

That thought remained on her mind while she showered and got dressed. When she opened the door to the hall, Clint was standing against the wall waiting for her. He was dressed in a pair of jeans and a chambray shirt. As usual, he looked great.

"Good morning," he said, smiling at her.

It was a smile that made her insides feel somewhat jittery.

"Good morning, Clint," she said, searching his expression in an attempt to decipher his mood.

"I know you haven't eaten breakfast yet, but I was

wondering if you would go riding with me this morning. I promise not to keep you out long."

"Sure," she said and shrugged.

They walked together through the house. The place seemed rather quiet, especially for a house full of guests. It was after eight in the morning. She had discovered over the past few days that the Westmorelands were early risers.

"Where's everyone?"

"Sleeping in late, I guess," Clint said.

"Oh."

When they walked outside she saw two horses were saddled and ready for them. Clint helped her mount Sunshine, the docile mare he had given her to ride, and then he mounted Royal. She glanced over at him.

"Where are we going?"

"To the south ridge," he said mysteriously.

She nodded. They hadn't ridden on that part of his property in a while. Thanks to Clint she felt comfortable riding and appreciated the slow pace he set for them. They rode in silence, enjoying the beautiful morning.

They had been riding for a while when Clint finally brought the horses to a stop. "This is a nice place to stop," he said, glancing over at her.

For what? she couldn't help wondering. *Was he going to ask her to leave the ranch? Had he figured out that the best way to end their farce of a marriage and quickly was to forget the annulment and file for a quick divorce instead?*

She watched as Clint dismounted from Royal and

tied him to a tree before coming back to help her off of Sunshine. He tied Sunshine to a tree, as well.

"Come on," Clint said, reaching for her hand. "Let's take a walk so we can talk."

She pulled her hand back. "Talking isn't necessary. I know what you want."

His brows drew together. "Do you?"

"Yes, I do," she said.

"And what do you think I want?" he asked, leaning against an oak tree.

She glanced around instead of looking at him and then she brought her gaze back to his.

"You want to skip the annulment and go straight to a divorce," Alyssa said.

Clint could only stare at her. What she had said was so far from the truth it was pitiful. What had happened last night at the ball had been an eye-opener for him. When Kim had said those insulting remarks his protective instincts had kicked in. He had immediately wanted to shield her from any kind of hurt, harm or danger.

Something else had also kicked in. His heart. He realized at that moment how much he cared for her. He loved her. And he wanted to always be by her side to protect her from the Kims and Kevins of the world. For him it wasn't a matter of lust, as he had first assumed. He realized now that his feelings for Alyssa were a matter of love. He couldn't imagine her leaving him or the ranch next week. He had no intentions of letting her go and the sooner she knew it the better.

"There will be no divorce, Alyssa. And there won't be an annulment," he said as he took a step toward her.

"What are you saying?"

A smile touched his lips and he reached into his back pocket and pulled out a small box and opened it. There was a beautiful wedding ring in the box.

"I'm saying that what I want is to marry you all over again. Make it truly right this time. Since the laws of Texas declare we're already man and wife, let's make it real. Let's renew our vows," he said.

He then got down on one knee and glanced up at her.

"Alyssa, will you continue to be my wife, till death us do part?"

Alyssa was shocked speechless. Tears flooded her eyes. She shook her head and tried wiping the tears away with her hand—the one Clint wasn't slipping the ring onto.

"But—but you can't want to stay married to me. You don't love me," she said.

Satisfied the ring was a perfect fit, Clint stood and smiled at her.

"Now that's where you're wrong. I do love you. I think I fell in love with you the first time we played our own special game," he said.

"Oh, Clint," she said, smiling through her tears.

He pulled her into his arms and murmured against her ear, "Is that a yes?"

She pulled back and smiled up at him. "That's definitely a yes! Oh, Clint, I will marry you again," she said.

"Thank you, sweetheart," he said. And then he was lowering his mouth to hers while pulling her closer into his arms. The kiss was long, deep and passionate. Clint knew that it wasn't enough, but he broke the kiss off anyway. He knew there was something else he had to tell her.

"You know when we left the ranch and you asked where everyone was?" he asked her.

She nodded. "You told me they were probably sleeping in," she said.

"I lied."

Alyssa lifted a brow. "They aren't sleeping in?"

"No."

A confused looked touched her features. "Where are they?"

"In the barn getting things ready."

He could tell by her expression that now she was really confused so he decided to explain things. "I told everyone last night that I planned to ask you to marry me today. Abby suggested that while we had everyone here, we might as well renew our vows today. We can always have a reception for the rest of the family later, preferably on my father's mountain in Montana when the weather gets warm," he said.

Alyssa truly didn't know what to say at first.

"Your family is doing that for me?"

Clint smiled. "They are doing it for us. They know how much I love you. I think they realized it before I did because all of them, with the exception of Cole and Reggie, have been there, done that. They know what it is like to fall in love with your heart even when your mind is still in denial," he said.

He leaned down and kissed her again and when she

wrapped her arms around his neck and returned the kiss, he knew that when they married this time around, it would be forever.

Epilogue

"You tricked me," Alyssa said.

She looked at herself in the full-length mirror before turning around and giving Casey an all-accusing look.

Casey laughed. "I did not. I just know my brother and figured he would get around to popping the question sooner or later. I just thought you should be prepared when he did. Like I said, he's slow. And since we were going shopping that day, I figured you might as well purchase a second dress just in case."

Alyssa shook her head. She had tried on several outfits for the ball and Casey had convinced her to buy the two she liked the best instead of just one. Now it seemed the second outfit, a beautiful off-white tea-length gown, would be the one she would marry Clint in. She had to admit that it was simply perfect.

"You look beautiful, Alyssa," Aunt Claudine said from across the room.

"Thanks, Aunt Claudine," Alyssa said lovingly to her aunt.

Her aunt's arrival had been another surprise the Westmorelands had sprung on her. They had contacted Claudine the night before and made arrangements for the older woman to fly in for today's festivities.

Alyssa still couldn't believe what the Westmorelands had accomplished in a single night. When she had been in her bedroom wondering how they felt about her after that embarrassing fiasco with Kim and Kevin, they'd huddled together somewhere with Clint and planned the ceremony for today. They were determined to make her one of them. And in her heart, she knew her marriage today would be more than just a renewing of her and Clint's vows. The marriage ceremony would affirm her love for Clint, but it would also proclaim her membership in the Westmoreland clan.

Tara Westmoreland glanced at her watch. "It's about time for you to make an entrance," she said, smiling. "The last thing you want to do is to keep a Westmoreland man waiting on his wedding day."

Alyssa smiled as she glanced around at all the women in the room. Westmoreland women, all of them, except for her aunt. "Thanks for everything. I already feel blessed having all of you in my life," Alyssa said. She had a feeling they knew what she meant.

"There're a few more where we came from," Shelly Westmoreland spoke up. "And they're all dying to meet you and send their love and regrets that they can't be here. We plan to have a reception on Corey's Mountain. With the exception of Delaney and Casey, we ladies became Westmorelands through marriage. What we discovered is a sisterhood that's very special and we welcome you with love."

Tears filled Alyssa's eyes. She was finally getting a family who would love her as much as she loved them.

Thirty minutes later, Alyssa was walking across the span of the room to where Clint, dressed in a dark suit, was standing beside his brother and father. She had asked Chester to give her away and he had truly seemed honored to do so. Casey was her matron of honor.

When she reached Clint, he smiled as he took her hand in his. She smiled back and together they faced the minister. Alyssa knew this was a new beginning for her and she would have a lot to tell her grandkids one day about how she was able to tame the wild and elusive heart of Clint Westmoreland.

* * * * *

COLE'S RED-HOT PURSUIT

Prologue

"I swear, Cole, if you weren't so preoccupied with staring at Patrina Foreman, you would have noticed that McKinnon was about to knock the hell out of Rick Summers just now for coming on to your sister," Durango Westmoreland said, joining his cousin near the punch bowl.

"Who?" Cole asked, finally taking his eyes off the woman across the room, the same one he'd been standing here watching since she'd arrived at the party given in honor of his sister, Casey.

"Rick Summers. He's been a pain in the—"

"No, I'm not talking about Summers. I'm talking about the woman. You said her name was Patrina…"

Durango shook his head, clearly seeing his cousin's

interest. "Her name is Patrina Foreman, but those who know her call her Trina. She's a doctor in town. In fact, she's Savannah's doctor and will be delivering the baby."

"Married?"

"She's a widow. Her husband, Perry, was the sheriff and was gunned down by an escaped convict almost three years ago. Trina and Perry had been childhood sweethearts so she took his death pretty hard."

Durango didn't say anything for a few minutes and then said, "If you're thinking what I think you're thinking, you might want to kill the thought. You're a Texas Ranger and Trina has sworn never to become involved with another lawman. Hell, to be totally honest, she hasn't done too much dating at all. Other than her work, Trina's life basically stopped when Perry died."

Cole immediately thought, *what a waste.* Patrina Foreman was a looker. She'd certainly grabbed his attention the moment she'd walked in the room. He couldn't recall the last time something so potent had happened between him and a woman. And there was no way he would let the party end without at least getting an introduction—especially when he'd felt the strong sexual chemistry between them when their gazes had caught and held. There was no way she hadn't felt it, as well, he was sure of it. And would even go so far as to place his ranger's badge on it.

"I think I'll go introduce myself."

Durango rolled his eyes on seeing the determined

look on Cole's face. "Okay, but don't say I didn't warn you."

A smooth smile touched Cole's lips when he glanced back over at Patrina and caught her staring at him. "I won't."

Chapter 1

Eleven months later

It seemed to require more effort than usual for Cole Westmoreland to open his eyes, and the moment he did, he wished he'd kept them closed. A sharp pain ripped through his body, starting at the top of his head and working its way down to the soles of his feet. To fight off the excruciating throb he tightened his hands into fists, and then it occurred to him that he was lying flat on his back in the middle of a bed that wasn't his.

He forced himself to gaze around a bedroom that wasn't his, either. In fact, he was at a loss as to whose bedroom it was. He closed his eyes against another sharp pain and wondered just where the hell he was.

He recalled getting off the plane at the Bozeman

Airport and renting a car to drive to his sister and brother-in-law's home on the outskirts of town. Casey and McKinnon weren't expecting him for another three weeks. His early arrival was to have been a surprise. He also remembered dismissing the car rental office's warning that an April snowstorm was headed their way. He'd assumed he would reach his destination before the storm hit.

But he had been wrong.

He'd been driving the rental car along the two-lane highway when out of nowhere, blankets of snow began falling, cutting visibility to zero. The last thing he remembered was tightening his grip on the steering wheel when he felt himself losing control of the car and then mouthing a curse before hitting something.

He reopened his eyes when he heard a sound. He forced his head to move, and his gaze locked on to the woman who entered the bedroom. *She definitely isn't my sister, Casey, so who is she?* He watched her place a basket of clothes on a table near the fireplace, and when she began folding up the clothes he studied her face.

She looked familiar and he searched his mind, trying to recall where he'd seen her before. He was not one to forget an attractive face, and even while flat on his back with pain racking his body, he was male enough to appreciate a pretty woman when he saw one.

And she was pretty.

She was tall. He figured her to be at least five-ten, and to his way of thinking, one gorgeous Amazon who could certainly complement his six-four. Her dark hair was pulled back in a ponytail. Her cocoa-brown face had high cheekbones, a pert nose—full lips that caught his gaze in a mesmerizing hold. He seemed to recall that he'd gazed at those same lips before and had gotten the same gut-wrenching reaction. Suddenly his stomach clenched in recognition.

Patrina Foreman.

They had met last year at a party given in his sister's honor by his stepmother, Abby, and McKinnon's mother, Morning Star. He and his brother, Clint, had flown in from Texas for the affair. Cole distinctly remembered how Patrina had kicked his libido into gear that night when he'd first seen her. The very air he'd been breathing had seemed to get snatched right from his lungs the moment their eyes had met. And then when his gaze had scanned her full-figured body, he'd been a goner. He was a man who appreciated a woman with some meat on her body, and Patrina's voluptuousness had been like an exploding bomb, sending all kinds of sensations rocketing through him.

According to his cousin, Durango, she was twenty-eight, and since he'd said that close to a year ago, she was probably twenty-nine now. And his cousin had also told him that Patrina was the gynecologist in town, and that she had lost her husband a few years back. A sheriff, her husband had died in the line of duty.

He'd also seen her in November at Casey and McKinnon's wedding, although she'd left before he'd gotten a chance to say anything to her. But the heated chemistry had still been there, even from across the room.

He continued to watch her fold the clothes and couldn't

help wondering why he was lying flat on his back on a bed in her home. He moved his mouth to ask, but no sound came forth. Instead, for some reason he didn't quite understand, he suddenly felt tired. The next thing he knew, he was succumbing to darkness once more.

Patrina Foreman hummed softly as she folded the last of her clothes. She took a sidelong glance at the man sleeping in her guest-room bed and noted he was still asleep. If he didn't wake up pretty soon, she would have to wake him and check his vital signs again. It was sheer luck that she'd come along Craven Road when she had; otherwise, no telling how long he would have remained in that car, unconscious. And with the weather as it was, she didn't want to think about what might have happened.

Once she'd seen that his injuries were minor, although the force of the impact had literally knocked him out, she'd managed to bring him around long enough to get him out of his vehicle and into hers. And then when she'd reached her ranch, it had been quite a challenge to get him into the house, since he wasn't exactly a small man. By taking advantage of the moments he regained consciousness, she'd managed to coax him into doing whatever she asked—like stripping down to his boxers and getting into bed under plenty of blankets to stay warm. She seriously doubted he would remember any of it, but she was certain it was something *she* would never forget.

She hadn't averted her gaze quickly enough and had seen his manly physique before he'd slipped beneath the covers. She had been nearly overtaken by emotions she couldn't even begin to name, emotions she hadn't had to deal with in quite some time. For as long as she lived, she wouldn't forget the sight of his broad shoulders, taut hips and long, masculine legs. She'd been shocked at how the fire of desire had flickered across every inch of her skin, and how her breath had gotten lodged in her throat.

She'd recognized him the moment she'd opened the door to his car to find him slumped over the steering wheel. Cole Westmoreland, a Texas Ranger who was related to all the other Westmorelands living around these parts. He was Corey Westmoreland's son, Casey Westmoreland Quinn's brother and Durango Westmoreland's cousin. She also knew he was a triplet to Casey and their brother, Clint, whom she'd heard had recently gotten married.

Because the roads were blocked and getting help for Cole would have been next to impossible, she'd made the decision to bring him here. So far he'd been an easygoing patient. It had been five hours since she'd gotten him settled. She figured that pretty soon he would wake up, if for nothing other than to go to the bathroom. And just in case he was hungry, she'd fixed a pot of beef stew.

She glanced out the window. The snow was still falling heavily. The phones lines were down and she could not get a signal on her cell phone. The battery-operated radio in the kitchen said it would be another two days before things let up. It was one of those rare blizzards these parts were prone to in April. While most of the

country was enjoying beautiful spring weather, Bozeman, Montana, was still in the clutches of what had been
a nasty winter. So at the moment the two of them were
stranded here at her ranch. She was glad she'd taken a
week off work—with no babies due to arrive this month,
she'd planned to spend her time reading and relaxing.
She hadn't counted on having a visitor.

Suddenly she felt an elemental change in the air that
had nothing to do with the weather. And then she heard the
sound of her name, a whisper so soft it caressed her skin
and almost made her shiver. She looked across the room
and found her gaze trapped with Cole Westmoreland's.

For an endless moment she stared into the dark depths
of his eyes before pulling in a deep breath. This very
thing had happened the first time she'd seen him last
year at a party given for his sister. It seemed that the
moment she'd entered the room that night his gaze had
connected to hers and held. Now he was looking at her
in a way she'd figured she would never experience again.
And her response to his stare was affecting her in a way
she wasn't prepared for.

"Water."

His request had her moving across the room to him
and the pitcher that sat beside the bed. She tried ignoring the way he was looking at her while she poured him
a glass of water. And then she placed her hand behind
his head for support while he took a sip, and tried not
to notice how warm he felt. He didn't have a fever. If
anyone did it was her. She could feel her body get hot
and tingly.

This was the first man she'd been attracted to since

Perry's death. She had dated but not on a regular basis, and none of the men had stirred her the way Cole Westmoreland had done before and was doing now. His gaze was sweeping slowly across her face, and to her way of thinking, it shifted and zeroed in on her lips and stayed there.

"Do you want more?" she asked after he had drained the entire glass.

His gaze returned to her eyes. "No, and thanks."

His deep, raspy voice floated across her nerve endings. Trying to retain control of her mind and senses, she eased his head back onto the pillow while trying to avoid thinking about the large, masculine body beneath the blanket. Even with the blanket's thickness she could make out his long, hard limbs. Elemental. Powerful. Male.

"Why am I here?" he asked, causing her to shift her gaze and look at him.

She lifted his wrist to take his pulse and could feel how erratically her own was beating. "Don't you remember?"

"No," he said simply.

That wasn't unusual and she nodded. "You were in a car accident and took a bump to the head."

"And how did I get here?"

"I came across you on my way home. I figured you must have been trying to make it to Casey and McKinnon's place before the storm hit. You're lucky I came along when I did."

"Was I unconscious?"

"Just about," she said, returning his arm to his side,

satisfied with his pulse rate but not with the way he was still staring at her mouth. "I was able to get you to co-operate, which is how I managed to get you out of the car and into mine. The same thing when I arrived here. Although you had to lean on me, I was able to manage you pretty well."

She couldn't help but smile when she said, "I was even able to get you to take off your clothes on your own and get into bed."

Cole nodded. He could believe that, since he'd never had a problem with taking off his clothes for any woman, and she definitely would not have been an exception. But he found it hard to believe that she alone had managed to get him in and out of her car. She wasn't a tiny woman, but compared to him, she was a lightweight. He was all solid and she was all soft curves.

"How long have I been here?" he decided to ask, not needing to dwell on her shape and size any longer.

"About five hours. You've been going in and out most of the time, but you've slept rather comfortably over the past couple of hours or so. But eventually I was going to have to wake you. When you take a hit on the head it's not good to sleep too much."

He nodded again, thinking, so he'd been told. There were two doctors in the Westmoreland family—his cousin Delaney and his cousin Thorn's wife, Tara.

"Are you hungry?"

He glanced up at her. "No. Thanks for asking," he said. He then glanced around the room.

"Power is out. I have a generator, so we have elec-tricity, but the phone lines are down and the signal for the cell phone is nonexistent. I don't have any way to let Casey or your father know you're here and all right."

His gaze returned to hers. "That's fine. Neither she nor Dad was expecting me for another three weeks, anyway. I was going to surprise them."

Patrina nodded. Casey lived a few miles down the road as did Durango and his wife, Savannah. Patrina had delivered their baby last September, a beautiful little girl they had named Sarah after Durango's mother. And Cole's father, Corey, lived on what everyone in these parts referred to as Corey's Mountain. She rarely saw Corey these days unless he and his wife, Abby, came down to visit their good friends, Morning Star and Martin Quinn, McKinnon's parents. But she usually ran into Casey at least once a week in town or just passing on the road.

"I've changed my mind."

His words intruded into her thoughts. She met his gaze and tried not to drown in the dark depths. She thought he had such beautiful eyes. She licked her lips. They seemed to go dry around him for some reason. Probably from her heated breath. "About what?"

"Food. I'm feeling hungry."

"Okay. I'll bring you some stew I've made."

"I can get up," he mumbled. "I'm not an invalid." Cole didn't like the thought of anyone, especially a woman, waiting on him. He felt fine. So fine that he'd almost slipped and said he was feeling horny, instead of hungry. Hell, just being this close to her had his heart thudding hard against his ribs, and had other parts of him throbbing.

"I would prefer that you didn't get up, Cole. You should stay put for a while. I checked you over and didn't feel any broken bones."

He lifted a brow. She'd checked him over? Hmm, he wondered if she'd felt something else besides no broken bones. As if she'd read his mind she quickly said. "I am a medical doctor, you know."

He couldn't help the smile that touched his lips. "You deliver babies and take care of womenfolk, right?"

"Yes, but that doesn't mean I can't take care of a man if I have to," she said as she turned to leave the room.

He couldn't help but chuckle at her tone. "Ah, that's good to know. I'm definitely going to remember that."

She glanced back over her shoulder. "Remember what?"

"That you can take care of a man."

The look she threw his way indicated he better be nice or else. And at that moment, he couldn't help wondering what that *or else* was.

Annoyed with herself for letting Cole rile her, Patrina moved around the kitchen to prepare him something to eat. The beef stew had been simmering and its aroma filled the kitchen.

Because she had grown up in these parts and was used to the cold, harsh winters, she was never caught unawares. She made sure her freezer and cupboards were always full, and she had installed the generator a few years back.

As she loaded a tray for Cole, she tried to recall the last time a man had stayed overnight in her home.

It probably was last year when her brother, Dale, had come in from Phoenix to attend McKinnon's wedding. At the same time she and Perry had been sweethearts, Dale and Perry had grown up in Bozeman the best of friends. More than once Dale had reminded Patrina that Perry had always said if anything ever happened to him, he would not want her to mourn him but, rather, have a rich and fulfilling life. She wished it could be that easy, but it wasn't. More times than not she went to bed missing the love she had lost.

A few minutes later she walked through the house and headed toward the bedroom carrying a tray loaded with food. In addition to the beef stew, she had made him a turkey sandwich and had also included a slice of the chocolate cake she had baked earlier in the week.

When she walked into the room she wasn't surprised to find the bed empty, even though she had asked him to stay put. Until she was certain he could move around on his own, she had wanted to be there to help him. The last thing she needed was for him to have a dizzy spell and fall.

The sound of running water confirmed her suspicions. He was taking a shower. She tried to force from her mind the image of him standing without any clothes on beneath a spray of water. She didn't know what was wrong with her. She didn't usually have such wanton thoughts. She was a doctor, a professional, but ever since she'd looked up to see Cole staring at her with those intense dark eyes of his, she'd been reminded that she was also a woman. He'd looked at her the same way that night last year at Casey's party. And the heat of his gaze had affected her in a way she hadn't been used to, and she'd quickly made the decision that Cole Westmoreland was someone she should steer clear of. In addition to being a man who could turn her life topsy-turvy if given the chance, she had also learned he was a lawman, and after Perry's death, she had vowed never to become involved with a lawman again.

"I was hoping to make it back to bed before you returned."

Patrina turned around and wished she hadn't. Cole stood in the doorway of the bathroom with a sheepish grin on his face. But what really caught her attention was the fact that he was completely naked, except for the towel around his middle. Of their own accord, her eyes raked his body. Why did he have to be so fine? So well built? She could just imagine running her hands over those hard muscular planes and—"

"The food smells good."

It occurred to her that she'd been standing there staring at him. She immediately dropped her eyes from his body and automatically licked her lips. "Well, since you're up and about, I'll leave this tray in here for you. There're also two pills for pain. You might not think you're hurting now, but you may experience some discomfort now that you've started moving around."

"Aren't you going to eat?"

What I'm going to do is get out of here before I do something real stupid, like cross the room and touch you to see if all those muscles are as hard as they look. "No, I have a couple of things to do in the kitchen. Go ahead and enjoy your meal." She turned to leave the room.

"Patrina?"

She turned back around before reaching the door.
She met his gaze. "Yes?"

"Thanks for everything. I see you even managed
to bring in my luggage from the car. I appreciate that.
Otherwise, I'd have to walk around your house without any clothes on."

She hoped he didn't notice the heated tint on her
face at the thought of him parading through her house
naked. "Well, I figured some things you can't possibly
do without, and clothes are one of them."

And then she quickly left the room.

She looks cute when she blushes, Cole thought as
he slipped into a pair of jeans and the shirt he'd taken
out of his luggage. He glanced out the window and saw
how hard the snow was still coming down and knew that
chances were he'd be her houseguest tonight, regardless of how either of them felt about it. He didn't have
a problem with it since a warm, cozy house was something he often craved, especially during those times as
a ranger when he'd been forced to brave the elements
during a stakeout.

But those days were long gone. His brother, Clint, had
been the first to retire as a Texas Ranger last year, and
then he had followed suit last month. With the money
he'd made from selling Clint his share of the ranch his
uncle had left to Clint, Casey and him, he'd made a
number of lucrative business investments. Thanks to the
expertise of his cousin, Spencer, the financial guru in
the Westmoreland family, one investment in particular

had paid off big-time. At the age of thirty-two Cole had been able to leave the Rangers a wealthy man.

He now had a stake in several business ventures, including the booming horse-breeding and -training business that his cousin, Durango, and his brother-in-law, McKinnon, had started a few years back. Clint had become a partner and after seeing the benefits of such an investment, Cole had recently become a partner, as well. But he preferred being a silent partner, so he could be free to pursue other opportunities.

One such opportunity was a chance to purchase a helicopter business that provided taxi service between the various mountains to the people who lived on them. Besides that, he and his cousin Quade, who was taking early retirement from the secret service, had discussed the possibility of them joining forces to start a network of security companies. Clint had expressed an interest, too, as if he didn't have enough to do already with his involvement in training horses and taking on a wife.

Cole smiled when he thought of his confirmed-bachelor brother being a happily married man. Alyssa was just what Clint needed and Cole was happy for him, but knew that for himself, marriage was not anything he wanted anytime soon, if ever. He preferred being single and all the benefits it afforded. And now that he was no longer tied to a regular job, he had plenty of time to do whatever pleased him.

And getting to know Dr. Foreman pleased him. He made her nervous, he could tell. It wasn't intentional—the last thing he wanted was a skittish female around him. But he was attracted to her. That was a "gimme" and had been from the first. Hell, when she had picked up his hand to check his pulse, he'd almost come out of his skin. Her touch had sent all kinds of sensations through his body, and he'd been reminded of a need so hot and raw that he'd had to momentarily close his eyes against its intensity.

Up close he'd seen just how beautiful she was, more than he had even remembered. He had this full awareness of her. Back in Austin, he was a man known to appreciate beautiful women and he could definitely appreciate her. Every full-figured inch of her.

He knew she was attracted to him, too. There were the usual giveaways—the way her breathing changed when they were close, the way she studied his body when she thought he wasn't aware she was doing so, and then there was the way she would nervously moisten her lips. Lips he was dying to taste, sample and devour. To say he was fascinated with her, enamored by her, hot for her and had been from the first would be an understatement. The woman had the ability to steal his breath away without even trying.

And just as he knew the attraction was mutual, he could tell she was fighting it, probably because she assumed he was still a ranger. Durango had warned him that because of what had happened to her husband, she didn't date lawmen. But then he recalled Durango also saying she didn't date much at all.

Well, I'm going to have to be the one to change that, he decided as he sat at the small table with the tray of food in front of him. He glanced around the room. It had a nice, comfortable feel without looking feminine.

The furniture was dark mahogany and the throw rugs scattered around on the floor were a nice touch. The bed was huge. It looked solid. Just the kind of bed you'd want to tangle with your woman on, between the sheets, on top of the covers, whatever suited your fancy.

In the distance he could hear the sound of pots and pans clinking as Patrina moved around in the kitchen. After taking the two painkillers she'd left, he tackled his stew. It was delicious. And she'd made him a huge sandwich. Man-size. Just like his desire for her.

When he finished the sandwich, Cole enjoyed the cake and coffee she'd also made. There was no doubt about it. The good doctor knew her way around a kitchen. His stomach was grateful.

The only thing he hated doing was eating alone, which was something he should be used to, since that was how he usually ate his meals. But it was hard knowing there was a pretty face he could look at in the other room.

"I came back to see if you needed anything else. Do you?"

He looked up at the sound of Patrina's voice. She was standing in the doorway. His gaze moved over her from head to toe, and he felt his blood pressure shoot to a level that had to be dangerous. She had a flawlessly beautiful face and a gorgeous body.

He took another sip of coffee while he continued to stare at her. Considering how much he was attracted to her, coupled with the fact that he hadn't slept with a woman in more than a year due to the number of undercover assignments he'd been involved in, what she'd asked was definitely a loaded question if ever he'd heard one.

He finally spoke. "Funny you should ask. Yes, there is something else I need."

Chapter 2

Patrina suddenly felt the weight of Cole's response on every inch of her shoulders. For some reason, she felt she needed to prepare for what he was about to say. Maybe she could tell from the way he was looking at her, with heated lust in his eyes. Or it could have possibly been the sudden shift in the air surrounding them, releasing something primal, something uninhibited, something better left capped, that warned her what could be coming. She just hoped he didn't say what she thought he was thinking.

Since Perry's death many men had attempted to date her—colleagues, friends of friends, guys Dale had introduced her to. None had succeeded. She preferred living an existence where she was not involved in a relationship, serious or otherwise, with any man. It was hard for some of her admirers to understand her position. They wouldn't take no for an answer. But none, she inwardly admitted, was as persistent as the man staring at her now.

She studied his expression and exhaled slowly. He'd made his statement and now it was time for her to ask what he meant by it. She walked farther into the room, paused by the table and asked her question. "And what else do you need, Cole?"

He didn't answer right away and she was aware that he was trying to decide if he really should. Good. Let him think about it. Some things were better left unsaid. She wasn't born yesterday and she had been a married woman at one time. She recognized the vibes, the tingle and the heat of lust. She knew enough about male testosterone and how it could get the best of a man sometimes. And she knew how not to become a victim when it got out of hand.

"I need company."

She blinked upon realizing that Cole had spoken. She studied his expression, searched his eyes. "Company?"

"Yes, company. I didn't like eating alone."

She had a sinking feeling that wasn't what he'd originally planned to say. She appreciated the fact that he had thought his answer through first. He didn't know her and there was a lot she didn't know about him. The only thing that was certain was the sexual chemistry between them. She was old enough and mature enough to recognize it for what it was worth. She was realistic enough to accept their attraction for what it was— wasted energy. The last thing she planned on doing was getting involved in an affair destined to go nowhere. She'd been married for five years to a wonderful man, was now a widow and wasn't interested in changing that status. Besides, Cole was a lawman, for heaven's sake.

"I told you why I didn't stay. I had things to do in the kitchen," she finally said, frowning and wondering if he was one of those self-absorbed men greedy for attention and looking for any willing female to give it to him.

"I want to get to know you better."

She saw the smile that touched his lips and the twinkle in his dark eyes. He was doing something to her, messing with her rational mind, while at the same time making breathing an effort for her. "Why?" she couldn't help asking.

He glanced out the window. "Because it looks like we're stuck in here together."

Patrina also fixed her gaze on the view outside the window. Snow was still falling, and according to the weather report on the radio, it wouldn't let up anytime soon. It would be this way for another couple of days. Whether she liked it or not, she was temporarily stranded with Cole Westmoreland.

She shook her head and quickly decided on a plan. "I think you should get back into bed and rest some. You're not out of the woods yet. I'm going to take this stuff to the kitchen and—"

"Promise." He met her gaze and she felt the lure in it. The automatic pull. "Promise you'll be back."

She knew she should fight it, resist it with everything she had. But then she felt she could handle it since she was used to men like Cole. She'd been raised with one and had spent a lot of her time watching him in action. Dale had been the consummate ladies' man. He'd used just about every charm he possessed, every pickup line in the book, to get girls. She glanced at the tray on the table. Good. Cole had taken the pain pills, which meant he would be getting drowsy in a little while. For the time being she would just humor him.

"Okay, I promise I'll be back."

She kept her promise and when she returned fifteen minutes later, he had gotten back into bed and… was wide awake. He evidently had more energy than she thought.

"I was beginning to wonder if you planned to return."

She took the wing chair across from the bed, folding her long skirt beneath her as she settled into it with a book in her hand. "I promised I would. I just wanted to catch the latest weather report on the radio," she said truthfully, although that wasn't the only thing that had detained her.

"And what did the report say?"

She sighed, not sure she wanted to tell him. "That we're in for a blizzard tonight and all day tomorrow."

He nodded. "Don't you ever get lonely living out here by yourself? Especially when the weather's like this?"

She shook her head. "No, because usually I stay overnight in town so I'll be available if my patients need me. It just so happens that I'm on vacation this week. I timed it so I would be taking time off when none of my patients were scheduled to deliver."

"And what happens if a baby decides to surprise its parents and arrive early?"

She laughed. "Trust me, it's happened before. But with this weather, they would just have to make their entrance into this world without me. There are other doctors on call when I'm not available."

"You delivered Durango and Savannah's baby."

She couldn't help the smile that touched her lips, remembering. "Yes, and that night I saw a side of Durango I thought I would never see."

"And what side was that?"

"The side that shows how much a man can actually love a woman and his child. I've known Durango for years, ever since I was a kid. Even before moving to Montana, he and his brothers and cousins used to visit your dad every summer on his mountain. Like McKinnon, my brother, Dale, was friends with all of them and none of us were surprised when Durango decided to come back to attend a university around here after finishing high school."

Cole nodded. He knew the story, having heard it a number of times. He couldn't help but admire a man like his father, Corey Westmoreland, who'd taken up so much time with his nephews. It hadn't been Corey's fault that Cole, Clint and Casey had grown up believing their father was dead. That was what their mother had told her triplets. Then on her deathbed a few years ago, she had confessed that their father was alive somewhere and hadn't died in a rodeo accident like they'd been told. The day after burying their mother, he and Clint had hired a private investigator to find their father.

Casey hadn't been all that eager and had struggled hard with their mother's cover-up. He was glad to see how his sister and father had grown close over the past year. The reason Cole had come to town now was for the big party that Casey and his father's wife, Abby, were planning for Corey's birthday at the end of the month.

Cole glanced over at Patrina. There was one question he was dying to ask her. "Are you involved with someone, Patrina?"

He saw her guarded expression and knew his question was unexpected. She stared down at the book in her hand and without looking at him, she asked, "Why do you want to know?"

"Curious."

She lifted her head and met his gaze and immediately he felt it the moment their eyes connected. The sexual chemistry was so tangible there was no way it could be misinterpreted. It was more than a mere meeting of the minds. It was a meeting of something a whole lot more powerful, and while one part of him was embracing it as a challenge, another part was thinking he needed to step back and grab control, since no woman had affected him this way before. He studied her and saw her tiny frown. While he might see their mutual attraction as a challenge, he could tell she saw it as a nuisance.

An assured smile touched his lips when he repeated, "So, are you involved with anyone?"

"No."

"Do you want to become involved?" He decided to go ahead and ask her, curious about her answer. If it was yes, then that made things easy for him. But if she said no, then that meant a different game plan, since he definitely wanted her and was a man known to get what he wanted.

She leaned toward him and a part of him wished she hadn't. His mouth nearly dropped open when his gaze shifted from her face to the V of her blouse. When she'd leaned forward, he could see the tops of her firm, round breasts and the taut nipples that strained against the material of her blouse.

"Read my lips, Cole Westmoreland. I have no desire to become involved."

His gaze shifted from her breasts to her lips and he wanted to do something more than just read them. A fantasy suddenly flashed in his mind. Something he intended to file away for the day he did take possession of those lips that were now formed into a pout. To his way of thinking, a downright sexy pout.

He then moved his gaze from her lips up to her eyes. She had been watching him the entire time. He wanted her to know just how taken he was with her. He wanted her to know he was a man determined. But what he saw in her eyes alerted him to the fact that she was a woman just as determined. Where he planned on breaking down her resolve, her intentions were not to make it easy for him. In fact, there was no doubt she intended to make it downright difficult. There was no doubt a confrontation between them would be of the most sexually intense kind.

"And what if I were to tell you, Patrina Foreman, that I want to become involved with you?"

He watched something flash in the depths of her dark

eyes as she pulled back. Anger. Fire. Heat. It could be all three, but it didn't bother him. He would eventually use them to his advantage. He'd never been fond of a woman who was too willing, anyway. A woman who didn't make things easy for him was the type he preferred and he couldn't recall when the last time was he'd encountered one such as that. One-night stands had become downright boring for him. In his last two sexual encounters, the women had been so eager they were the ones who'd asked him to take them to bed, claiming he wasn't moving fast enough to suit them.

"I would tell you that you were wasting your time. Take a good look at me, Cole. Do I look like a woman who could be easily swayed?"

Now that she'd given the invitation, he decided to take her up on her offer. He took a good look at her, not that he hadn't checked her out pretty much already. His gaze leisurely swept over her. She had a full figure, well endowed in all the right places, a real sexy and feminine body even in clothes. He didn't want to think how it would look out of clothes.

"Do I look like a woman who elicits uncontrollable lust in a man?"

Yes, he would say she did, but evidently she had other ideas. "What is the point you are trying to make?" he asked, deciding they needed to cut to the chase.

Her frown deepened as she stood up from the chair. "The point I'm trying to make is that I know your type. I'm sibling to one. You are man. I am woman. This thing, this attraction between us, is only a fluke. It's temporary. It's meaningless. For you it's just a whim.

Men like you have them most of the time. It's an ingrained part of your nature. Women of all shapes and sizes flock to you. Throw themselves at your feet, plaster themselves across your bed, spread themselves for you to enjoy. And when it's all over, you wear a satisfied smirk on your face and walk away. In your mind you're thinking, next. And for you there is a next. And a next. I don't intend to be any man's *next*."

He considered her words—at least he tried to. It was hard when her breasts were heaving with every single word she spoke, every movement she made. And when she had placed her hands on her hips to glare at him, he had shifted his gaze from her breasts to her hips. Flaring, wide, absolutely plentiful. He could imagine himself...

"Women my size are a joke to men like you."

His head snapped up at that. "Excuse me?"

Her eyes narrowed. "You heard what I said. Men like you, cover-model potential, are drawn to women who are also cover-model potential. Granted, I might be your flavor of the moment, but don't think you can show up in town, bored with what you left behind in Texas and decide to sample the local treats while you are here in Montana."

Cole stared at her. Okay, she was partly right. While he had gotten bored with the easy lays and had thought it would be nice to find a woman interested in a couple of quickies while he was here visiting, he hadn't intentionally set his sights on her. That is, until he'd found himself in her house and in her bed. Opportunities weren't something he liked missing. He had to admit that he saw her as an opportunity to take care of an eleven-month sexual drought.

But the part she'd said about him being cover-model potential who would only be drawn to a woman who looked like a supermodel was so far from the truth it was a shame. He liked women. And when it came to them he didn't discriminate as to weight, size, creed or color. He liked them all. He appreciated them all. And if he had the energy he would try to please them all. Hell, he was single. He wasn't tied to anyone and didn't intend to be. He didn't take anything from a woman she didn't want to give, and most women let him know up front that they were in the giving mood.

Okay, it seemed Patrina wasn't in the giving mood. But there was a thing called seduction, and it was something he was pretty good at. Another thing he was good at was reading people, and he was focusing on reading what her lips weren't saying. She was so full of sensual emotions, such an abundance of sexual heat, it wasn't funny. Whether she recognized the signs or not, she was a woman who needed a roll in the hay as much as he did. He'd bet she hadn't engaged in any type of sexual activity since her husband died. Her reaction to him was a telltale sign. Although at the moment she was fighting it, specifically, fighting him, he didn't plan on letting her get away with it. In the end, she would thank him. Suddenly Cole felt an overpowering urge to prove his theories about her.

And Patrina, it seemed, had this far-fetched notion that he wasn't really attracted to her. Maybe he ought to invite her to stick her hand under the bedcovers to see…and to feel just how attracted he was to her.

"Now, did I make myself clear?"

He stared at her for a long moment before replying, "Yes, you did. Now I think I need to make myself clear, as well."

She blinked. Then she frowned at him before saying. "All right. Go ahead."

Refusing to lie flat on his back any longer, he kicked the covers aside and eased out of bed. Surprised, she took a quick step back and he noticed how she tried averting her gaze from the crotch of his boxers. "I don't force myself on women, Patrina, so don't feel you aren't safe around me. But I do know that I can pick up the scent of a willing woman a mile away, and regardless of the fact that you're trying like hell to fight it, you *are* willing. Hell, you are so willing, certain parts of my body have shifted into ready mode just waiting for you to say the word. I won't force you, but at some point in time I'm going to give you just what you need or what you possibly don't know you need."

Her glare sharpened. "Oh, you see me as a sex-deprived widow, is that it?"

He considered her words and a slow smile touched his lips. "No, I don't see you that way, but before it's all over I will definitely make you a very merry widow. When I look at you I see a very sexy and desirable woman who—for whatever reason—has been denying herself the company of a man. Maybe it's because you're afraid to get close to another male after losing your husband, or it could be you're scared to let yourself go, uncomfortable with the thought of becoming a fulfilled woman in someone else's arms. I want to think that perhaps fate is the reason we ended up stranded here together, and only time will tell. But I will make you this promise. It won't be me who makes the first move. It won't be me who eventually asks us to share a bed. It will be you."

"When hell freezes over!"

His smile widened. "Take a look out the window, baby. To my way of thinking, it's getting there."

Patrina breathed out a long, frustrated sigh. She didn't know just what to make of Cole and she was trying real hard to control a temper she didn't know she had until now.

Where did he come off assuming she was open game? She had done a good deed by rescuing him from the storm and bringing him to her place to recover, not for him to pounce on her when he thought he had the first opportunity to do so. Okay, she would be the first to admit the vibes between them were strong. Stronger than she'd had with any man, but evidently they were sending out the wrong message. There was no doubt in her mind that a man who looked like him probably had women throwing themselves at him all the time; however, that was no reason for him to assume she wanted to be one of them. He thought he could turn her into a merry widow; the very thought was absurd. Besides, even if she was the least bit interested in him, which she wasn't, he would be the last person she'd want to become involved with. He was a Texas Ranger, a lawman, and she had decided the day she had buried Perry that she would not get involved with another lawman again.

"You have nothing else to say?" he asked.

Her lips twisted as she glared at him, trying to stay in control of her anger. "What do you expect me to say? We met last year briefly, but you assume you know me and everything about me. Someone must have told you that you're God's gift to women, a man who assumes every woman, regardless of shape, size or color, is looking for a romp between the sheets. You've been in my house less than eight hours and already you're making a play for me. Is this how you show your appreciation for my warm and caring hospitality?"

Cole frowned. If she thought she was going to turn the tables on him by making him feel guilty about anything, she was wrong. The bottom line was, he was man and she was woman. Neither of them was involved with anyone, and desire was flowing so thickly between them you could turn it into mortar to lay bricks. He wanted her, and whether she admitted it or not, she wanted him. Surely she couldn't fault him for finding her desirable, for wanting to take her to bed. Okay, he might have come on too strong, too quickly, but hell, she was the one looking at him with those hungry eyes when she thought he wasn't looking. He merely wanted her to know that when and if she decided to make a move, he was more than ready.

"Like I said, Patrina, I've never forced myself on a woman and I don't plan to start now. The last thing I want you to think is that I don't respect you, because I do. What's going on between us has nothing to do with respect. It's about the fulfillment of wants and needs. From what I've gathered, you've put yourself on a shelf and I'm at a loss as to why when you're so beautiful and desirable."

He leaned closer. "It's time you're taken off the shelf and I'm just the man who's bold enough to do it, and if that pisses you off, then so be it."

Her glare darkened. "How dare you!"

"How dare I what? How dare I be bold enough to remind you that you're a woman? Something you seem to want to forget? Well, look at me, Patrina, and what you'll see is a man who finds nothing wrong with noticing a woman as a woman and bringing it to that woman's attention if I have to."

Patrina tilted up her face, opened her mouth to tell him just what she thought of what he'd said when he suddenly leaned in even closer, and before she could draw in her next breath, he covered her mouth with his.

She thought of putting her strength into a shove to push him back, but the deep growl she heard from within his throat stopped her at the same time his tongue was eased into her mouth. What she hadn't expected were the sensations that tongue taking hold of hers evoked.

Anger quickly became curiosity, which immediately shifted to something she hadn't felt in so long she'd almost forgotten it existed—sexual hunger. And before she could stop it, it took control of her mind, body and senses. And as if that wasn't enough she felt one of his hands touch the center of her back to draw her closer into his heat.

His heat was as hot as anything she'd ever experienced, and he was sipping her up like he was obsessed with the taste of her. Willing her mind or body to resist him was not an option. Not when every fiber of her being was tuned in to his mouth and what he was doing to hers, so exquisitely poignant she wondered where he'd learned to kiss that way. He took, but at the same time he gave. There was no doubt that he was experienced when it came to the art of lovemaking. He was stirring to life within her sensations that were infusing every cell in her body, every nerve ending. The man was basically devouring her alive, and with a possessiveness she felt all the way to the bone.

And then it suddenly occurred to her that she was kissing him back. That hadn't been her initial plan, and then it quickly dawned on her that she really didn't have a plan. At the moment she was a willing participant who was handling Cole's assault on her mouth in the only way she knew how. Complete surrender.

Later she would rake herself over the coals for allowing him such liberties, for letting him turn her brain into mush, for making her feel things she hadn't felt in years. But for now, she wanted to savor, to relish and to enjoy the feel of being in a man's arms and being kissed by him this way. He was stoking a fire that had burned out long ago. And as she sank deeper into the strong arms that held her, she felt a flame being stirred from that fire, which only heightened her senses of him as a man.

Suddenly he pulled his mouth away and she watched as he clutched the bedpost as if what they'd shared was more than he'd bargained for, too. She took that opportunity to take a step back.

Cole drew in a deep breath. His head was spinning. His brain felt intoxicated and his body felt wildly alive. And all from a kiss. Whether Patrina admitted it or not, that kiss had served a very important purpose. It proved a number of things, but mainly that they were hot for each other. He opened his mouth to tell her just that, but she shoved an upraised finger in his face.

"Don't say it. Don't even think it," she warned. "It was just a kiss. It meant nothing."

He gave her a sharp look, zeroing in on lips that had just gotten thoroughly kissed. She wasn't being completely honest with herself or with him if she wanted to claim that the kiss had meant nothing when they both knew just the opposite. It *had* meant something.

"Think what you want, but I've proved a point," he said, deciding he'd had enough energy-draining activity for one day. Easing down on the bed, he ignored her glare as he slid back under the covers.

"And I've also done something else, as well," he said. Knowing he had her too mad to ask what that something else was, he then said, "I've initiated my plan to move you off that shelf. Although you're still there, you're no longer in the same spot. I've shifted you away from the side that's been cold for some time to a side better suited for you. And that, Patrina, is the hot side."

She stared at him like he'd totally lost his mind. But that was fine. She could think whatever she wanted, he thought as he closed his eyes. Like he'd said, he had proved a point, and besides, he had tasted her hot side.

And damned if he didn't like it. He liked it a hell of a lot.

Chapter 3

"Good morning."

Standing at the kitchen counter, Patrina paused, trying to get her thoughts and emotions under control before turning to face Cole. When she had awakened last night it was to discover she had fallen asleep in the chair next to the bed where he slept.

She had eased from the room to take a shower before climbing into her own bed and then had trouble sleeping, knowing he was in the room across the hall. Twice during the night she had gotten up to check on him and had seen he was still sleeping peacefully—and looking nothing like the man who was destined to turn her life upside down when awake.

She could vividly recall the first time she had seen him last year at Casey's party. The moment their gazes had connected she had felt something strong, so elemental, and it had shaken her to the core, nearly corrupted her nervous system and made her realize for the first time since Perry's death that she was capable of being attracted to another man. She had been totally confused by the intensity of that attraction and had been too taken aback by it to try to figure things out at the time.

Her intention had been to avoid Cole all evening that night at the party; however, that was something he would not let happen, and he'd finally cornered her and introduced himself. Like everyone else in these parts, she had heard about Corey's triplets, but other than Casey, she hadn't met them. Clint and Cole looked so much alike they could be identical, but there was something about Cole that stood out. Maybe it was his features, which were so compelling they'd taken her breath away the moment she'd seen him. Or it could have been the shape of his mouth—so intensely sexual it made you think of stolen kisses or had you not thinking at all. And then maybe, just maybe, it was the dark eyes that seemed capable of stripping you naked when they looked at you. Whatever it was, she had quickly reached the conclusion that like her brother, Cole was a ladies' man constantly on the prowl and she was a woman who refused to become his prey.

She had gotten the same impression about him when she'd seen him again six months later at Casey and McKinnon's wedding. The moment he had walked into the church and their gazes had connected, just like before, sexual chemistry, thick enough to almost smother you, had flowed between them all the way across the aisle of the church. Knowing she couldn't take the chance of him catching her at a vulnerable moment, she had left the church immediately after the wedding was over and skipped the reception, giving him no chance to exchange a single word with her.

Now, less than six months later he's a guest in her home.

Deciding it was time to acknowledge his presence, she plastered a smile on her face and turned around. "Good morning, Cole. H-how…"

Her words faltered as her gaze zeroed in on him standing there, casually lounging in the doorway that separated the kitchen from the dining room. He was shirtless and wearing a pair of jeans that rode low on his hips and looking sexier than any man had a right to be. And he was barefoot, which gave him an at-home look. A sprinkling of dark hair covered his muscular chest— and it was a chest so well defined she tried thinking of numerous reasons she should rub her hands across it.

It suddenly dawned on her that she was standing there staring at him, and just as she was raking her gaze over him, he was doing the same with her. She was wearing a pair of slacks and a pullover sweater and she didn't want to admit she had taken more time with her appearance than normal. The snow still hadn't let up outside, but she definitely felt heat on the inside.

"Something smells good."

His words were like a caress to her skin and she quickly turned back to the counter and leaned forward to reach down to get a frying pan out of the cabinet below, figuring she had ogled him long enough and any more was only asking for trouble. "I hope you're hungry," she said over her shoulder as she straightened.

"I am."

From the sound of his voice she could tell he'd moved into the room. In fact, he sounded as if he was right at her back. She was too nervous to turn around to see if that was the case.

"How do you like your eggs?" she asked.

"Um, I'm sure I'll enjoy them whatever way you prepare them."

It seemed he whispered the words right close to her ear. She swung around with the skillet in her hand only to have the front of her body hit smack up against his.

Before she could ask why he was standing so close, he reached out and took the skillet out of her hand. His lips curved into a smile. "Can't have you thinking of using this as a weapon," he said, placing it on the counter. He then leaned in closer. "I want to thank you for everything."

His mouth was almost touching hers and once she could release her gaze from his lips, she forced herself to wonder what exactly he was thanking her for. The kiss they had shared yesterday possibly? She doubted it since she figured his lips had kissed countless other women, and most, she was certain, had been more experienced in doing that sort of thing than she was. "What are you thanking me for?"

"For bringing me here, taking care of me and putting up with my straightforwardness about certain things."

Straightforwardness or arrogance? She quickly thought and knew just what *certain things* he was referring to. "I'm a doctor. I'm used to putting up with all kinds of people and their attitudes and dispositions."

"You're also a woman, Patrina," he said, looking her straight in the eye as he leaned in even closer. "And that's something I feel compelled to remind you of."

She noticed his gaze was lowering to her lips and a faint shiver ran down her spine. She could almost feel the heat radiating from him and licked her lips again. Instinct warned her to take a step back or be robbed of her concentration, but she couldn't since the counter was at her back.

It hit her then what his response to her had been. Why did he feel he should remind her of anything? The first time they had spent more than five minutes in each other's presence was yesterday. It wasn't like they really knew a lot about each other for him to decide on something like that. Stubbornness stiffened her spine. "You don't need to feel compelled to do anything, and basically you have no right. Besides, being a woman isn't anything I can forget."

He shrugged. "No, but it's something you evidently seem determined to ignore and I refused to let you do that. I want you to feel the passion."

She narrowed her gaze at the same time she opened her mouth to tell him that she had no intention of feeling anything when suddenly he swooped down and connected his mouth to hers. At first, everything inside her tensed, went on full alert, but then she relaxed and her mouth clung to his, and just like the day before, she automatically began kissing him back.

The hot fever she felt she had yesterday gripped her

in a way that had her wondering what she was doing and just what she was letting him do to her. She was actually melting under each stroke of his tongue and could feel the swell of her breasts pressed against his bare chest—that same chest she'd ogled just seconds earlier. Everything at that moment seemed so right, although in the back of her mind she knew it was all wrong. The texture of his mouth was manly, his flavor provocative, and the longer he kissed her, the more he was drawing her in, tempting her with a degree of desire she had forgotten could exist between a man and woman. This kiss was doing a mental breakdown of her senses in a way that had her moaning deep in her throat.

He was kissing her with a hunger she felt all the way to her toes and he refused to let up. Instead, he took her tongue in a relentless hold, as if savoring it, tangling with it, gave him immense pleasure. It was certainly giving her more pleasure than she had counted on. She'd never imagined something could be so intense until he'd kissed her last night, and this one was no different. If anything, it had even more fire.

Then suddenly his mouth softened on hers, just moments before he broke off the kiss. She let out a soft moan before automatically lowering her face onto his chest, not ready to look him in the eye while giving herself time to catch her breath. She ignored the warm feel of his hand gently caressing her back as if trying to soothe new life into her and wanted to protest that she was fine with her present life. She didn't want this— the passion, the awakening feelings that bordered on sensations she wasn't used to, sensations she had gotten over long ago. What she desperately needed was a chance to be alone, but since the weather was still ugly outside, she knew such a thing was next to impossible. Cole wasn't going anywhere and neither was she.

Cole was deep into his own thoughts as he continued to hold her, gently rubbing her back, while neither made an attempt at conversation. Just as well, since he figured the kiss—the second one they'd shared—had said enough. But then, it might not have. Patrina, he was discovering, was stubborn when it came to acknowledging some things. "I could have kept right on kissing you, you know," he said in a low voice, close to her ear. He figured she needed to know that.

He felt the faint tremor that touched her body, once, then again before she lifted her head and looked at him. The darkness of her eyes touched him in a way he found unnerving, and then with little or no control on his part, he lowered his head and gently brushed his lips across hers, feeling her shiver again in his arms.

"You're trying to be difficult," she accused breathlessly, while narrowing her gaze at him.

Her words, as well as her expression, brought a smile to his lips. She wasn't happy with him, but he was more than happy with her. He simply liked stoking her fire. "No, what I am is persistent," he corrected, drawing her closer. "I figure that sooner or later you'll come around to my way of thinking."

"Don't hold your breath."

Cole knew she really didn't have a clue about what she was doing to him. He felt his erection throb and quickly decided that maybe she did. There was no way she wasn't aware of how aroused he was. They were standing so close their bodies seemed to be plastered together. And for a moment he felt something, a fierce tightening in his gut, as well as a hard throb in his lower extremities that reminded him once again, and not too subtly, that he was a full-blooded male. And a hot one at that.

He was standing with his legs braced apart so that his thighs could snugly embrace hers and figured his aroused body part, which was unashamedly pressed against her center, made what was on his mind a dead giveaway. He tried dropping his gaze from hers and decided it wasn't a good idea when his eyes came to rest upon the necklace she wore around her neck. It was a gold heart and its resting place was right smack between her breasts. Nice plump breasts.

Feeling his gut tighten even more, he lifted his gaze and studied the look in her eyes, quickly reaching the conclusion that nothing had changed. The desire between them was strong, intense as ever. But talk about someone being difficult, as far as he was concerned, she could be hailed as queen. He would, however, enjoy breaking down her resolve.

Deciding he had made his point for now, he released her from his arms and took a step back. "Do you need my help fixing breakfast?"

She tilted her head at an angle that showed the perfection of her neck and the moistness of the lips he had kissed. "No, I don't need your help. You can sit in the living room and I'll call you when it's ready."

Cole chuckled as he crossed his arms over his chest.

It was either that or he'd reach for her again and pull her into his arms and kiss her. "In other words, you want me out of the way."

"Yes, that's what I want."

"All right."

She eyed him like he'd given in too easy. "What?" he asked, smiling.

She lifted a brow and then, as if she didn't want to discuss anything with him any longer, she said, "Nothing. I'll call you when everything's ready." She then turned to the counter and presented her back to him.

He was tempted to reach out and brush her hair away from her neck and leave his mark there, but knew she wouldn't appreciate him doing something so outrageously bold. Hell, the back of her didn't look so bad, either. The denim of her jeans fit snugly over her shapely bottom. He forced his heart to beat at an even pace.

He smiled as he moved in the direction of her living room. Once there, he decided not to sit down as she had suggested. Instead, he glanced around, checked things out. The living room, like the other parts of the house, was nicely furnished and the furniture was solid and sturdy, the kind that was made to last and fit perfectly in this environment. Considering the weather in these parts, undoubtedly, it had to.

A thick, padded sofa and love seat made of rich leather looked inviting, and the throw rugs scattered about on the floor gave you the option of curling up in front of the fireplace. But one glance out the window brought forth a dreary picture. He often wondered how his father could endure the harshness of Montana's cold weather, high on his mountain, especially those days before Abby had returned to his life. But what of those times when he'd been up there alone, those harsh and cold winters when Corey Westmoreland had lived his life as a lonely man, pretty much the way Patrina was living hers—a lonely woman. A part of him wondered what right he had to make the assumption that her life was lonely. She had her work, which he figured she enjoyed, but still he felt she needed more. Like he'd always felt his mother had needed more.

He recalled as a little boy watching his beautiful mother deny herself the chance of falling in love again and living a happy life. Instead, she'd clung to the story she'd fabricated for her children and everyone else that her husband—the only man she could ever love—had died in a rodeo accident. Although Cole and his siblings had discovered later that Corey Westmoreland wasn't dead, in a way he was to Carolyn Roberts, since she had known she would never be the woman to have his heart.

Cole could recall a number of good men who'd come calling on his mother, trying to gain her interest, like his fourth-grade teacher, Mr. Jefferson. But none had been able to awaken the love she'd buried long before her triplets were born. She had died without the love or companionship of a good man. She had died in that same spot on the shelf where she'd placed herself for more than thirty years. And for a reason he didn't want to dwell on, he didn't want that for Patrina. Although he was not interested in a serious relationship with any woman, he had no problem being the one to initiate her return to a life filled with excitement, one filled with fun where she would want to take a part in all the things that went with it—such as sharing her bed with a man.

Cole moved in front of the fireplace and saw the framed photographs lined up on the mantel. His gaze went immediately to one in particular and knew he was seeing Patrina on her wedding day with the man who'd been her husband. From what he remembered Durango telling him, Patrina had been married five years before her husband was killed. After that she had thrown herself into her work. For some reason he couldn't help standing there staring at the photo for a long period of time.

According to Durango, Perry Foreman had been a good friend and a first-class lawman whose life had been shortened, taken away needlessly and way too soon, leaving a grieving wife behind. How long had it been? Over three years? He couldn't help wondering at what point the grieving stopped. When did a person decide to start living again?

He moved his gaze to another framed photograph. It was of Patrina with two other women. They were older women and he could see a strong family resemblance in their faces, notably the eyes and jaw. Her mother and grandmother, perhaps? He hadn't asked her about any living relatives. He knew about her brother, Dale, since they had met at Casey and McKinnon's wedding.

"I just put the biscuits in the oven. They won't take long to bake."

He turned at the sound of her voice. She was standing in the doorway that separated the kitchen from the living room and was about to turn back around when he said, "Wait a second. Who are these two women in this photo with you?"

He watched as her mouth curved in a smile, and its vibrancy almost dulled his senses. This was probably the first genuine smile she'd given him. "That's my mother and grandmother," she said, coming into the room and standing what he guessed she figured was a safe distance from him.

"Are they still living?"

He saw the sadness that crept into her eyes. "No, both are gone. I miss them." Then a slight smile touched her lips. "Everybody misses them. They were the town's midwives and so was my great-grandmother. That's four generations of Epperson women delivering babies around these parts. I don't know of many people born on the outskirts of town who weren't delivered by them. Although they trained me to follow in their footsteps, I decided to go to medical school to offer my patients the best of both worlds."

He nodded. "Dale is all the family you have?"

She chuckled and the rich sound carried through the room. "Yes, and trust me when I say that he's enough."

From the tone of her voice he could tell she shared a close relationship with her brother, the same kind he shared with Casey and Clint.

"I take it this is your husband in the other photo."

She didn't say anything for a moment, just stared at the photo. "Yes," she finally said. "That's me and Perry on our wedding day. He was a good man."

"So I heard. Durango and McKinnon liked him."

She put her hands in the pockets of her jeans and

leaned against the corner of the fireplace. "Everybody liked Perry. He was that kind of person, real easy to like. And he was a good sheriff." She was quiet for a short while before adding, "He should not have gotten killed that night."

"But he did," he decided to remind her, not that he was insensitive to the pain he heard in her voice, pain she hadn't let go of even after three years. But he was thinking more along the lines of the life she was now denying herself. He didn't understand why he felt the need to push the issue every chance he got, but he did.

"You don't have to remind me of that, Cole." She straightened her stance and all but snapped, "And Perry dying is one of the reasons I will never become involved with a lawman again."

His brows rose, not in surprise since that was something else Durango had shared with him, but because of the determination he heard in her words. As far as she was concerned her mind was made up, pretty well set on the matter. "Why?" he decided to ask, wanting to hear her reason from her own lips. "Because he died in the line of duty?"

"Yes. It was a senseless death and as far as I'm concerned that reason is good enough."

Before he could say anything to that she walked back into the kitchen. He hated telling her, but that reason wasn't good enough. She refused to believe that men who entered the world of fighting crime do so knowing their lives could be taken away at any time, but the chance of doing good, even for a short while, outweighed the risk of becoming a casualty. He had en-

joyed his life as a Texas Ranger and although he knew
the good guys didn't always win, they did make a difference. The only reason he and Clint were no longer
rangers had nothing to do with the risks involved with
the job, but had everything to do with taking advantage
of other opportunities that had come their way.

"Everything is ready now, Cole."

The sound of her voice touched him in a purely elemental way. It was intensely feminine and he liked hearing it. "I'll be there in a minute," he called back to her.

As he began walking toward the bedroom to put on
a shirt, he figured any other man would respect her
wishes and let her live whatever kind of life she wanted,
but he wasn't just any other man. He was a man very
much attracted to her. He was a man of action and not
someone who did anything on an idle whim. And at the
moment, it seemed that he was the one who was able to
push her buttons. The two times they had kissed, he had
tasted her passion and her hunger, had almost drowned
in it. She had enjoyed kissing him as much as he had
enjoyed kissing her. There was no mistake about that.
Letting her remain on that shelf was not an option. She
was a woman who was meant to give and receive pleasure and he intended to do everything in his power to
convince her of that.

Chapter 4

Patrina was conscious of Cole the moment he entered the kitchen. She didn't look up from placing the food items on the table; instead, her thoughts dwelled on the last time she'd shared breakfast in this house with a man who wasn't Dale. It definitely had been a long time.

She heard the water running and knew he was at the sink washing his hands. "Everything looks good, Patrina."

Knowing he was so close at hand was making it impossible for her to relax. The man had more or less stated that he planned to seduce her, or would at least try. She bet he figured that two kisses in less than twenty-four hours wasn't bad. She was determined he wouldn't make it to number three. "Thanks, Cole. Everything is ready."

"Aren't you going to join me?"

He had come to stand close beside her and his nearness almost startled her. She hadn't heard him move. "I'd love to have some company," he added.

She looked up. His jeans still hung low on his hips, but at least he had put on a shirt. She was grateful for that. She then met his gaze. "I have things to do."

"You have to eat sometime." And then he moved slightly closer and asked, "Why do I get the distinct impression that you're afraid of me? Or is it that you're afraid of what I do to you? What we do to each other?"

She looked at him. At his facial features that were so intensely handsome they made her ache, at his eyes so impressively sexy they sent a shiver racing through her. She wanted to feel irritation, but felt a throb of desire instead. She breathed in deeply, fighting the impulse to do something really foolish like accept things as they were between them and go ahead and savor the moment. She held back. A part of her was fighting to draw the line, especially with him, although she was finding it harder and harder to do so.

"Tell me. Why are you so persistent about that?" she demanded softly.

"Because of this," he said in a voice just as soft, while reaching out and taking her hand in his. "Feel it. Feel the passion."

The moment they touched, she gasped, and although she tried valiantly to fight it, she felt currents of electricity dart up her spine. Warm sensations began flooding her insides while goose bumps formed on her arm. Her stomach began tightening, and her nervous system seemed to be on overload. She met his gaze, became locked into it and saw hot desire in the dark depths of his eyes.

She blinked, hoping she was mistaken by what she saw. It was the same look he'd given her from the first. The longer his gaze held hers, the more convinced she was that she was not mistaken.

He smoothly withdrew his hand from hers, dropped it to his side before saying, "I think I've made my point."

Whether he made it or not, it was a point not too well taken. One she intended to ignore. "Think whatever you want, Cole. I suggest you sit down and eat before your food gets cold."

"Ladies first."

She regarded him steadily as she took the chair that he held out for her. "Thanks."

His mouth curved into a sexy smile. "You're more than welcome."

It was then that she realized she had done exactly what he'd wanted by sitting down to eat with him. He sat across from her and followed her lead and said grace. Then he began helping himself to everything. There was plenty of food. She'd served biscuits, sausages, eggs, bacon, orange juice and coffee. One thing she'd quickly found out about him was that he enjoyed eating.

He took a sip of coffee. "You make the best coffee. Hot, strong, not too sweet. Just right."

She didn't want to say that's how Perry had liked his coffee. She had an instinctive feeling he wouldn't appreciate hearing it.

"Your television works, right?"

She glanced up and looked across the table at him. "Yes."

"Why don't you have it on?"

She shrugged before biting into a piece of bacon. "I usually don't have time to watch television. Not nowadays, anyway. I'm too busy with the work I do at the hospital and the clinic. Besides, there's nothing on most of the time other than those reality shows or cop shows. I can do without either."

"You mean you're not a *CSI* fan?" he asked, smiling, before taking another sip of his coffee.

"I don't want to have anything to do with anything connected to law enforcement and that includes watching it on television."

"I'm sure your position on that hasn't made your local police department happy."

She placed her fork beside her plate and glared at him. "Don't try twisting my words. I'm not saying that I don't support or appreciate what they do. I was a lawman's wife too long not to. All I'm saying is that it's a life I don't want to be a part of ever again."

Cole didn't say anything but couldn't help wondering if her words, like the ones she had spoken earlier, were meant to deter him since she assumed he was still a Texas Ranger. No one in his family, not even his father and sister, knew he had left the agency. He planned to surprise them with the news when he saw them at his father's birthday party. Of course Clint knew, and because they were working on a business deal together, his cousin Quade was aware of it.

He had seen no reason not to mention it to Patrina—

until now. With what she had just said and the statement she'd made earlier, he felt the need to prove to her that what he did for a living didn't matter when it came to the passion sizzling between them. One had nothing to do with the other.

"You're free to watch anything on television you like, Cole. I'm into a good book, anyway."

He glanced over at her. "A Rock Mason novel?"

She smiled as she leaned back in her chair. "Yes, a Rock Mason novel."

He couldn't help but smile since they both knew that Rock Mason was actually his cousin, Stone Westmoreland. Stone's wife, Madison, had given birth to a son a couple of months ago. "Have you figured out who's going to be the next victim yet?" he couldn't help asking her. Stone was an ace when it came to writing thrillers.

"No, not yet. The book's definitely a page-turner, though. Stone has another bestseller under his belt."

They didn't say anything else for a while as they continued to eat. At one point Patrina risked glancing across the table at Cole to find him sipping his coffee and staring at her. She quickly refocused on her food.

"Is there anything you need me to do, Patrina?"

She quickly glanced up and met his gaze. "Anything like what?"

He shrugged. "Chop wood for the fireplace, help wash the breakfast dishes, go outside and play in the snow…you name it and I'm all for it."

The thought of the last item made her chuckle. She couldn't see the two of them doing something as outrageous as playing outside in the snow. "There's already enough wood chopped. Dale took care of that when he was passing through last month. As far as the dishes are concerned, I plan to just rinse them off and place them in the dishwasher."

"And the offer for us to go outside and play in the snow?" he asked, still staring at her.

"I'll pass on that one. It's too cold outside."

"You of all people should be used to it," Cole said, chuckling. "Come outside with me. I dare you."

She shook her head. "Don't waste your time daring me because I'm not going outside. Besides, you still need to take it easy."

"I feel fine," he assured her. Without breaking their gazes he pushed his chair away from the table and stood. "Why don't you go get comfortable and start on your book while I load up the dishwasher?"

"Cole, you don't have to do that."

"But I want to. I need something to keep me busy. Go ahead and start reading your book."

"I started reading it last night."

He nodded as he began gathering the dishes off the table. "I know. I woke up a few times and saw you sitting in the chair reading. Then I saw you'd fallen asleep with the book in your hand. The last time I woke up and glanced over at the chair, it was empty."

Patrina gave a small, dismissive shrug. "The chair was getting uncomfortable and I needed to get into bed."

He paused for a moment and looked over and met her gaze. "You could have shared mine. I would not have minded and would gladly have moved over and made room for you." He resumed collecting the dishes.

She let out a deep sigh. "You don't plan on letting up, do you."

He didn't bother looking at her when he said, "I've already explained the situation to you, Patrina. Nothing has changed. In fact, I'm more determined than ever." He walked over to the sink and began placing the dishes in it.

"Why?"

With that one question, one word, he turned around, and she was amazed at how intensely she could feel the direct hit of his gaze. "We covered that already," he said, speaking in a calm and rational tone. "You already know why. But if you need reminding, the simple fact is, I want you and you want me."

"And what if I said I *don't* want you? That I don't have any sexual interest in you whatsoever?" she said, getting to her feet and glaring across the room at him.

"Then I'd say you were lying or that you're a woman who doesn't know what she wants."

Patrina took offense. "Nothing is going to happen between us, Cole," she said, determined to stand her ground.

"You want to bet?" he challenged. "You felt the same thing I did when I touched your hand earlier. And it was there in the kisses we've shared. Deny it all you want, sweetheart, but even now I can feel your heat. I can almost taste it. And eventually, I *will* taste it," he said.

"You think I'm a woman who can't resist your charms?"

He crossed his arms over his chest and leaned back

against the counter. His gaze roved over her from head to toe before he said, "No, but I do admit to being a man who can't seem to resist yours."

Thinking that he apparently liked having the last word, and seeing no reason to continue a conversation with him that was going nowhere, Patrina walked out of the kitchen. Once in the living room she forced herself to breathe in deeply. Of all the arrogant men she'd ever encountered, Cole Westmoreland took the cake.

And the nerve of him to claim that he was a man who couldn't resist her charms. Yeah, right. Did he actually expect her to believe that? Suddenly a tightness tugged deep in her stomach. What if he was telling the truth? What if the desire they felt for each other was just that strong? Just that powerful? What if it became uncontrollable?

She quickly did a mental review of everything that had happened since she'd brought him into her home, especially that time while, when folding up clothes, she'd looked up to find him staring at her. Could two people actually connect that spontaneously? Could they suddenly want each other to a degree where they would lose their minds, as well as their common sense, to passion?

She was definitely out of her element here. She and Perry had been childhood sweethearts, had known each other since junior high school when his family had moved into the area. There had never been a rushed moment in their relationship. He was easygoing and patient. The fact that they'd made love for the first time on their wedding night attested to that. All those years when they had dated, they had managed to control their overzealous hormones with very little effort. With Perry she had never felt pressured or overwhelmed. And she'd certainly never felt the intense sexual chemistry she felt with Cole. But still…

Just because they were attracted to each other was no reason to act on that attraction. Of course Cole saw things differently and was of the belief their attraction alone was enough reason to act on it. He was clearly a man who had no qualms about indulging in a casual relationship and expected her to follow suit. Well, she had news for him. There wasn't that much passion in the world that would make her consider such a thing.

Leaving the living room, she went into her bedroom and in a bout of both anger and frustration, she slammed the door shut behind her. She crossed the room and snatched the book off the dresser. *Fine!* Let him spend some time alone since he only saw her as a body he was eager to pounce on. Maybe if she ignored him, that would eventually knock some sense into him.

Stretching out on the bed, she opened her book and began reading. She refused to let Cole get on her last nerve.

He'd have to be an idiot not to know he'd made Patrina mad again, Cole thought, as he loaded the last plate into the dishwasher. And if she thought ignoring him would do the trick, she was sadly mistaken. She had to come out of hiding sooner or later. He had enough to keep himself busy until she did. He loved working word puzzles and had a ton of them packed in his luggage. There was nothing like stimulating his mind, since thanks to Patrina the rest of him was already there.

Feeling frustration settling in, he walked over to the window and stared out at the still-falling snow. But despite its thickness, in the distance he could see the mountains, snow-covered and definitely a beautiful sight, postcard perfect.

Deciding he would forgo watching television and start on those word puzzles, he walked out of the living room toward the guest room. He paused a moment by Patrina's closed bedroom door, tempted to knock. But then he decided he was in enough hot water with her already. It was time to chill and allow her time to come to terms with everything he'd said to her. Besides, she couldn't stay locked up behind closed doors all day.

A smile touched his lips when he thought of a way to eventually get her out of there. She had to come out and eat some time.

Patrina glanced over at the clock and then stretched out on the bed to change positions. It was late afternoon already and a glance out the window showed it was snowing more heavily than before.

She couldn't believe she had been reading nearly nonstop since the morning, but at least it had given her time by herself. The last thing she'd wanted was another encounter with Cole. There was no doubt in her mind that he had his mind set on wearing down her defenses, and she intended to resist him every step of the way.

Suddenly she sat up in bed and sniffed the air. A

delicious aroma was coming from the kitchen. She got out of bed and opened the door and found the scent was even stronger. Curious, she walked out into the hall and headed for the kitchen. Once there she paused in the doorway. Cole was standing beside the stove stirring a pot, and even with a huge spoon in his hand and an apron tied around his waist, she was fully aware of his potent masculinity.

"What are you doing?" she couldn't help asking.

He glanced over at her and smiled. She tried not to notice what that smile did to her insides. She breathed in to stop her stomach from doing flips. "I thought I'd be the one to prepare dinner tonight," he said, giving her a thorough once-over, and making it obvious he was doing so.

She tried ignoring him. "I didn't know you could cook."

He chuckled. "There's a lot you don't know about me, but yes, I can cook and I like doing it. By the time the table is set everything will be ready. I thought I'd try some of my Texas chili on you."

She leaned against the counter. "It smells good."

"Thanks, and later you'll agree that it tastes as good as it smells."

She rolled her eyes. The man was so overly confident it was a shame. "What do you need me to do?"

"Nothing. I have everything taken care of. The rolls are about ready to come out of the oven and the salad is in the refrigerator. Did you enjoy your rest?"

A part of her felt guilty knowing that while she'd been stretched across the bed reading, he had been busy at work in the kitchen. "Yes, but you should have let me help you."

He chuckled as he took the rolls out of the oven. "No way. I got the distinct impression this morning that you'd had enough of me for a while and needed your space."

He had certainly read things correctly, she thought, moving to the sink to wash her hands. "The least I can do is help by setting the table."

Not waiting for him to say whether she could help or not, she went to the cabinets to take down the plates. After all, it was *her* kitchen.

"Did you finish your book?"

She glanced at him over her shoulder and became far too aware of his stance. He was no longer standing in front of the stove, but had moved to lean a hip against the counter. She was totally conscious of the sexy way his jeans fit his body, and it made her suddenly feel warm. Then there was the way his shirt stretched across a muscular chest and the way—

"Well, did you?"

She blinked upon realizing he was asking her something. The deep baritone of his voice vibrated along every nerve in her body. "Did I what?"

He smiled in a way that was just as sexy as his stance. "Did you finish the book?"

"Not yet. But things are getting pretty interesting," she said quietly, thinking it wasn't just happening that way in the book. She met his dark gaze and felt shivers go up her spine.

"Are you going to set the table?"

Patrina looked down and then it hit her that she was standing there holding the plates in her hands and staring. "Yes, I'm going to do it," she said, pushing away from the cabinet. He moved at the same time she did and the next thing she knew they were facing each other. He took the plates out of her hands and placed them on the table.

He then gave her his complete attention. "I know you needed your space, but I didn't like it," he said huskily.

She didn't know what to say, so she just stood there and stared up at him, finding it hard not to do so. In fact, she was finding it hard to concentrate on anything at the moment—except the perfect specimen of a man standing in front of her.

"Why didn't you like it?" she heard herself asking, and nervously licked her lips. She couldn't help noticing how his gaze latched on to the movement of her tongue.

"Because I would have preferred you spend time with me," he said in a barely audible voice.

Although she already had an idea, she asked, anyway. "Doing what?"

His sexy smile became sexier when he said, "Word puzzles."

She blinked again, not sure she'd heard him correctly. "Word puzzles?"

He nodded slowly. "Yes, I'm good at working them."

As far as she was concerned, that wasn't the only thing he was good at working. He was definitely doing a good job working her. Her body was tingling from the mere fact that he was standing so close. It wouldn't take much to reach up and loop her arms around his neck, and then pull his mouth down to hers and then...

"Don't think it, Patrina. Just do it," he whispered throatily, leaning in closer.

Their gazes locked and she wondered how he'd known what she'd been thinking. It must have shown in her eyes, or it could have been the sound of her breathing. She couldn't help noticing it had gotten rather choppy.

"You're hesitating. Let me go ahead and get you started," he whispered in a raspy voice before reaching out and cupping her face in his hands, And at the same time he shifted his body, specifically his hips, to press against hers, aligning their bodies perfectly.

Whenever he touched her, her body would automatically respond and it didn't behave any differently now. But she couldn't explain the degree with which it was doing so. Desire was rushing through her with a force that nearly left her breathless and the nipples of her breasts were feeling taut, tender, sensitive. Heat flared low in her body, making it hard to think, so she was doing what he had asked her to do several times. She was feeling the passion.

She could feel the heat of his gaze as his mouth inched closer to her lips; she could feel the hard evidence of his desire that was pressed against her abdomen. And she could also feel the touch of his hand on her face, warm, strong and steady.

Then their lips touched and she no longer felt the passion, she tasted it. It had a flavor all its own. Tart, tingly and so incredibly arousing it had her heart pounding relentlessly in her chest as he continued to kiss her with a single-minded purpose that went deeper than anything she'd ever felt before. It was a primal need she didn't know she was capable of.

And then she noticed his hands were no longer on her face but had moved to her rear end. He was pressing her closer to him, letting her feel the state of his arousal. Instinctively she moved her hips against it and he took the kiss deeper.

Not bothering to question why, she gave in to her needs, needs he was forcing her to admit she had. His tongue aggressively dueled with hers and she wrapped her arms around his neck to lock their mouths in place. With her firm grip the only thing he was capable of doing was changing the angle of the kiss and in doing so, she heard him groan deep in his throat.

One of them, she thought, had on too many clothes and quickly concluded it had to be him. She felt his hard erection pressed against her, and now she wanted to really feel it, to touch it, take it in her hand and hold it. As if her hands had a mind of their own, they moved from around his neck and reached down and began pulling out his shirt before lowering his zipper and then reaching for his belt buckle with an urgency she couldn't control.

And then the buzzer on the stove went off.

For her it had the effect of ice water being tossed on a hot surface, and she pulled away from him with such speed that she almost tripped in the process. He reached out to keep her from falling, but she jerked away and turned her back to him. But not before she saw that his

shirt had been pulled out of his pants and that his zipper
was down. Embarrassment flooded her face in knowing
she had done both and had intended to go even further.

"Patrina?"

She refused to turn around to let him look at her. A
part of her wished that somehow the floor would open
up and swallow her whole. How in the world had she
let things get so out of hand?

"Patrina, turn around and look at me."

"No," she said over her shoulder as she began moving toward the living room. "I don't want to look at you.
I want to be left alone."

"What you are, Patrina, is afraid," he said, and from
the sound of it, he was right on her heels, but she refused
to slow down to see if he was or not. "You are afraid
that you might give in to your passion, continue to feel
it and be driven to admit to the very thing you're trying so hard to deny."

That did it. She suddenly stopped and turned and he
all but ran into her and made her lose her balance. She
tumbled onto the sofa and he went with her, and when
her back hit the leather cushion, he ended up sprawled
on top of her, his face just inches from hers.

She opened her mouth to scream at him to get off
her, but no words formed in her throat. Instead, her
gaze latched on to a pair of sensual lips that were so
close to hers she could feel his heated breath. When she
shifted her gaze, she also saw vibrant fire lighting the
dark depths of his eyes. Looking into them seemed to
have a hypnotic effect and she felt her entire body getting hot all over.

He didn't say anything. He continued to look at her with the same intensity as she was looking at him, and she found herself wondering why she'd never shared something of this degree, something of this level of intimacy with Perry. There had been plenty of physical contact between them and she had enjoyed their kisses, but they hadn't been full of fire like the ones Cole delivered. In analyzing things now, it seemed that she and Perry were too close as friends to become so intimate as lovers. He had to be the kindest and gentlest man she'd ever known and those characteristics extended into their bedroom. When they had made love it seemed like he'd been intent on keeping their level of intimacy at a minimum. It was as if he'd thought of her as a piece of crystal, something meant to be handled carefully or else it would break.

Cole wasn't treating her like a piece of crystal. He was treating her like a woman he thought could deliver passion to match his. Personally she thought he was expecting way too much from her. But then he had a way of making her body tingle just by being near her. And a part of her believed that he couldn't give any woman just a minimum level of intimacy. A man of his sensual nature was only capable of delivering a level that would go way beyond the max. It would be off the charts. The thought of that made her breath catch in her throat.

She noted he was still staring at her. She also noted his lips were moving closer. Then they paused as if they refused to move any farther. And she became aware of what he was doing. He was leaving the decision to take things beyond what they were right now to her. He wouldn't push her any further.

The look in his eyes made sensations stir within her, made her blood flow through her veins in a way that just couldn't be normal. They were lying on the sofa fully clothed, yet she could still feel his heat. Not only was she feeling it, she seemed to be absorbing it, right through her clothes and into her skin.

She could no longer question what he was doing to her or why. She wasn't dealing with a mild-mannered man like Perry. At the moment there wasn't a single thing refined about Cole that she could think of. He was a man who went after what he wanted without any finesse or skilled diplomacy.

They didn't say anything for a long moment. They continued to lie together and stare at each other, fueling the fire between them, a fire destined to become an inferno. She felt the full length of him, every muscle of his perfect physique, pressed against her, and she began to fall deeper and deeper into a sea of sexual desire. Then she heard herself give a little moan before looping her arms around his neck to bring his mouth down to hers.

The moment their lips touched, his tongue entered her mouth like it had every right to do so, and like those other times, it took over not only her mouth but her senses. He was kissing her with pure, unadulterated possession. And as if she'd been given her cue, she kissed him back with a fervor she didn't know she had until meeting him.

Moments later, and she wasn't sure just how much later, he broke off the kiss and pressed his forehead against hers as if to catch his breath. She needed to catch her breath, also. And then as if he couldn't help himself, he shifted their bodies sideways and then leaned forward and placed a brief, erotic kiss on her lips that caused a stirring in her stomach, an urgency that seemed to consume her.

For a long moment they lay there in silence while he held her, then both got to their feet. A slow smile curved his mouth. "I think we should go into the kitchen and eat now," he said in a warmly seductive voice as he pulled her closer into his arms.

"And then," he added while holding her gaze with an intensity that made her shudder, "what takes place after dinner will be strictly your call."

Chapter 5

Cole glanced across the table at Patrina. She hadn't said much since they had begun eating. He figured what he'd told her moments ago in the living room had given her something to think about.

She was stubborn, filled with more spirit and fire than any woman he'd ever met. Considering those things, she probably would still not admit to wanting him, and definitely would not act on it, although they had kissed about four times now. And they hadn't been chaste kisses, either, but the kind that set your body on fire. Hell, his body was still burning and he was hard as a rock.

At least if nothing else he was proving to her that she was indeed a sensual woman, something else she still probably wanted to deny. All and all, he felt that when it came to Patrina Foreman, he still had one hell of a challenge on his hands. The good doctor just refused to acknowledge what was so blatantly obvious. She needed a good roll in the hay just as much as he did. He refused to let up trying to convince her that indulging in a couple of sexual encounters with him was just what she needed.

Deciding the silence between them had lasted long enough, he figured it was time to get her talking. She was very dedicated to her job, so he decided to begin there. He leaned back in his chair, took a sip of his wine and asked, "What exactly do you do at that clinic, Patrina?"

It took her a while but she finally lifted her head and looked at him. And then she was frowning. "Why do you want to know?"

He shrugged. "Because I'm interested."

She gave a doubtful snort, which meant she didn't believe him. He understood what she was doing. For a little while she had let her guard down with him and now she was trying to recover ground and put it back up. "And why would you be interested?"

He had an answer for her. "Because I'm interested in anything that involves you," he said, completely honest and totally unfazed by the cold look she was giving him.

It was hard to believe that less than an hour ago she had been warm and willing in his arms. She'd kissed him with as much passion as he'd been kissing her. The memory of their tumble onto the couch and the way their lips had locked still had heat thrumming through him. He was in worse shape now than before mainly because he had gotten a good taste of that bottled-up passion and was determined to get her off that damn shelf now more than ever.

"So tell me," he said when she refused to start talking. "I'm really interested in what you do at that clinic, so tell me."

"What if I don't want to?" she asked through tight lips.

He smiled. "Um, I can think of several ways to make you talk."

Evidently the ones he'd been thinking of crossed her mind, too, and she quickly dropped her gaze and began studying her glass of wine. Then she said, "It's a women's clinic that provides free services, which include physicals, breasts exams, pap smears, pregnancy testing, comprehensive health education, as well as many other types of needed services."

"How often are you there?"

She shrugged. "It's voluntary and I'm there as much as I can be, usually at least a few hours each day. I wish I could do more. Funding is tight and the medical equipment we need isn't cheap. We depend on private donations to ensure ongoing services for women who lack access to adequate health care."

"Pregnant women?"

"*All* women. Last year, our outreach program provided services to over a thousand homeless women. We believe all women deserve excellent health care, regardless of their ability to pay, and…"

Cole listened as she continued talking and could tell that her work at the clinic was something she was very passionate about. But then, he had discovered that she was a very passionate person…and very expressive. He couldn't stop looking at her while she was speaking and how she used her hands to get several points across. She had nice hands and he would do just about anything to feel those hands on him. She'd come close, had even unzipped his pants before that damn timer on the stove had gone off. Hell, he wished he'd remembered to turn the thing off when he'd taken the rolls out of the oven.

His gaze moved from her hands over her face, scanning her eyebrows, cheekbone and nose before latching on to her lips. Damn, they were kissable lips and he wouldn't mind tasting them again. But what he really wanted was her naked and in bed with him. He wanted to move in place between her lush thighs and get inside her, move in and out, see the expression on her face when he made her come. Feel the shuddering power of his release when he did likewise.

"Sorry…" She paused and drew in a quick breath. "I didn't mean to go on and on like that. I kind of get carried away."

Her words pulled him back in. "No reason to apologize," he quickly said. "I found everything you said interesting." *At least I did when I wasn't thinking about making love to you.*

"Since you cooked, the least I can do is take care of the dishes," she said, getting to her feet.

He could tell she was nervous about what she perceived as his expectations on how the evening should end. When she reached for his plate, he grabbed hold of her hand and gently gripped her fingers with his. "I don't like it when you seem afraid of me, Patrina." He felt the shiver that passed through her and then that same shiver passed through him.

She tried pulling her hand free but he kept a tight hold and wouldn't let it go. "I'm not afraid of you, Cole. I'm just unsure about a lot of things right now."

"Don't be unsure of anything," he said quietly. "Especially when it involves us."

He watched as she drew a deep breath and then released it before saying, "But there is no *us*, Cole."

He regarded her for several silent seconds, saw the determined glint in her gaze, the stubborn set of her jaw. "You didn't think that a couple of hours ago on that sofa. Need I remind you of what almost happened?"

She tugged her hand from his and narrowed her eyes. "It was a mistake."

The corners of his mouth curved into a smile. "It was more like satisfaction to me. I could have kept on kissing you and you could have kept on kissing me." He was tempted to go ahead and tell her, anyway, in blatant, plain English of the most erotic kind just where all that kissing could have led, but he decided not to. The fiery spark in her eyes was a clear indication that she wouldn't appreciate hearing it. She wasn't too happy with him right now, which meant they were back to square one.

"Look, Patrina, if it makes you happy, I'll help you do the dishes and then we can go to bed." At her piercing glare he quickly said, "Separate beds, of course. This has been a long and tiring day for me." And that, he thought, was putting it mildly. Spending another night with a hard-on was something he wasn't looking forward to. "But then, if you want to share my bed I have nothing against it," he said in a low voice that sounded like a sexual rumble even to his own ears.

"I'm sleeping in my bed tonight and you're sleeping in yours," she said, as if saying it to him would make it happen.

"If that's the way you want things."

"It is."

"Then at least let me help you with the dishes," he said, taking another sip of his wine, resisting the urge to reach out to take her hand in his again, tumble her into his lap, pour some of the wine down the front of her blouse and be so bold as to lap the wine up with his tongue.

"I can handle the dishes on my own," she said, breaking into his thoughts while stacking up the plates. "I don't need your help."

He stood and slid his hands into the pockets of his jeans, thinking she had to be the most stubborn woman he had encountered in a long time. "Fine, I'll leave you to it, then."

She regarded him carefully, as if she didn't believe for one minute he would give in to her that easily. When she saw that he was, she said, "Good."

He moved away from the table, but before he walked out of the kitchen he turned to her. "No, what would be good in my book—actually better than good—is sharing a bed with you."

Patrina released a deep, frustrated sigh of relief the moment she heard the shower going in the guest room. That relief was short-lived when her mind was suddenly filled with visions of a naked Cole standing under a spray of water.

She closed her eyes, fighting off the forbidden thoughts, refusing to let her mind go there, but it seemed to be going there, anyway. She couldn't forget how they had tumbled onto the sofa, how his solid, muscled body had been on top of hers, how his firm thighs had worked themselves between her legs in such a way that denim rubbing again denim had been an actual turn-on.

It didn't do much for her to remember how she had latched on to his mouth to finish what had started in the kitchen. Once again he had reminded her just how much of a female she was. Just how much passion she had been missing out on—both before and after Perry's death.

She quickly opened her eyes, not wanting to go there, refusing to think about it. Perry had been simply great in the bedroom; he'd just handled her a lot differently than Cole would—if given the chance. But she refused to give him the chance and the sooner he realized that, the better off the both of them would be.

She and Cole were playing this vicious game of tug-of-war where he was determined to come out the winner. And she was just as determined that he be the loser. Considering the kitchen scene earlier when she had come close to touching him in an intimate way, as well as the tumble onto the sofa, she would go so far as to admit that for a little while, she had gotten caught up in passion and had allowed him to break down her defenses. But she had recovered, was of sound mind, on top of her game, and simply refused to let him get an advantage again. She had to show him that she wasn't just some naive country girl.

She wasn't born yesterday and was well aware that it was all about sex to him. Nothing more than a quick tumble between the sheets. But then, knowing Cole, she suspected there would be nothing quick about it. He would draw it out, savor every second. He would strive to make her experience things that she had never experienced before, even during her five years of marriage. Already his kisses had taken her into unfamiliar territory.

Okay, she would be the first to admit that curiosity and desire had almost gotten the best of her, had almost done her in, but she was back in control. Talking about the clinic had helped. It had made her remember just how many women she'd counseled about the importance of being accountable for their actions and whatever decisions they made. It was time for her to take a dose of her own medicine.

It didn't take her long to finish the dishes and sweep the floor, deciding to have both done before Cole took a notion to return. She would retire early tonight and finish reading her book. But first she wanted to listen to the weather report. She needed to know just how much longer it would be before Cole was able to leave so she could get her life back to how it had been before he arrived—all work and no play, filled with apathy, definitely lacking passion. Before he had set foot in her house, the only desire she had was for the work she did at the doctor's office she owned and at the clinic. She would admit she lived a boring life. *Would it really be totally wrong, absolutely insane to sample some of what Cole was offering, and for once to forget about everything and everyone other than myself and my own needs?*

He said he wanted her and she had no reason not to believe him, especially once it appeared he had been aroused all day, at least whenever he was in her presence. She was a medical doctor, so she recognized the obvious signs. But then, she was a woman, as well, and given that, she had done more than noted the signs. For a while she had gotten caught up in it, gloried in the fact that he found her so desirable he couldn't control his body's reaction.

The thought that she could do something like that to a man, especially a man like Cole, was totally mind-boggling. Maybe she should rethink her position, give in to her desires, to see where it got the both of them. It wasn't like he was a permanent resident of Bozeman, so chances were that when the weather cleared for him to leave, she probably wouldn't be seeing him again while he was visiting Casey. She knew about the huge party Casey and Abby had planned for Corey later in the month, and she had every intention of attending. Even if she and Cole did share a bed before he left, by the time the party happened, she should be able to put the affair behind her so that when she saw him again, she wouldn't have a flare-up of passion, at least not of the degree she was having now. So maybe sleeping with him—to work him out of her system—wasn't such a bad idea.

Deciding she'd drunk too much wine at dinner for her to be considering such a thing, she moved across the kitchen to turn on the radio, as well as to put on a pot of coffee. She needed to sober up her brain cells.

Not much later she was standing at the window looking out with a cup of coffee in her hand. It was dark outside and still snowing. According to the weather report, things should start clearing up by late tomorrow evening or early the following day. That meant that this could be the last night Cole would have to stay under her roof. There was a chance he could leave for Casey and McKinnon's place before dark tomorrow. Then she could have her house all to herself again. She wouldn't have to worry about dressing decently if she didn't want to, or having a man underfoot. Nor would she have to worry about her hormones going wacky on her from a purely male dimpled smile or a dark lustful gaze.

"Is it still snowing?"

She quickly turned, sloshing some of the hot coffee on her hand. "Ouch."

Before she knew what was happening, Cole had quickly crossed the room to take the cup out of her hand and place it on the counter. "What are you trying to do? Burn yourself?" he asked in a deep voice filled with concern.

"You startled me," she accused.

"Sorry. I didn't mean to."

She tried ignoring the sensual huskiness in his voice. "Well, you did."

It was then that she noticed what he was wearing. In her opinion it was very little. He was barefoot with only a pair of boxer pajama bottoms, similar to the ones Dale liked to wear, but she never had reason to notice how snug they fit Dale. They were a silk pair and she was sure they belonged to a set. So where was the top part? Or at the very least, a matching robe.

Maybe she should at least be grateful that he was wearing anything at all, since some men preferred sleeping in the nude. But then, this wasn't his house. It was hers and under those circumstances he didn't have a choice in the matter.

But still…even with the boxer shorts there were a few things she couldn't help but notice. Like the fact he was still aroused. The cut of the boxers made that much completely obvious. She didn't want to stare but she found that she couldn't help herself. He was huge and as packed as any man had a right to be and then some. She subconsciously clamped her inner thighs together at the thought of something that size going into her. There was no way she wouldn't get stretched to the limit.

"So what do you think?"

She blinked and quickly shifted her gaze to his face. "About what?"

"The weather," he said, his dark gaze holding hers.

She couldn't help wondering if they were really discussing the weather. Regardless, she intended to play right along. "It's my understanding it should start clearing up tomorrow."

There was a bit of silence, then he said, "That means I'll be able to leave."

"Yes. I'm sure Casey will be glad to see you."

"Just like I'm sure you'll be glad to be all alone again."

Patrina suddenly felt a shiver of apprehension run up her spine. Would she really be glad to be all alone again?

"There's a full moon in the sky," he said quietly.

It was then that she noticed he was no longer looking at her but was looking out the window and up at the sky. She pondered his comment and wondered if it had any specific meaning. When she couldn't think of one she said, "And?" She figured there had to be more.

Although he didn't look at her, she saw his smile. "According to Ian, each full moon has a different meaning and a magical purpose," he said as he continued to gaze out the window and look at the sky.

Ian was Cole's cousin and considered the astronomer in the Westmoreland family because he had a degree in physics and had once worked for NASA. Ian was now the owner of a beautiful casino on Lake Tahoe. "And what do you think is the meaning of this full moon?" she couldn't help but ask.

He turned to her. "A full moon in April is the Seed Moon. It's the time to plant your seeds of desire in Mother Earth."

She raised a suspicious brow. "And you distinctly remember Ian saying that?"

His smile widened as he turned back to the window. "No. He gave me a book and I distinctly recall reading it."

"Oh." *Planting seeds of desire in Mother Earth.* She wasn't about to ask how that was done. But she couldn't deny it had her thinking, making a number of possibilities flow through her mind. Planting seeds of desire sounded a lot like setting someone up for seduction.

"Like I told you yesterday," Cole began, breaking into her thoughts, "neither Casey nor my father was expecting me this soon and they don't have any idea what day I arrived, so if you prefer, I won't let them know I spent some time here, stranded during the snowstorm with you."

"Why should it matter?" she asked. "Nothing happened between us."

He looked at her, raised an arched brow. "Nothing?"

She shrugged. "Okay, we kissed a few times."

"Yes, we did, didn't we?" he said softly, his gaze latched on to her lips. His dark eyes then shifted and held hers and she began to feel a sharp ache below her stomach.

"Yes," she finally answered. "We did."

"Want to do it again?"

That was one question she hadn't expected, yet she should not have been surprised that he had asked it. In the past thirty hours, she had discovered that Cole Westmoreland was a man who did or said whatever pleased him.

She opened her mouth to say that, no, she didn't want to do it again, then immediately closed it, thinking who was she kidding? She enjoyed kissing him and, yes, she wanted to do it again since it probably would be the last time she did so. He would be leaving tomorrow and chances were their paths wouldn't cross again—at least not in such an intimate setting.

She glanced out the window, thinking that the most sensible thing to do was turn and escape to her bedroom and not have any more contact with him. But for some reason she didn't want to think sensibly. She really didn't want to think at all, and the only time she couldn't think was when she was in his arms sharing a kiss.

"Patrina?"

She returned her gaze to his. "Perhaps," she said softly.

He arched a brow. "Perhaps?"

She nodded. "Perhaps, I want to do it again."

He gave her a level look. "Don't you know for certain?"

Patrina heard the slight tremor in his voice. "Well, maybe I prefer that you take your time and convince me that I do."

Her words seemed to hang between them as they stared at each other, and for some reason, all she could think about was his mouth making her pulse race. And then he broke into her thoughts when he said in a gentle yet throaty voice, "I hope you understand what you're asking."

Oh, I understand all right, but it'll only be limited to kissing. She could handle that. Her throat suddenly felt tight, constricted, but she managed to force through enough sound to say, "I understand what I'm asking, Cole."

As soon as she stated her affirmation, she was pulled into strong, muscular arms.

Chapter 6

The first thing Cole wanted to do was taste her. He couldn't resist. Just one quick taste and then he would go about his business, taking his time to convince her that they needed to kiss again and again—definitely a lot longer each and every time.

His mouth brushed hers, just long enough to snake out his tongue and caress her bottom lip with its tip. He heard her sharp intake of breath and quickly pulled back on her moan. He did it again, a second longer this time, a little more provocatively when he wiggled the tip of his tongue while caressing the tantalizing surface of her upper lip.

He withdrew when she released another moan, this one throatier than the last and saw that her eyes had closed and her lips were moist from where his tongue had been. He liked the look of it. He also liked the look in her eyes when she reopened them to stare at him. He saw something hot and sensuous in their depths and fought for control not to say the hell with it and pull her into his arms and give her a long, hungry kiss.

Deciding to take the degree of her desire, as well as his, to another level, one that he could sufficiently handle, he reached out and with the tip of his finger, traced a path from her moist bottom lip down past her jaw to where her pulse was beating wildly in her throat. She said nothing while watching him attentively, but he could hear the unevenness of her breathing.

And then his lips and tongue replaced his finger while they moved all over her face, wanting to leave his mark everywhere on her features. And when he felt a shiver pass through her, he knew she was ready for something heavier and pulled her closer into his arms and greedily claimed her mouth in a long, slow kiss that made shivers run through her body even more than before.

Moments later, he pulled back and whispered the question close to her moist lips. "Want to try another one?"

Instead of answering, she nodded, and then he was back at her lips, devouring them in a way that shook him to the core. Never had his tongue been so ravenous for a woman's mouth; never had his palate been so famished. He could go on kissing her all night, but he wanted each one to be slow, long and fulfilling. And from the sound of her moans, they were.

He thought that this type of seduction suited her per-

fectly. Something slow and detailed while stirring her
passion. With each stroke of his tongue he was able to
discover just what she liked, what she had never experienced before and just what she wanted him to do again.

He also discovered what part of her mouth gave her
the most pleasure, what part of it his tongue touched
that made her moan the loudest, made her desire the
strongest. He knew he could make her come just from
kissing her if he were to turn up the heat a notch, and a
part of him was pushed to do just that. That would lead
into him giving her another type of kiss while at the
same time experiencing a different taste of her.

The thought of doing so made his body harden even
more, made his erection throb in a way that had him
clutching for breath. All she'd given him was the liberty to kiss her. However, he intended to show her that
when it came to kissing, there was no such thing as
limitations. Kissing came in several forms and it could
be done to a number of places, not confined just to the
lips. No parts of the body were exempt. When she'd af-
firmed her understanding, he doubted that she knew the
full extent of where it could lead. But he, on the other
hand, understood perfectly and intended to take whatever kisses he delivered to the highest level possible.

He eased down on the windowsill, found it sturdy
enough to hold his weight and pulled her to stand between his open legs, which put him eye to eye with her
chest. He drew in a tight breath when he noticed how
the nipples of her breasts were straining against her
blouse as if begging to be freed. And he had no qualms
about obliging the pair.

Still holding Patrina's gaze he began undoing the buttons, and each one exposed more of her black lacy bra. When all the buttons were undone, he eased the blouse from her arms and shoulders.

"You're only supposed to kiss me," he heard her remind him in a ragged voice.

"I know and I shall," he said throatily, letting his fingers move to the front clasp of her bra. "But kissing comes in many forms."

Then with a flick of his fingers her bra opened and her breasts burst forth. His mouth and hand were on them immediately, lightly cupping one while his mouth greedily devoured the other. He knew the moment she lifted her arms and held his head to her breasts, evidently thinking if she didn't do so he would stop. But there was no way he could stop. The taste of her was being absorbed into everything about him that was male, and her luscious essence—hot and enticing— was playing havoc with his senses.

She moaned his name over and over, and the more he heard it, the more he wanted to make her say it that much more, with even more meaning. He decided to put his other hand, the one that was free at the moment, to work and knew just where he wanted it to be and what he wanted it to do.

Reaching down he found the snap to her slacks and slowly worked it free to open it. She was so wrapped up in what he was doing to her breasts that she was unaware of what he was doing to the lower part of her body. He tugged her pants apart at the waist and the moment he did so, he inserted his hand inside and his fingers inched past the flimsy material of her panties to cup her feminine mound. He felt her body go still at the intimate touch and he freed the nipple in his mouth long enough to glance up and meet her gaze.

"Wh-what are you doing?" she asked in a strained voice, but she didn't pull away.

He chose his words carefully and spoke softly. "Like I said earlier, kissing comes in several forms. Will you trust me tonight to introduce you to a few of them?"

She said nothing as her gaze held his and he knew she was trying to come to terms with what he was saying, trying to decide just what she should do. He realized in asking her to trust him that he was asking a lot of her when she had no idea what he intended to do. And at that moment, he couldn't help wondering what was going on in that pretty little head of hers.

Patrina stood there and stared down at Cole, specifically at his mouth, which had been suckling at her breasts. She recalled how earlier those same lips and tongue had driven her crazy with desire, had her body still tingling. And now he wanted to use his mouth on her again, in other places, and she had an idea where.

During the five years of their marriage, she and Perry had never engaged in what she knew Cole was hinting at, and she couldn't help the sensations that flooded her stomach at the thought of participating in such an intimate act with him. To say she'd never been curious about it would be a lie, and now Cole was offering her the chance to indulge. Should she take it?

As if sensing that she was on the borderline, his fingers slowly began to move and the heated core of her began throbbing at the intimate contact. He was stroking new life into that part of her, creating a need she'd never known she had.

Her gaze shifted from his mouth to his eyes, which were boring into hers with an intensity that almost took her breath away. "Tell me," he whispered softly. "Tell me I can kiss you here," he said, and at the same time he inserted a single finger inside her to let her know just where he meant.

She sucked in a deep breath, suddenly feeling exposed, vulnerable and filled with a fire, the degree of which she hadn't known was possible for her. And it was taking over her senses, literally burning them to a cinder and making her act the part of someone she really didn't know. She could only close her eyes against such intense desire.

"Patrina."

She opened her eyes to meet his intense gaze and the look she saw there took her breath away. He wanted her. He *really* wanted her. Probably just as much as she wanted him. He wanted to introduce her to something new and different and she knew that she wanted the same thing.

"Yes," she whispered softly. "You can kiss me there."

She saw the smile that touched his lips and he didn't waste any time pulling her slacks down past her knees and taking her panties right along with them, leaving her feminine mound fully exposed for his private viewing. She closed her eyes but knew the exact moment he dropped to his knees in front of her and felt the strong hands that gently parted her thighs. She fought to remain standing when she felt him bury the bridge of his nose in the curls covering her mound, and she fought to retain her ability to breathe the moment he inserted his tongue inside her.

And like a meal he just had to devour, he tightened his hold on her thighs to keep her steady while his mouth went to work on her, the tip of his tongue piercing her with desire so strong and deep she cried out from something so totally unexpected, as well as something so profoundly intense.

She opened her eyes for a heated second and looked down only to see his head buried between her legs. Each and every stroke of his tongue was precision quick, lightning sharp, and was sending her over the edge in a way she'd never gone before.

She bit her lip in an effort not to cry out again, but cried out, anyway. She felt her knees buckling beneath her, but the firm grip of his hands on her thighs kept her standing. She grasped the sides of his head, telling herself she needed to pull him away, but instead, found she was placing pressure to keep him right there. He was exploring the insides of her body, the areas where his tongue could reach, and she was too overcome with passion to stop him. In fact, she heard her whispers of "Don't stop" over and over again.

Then suddenly, she felt her entire body filled with electrified sensations that ripped through her with a force that had her screaming his name, and she couldn't do anything but ride the incredible waves that were carrying her to some unknown destination. Frissons

of pleasure attacked every cell of her body before she
shook with the force of an orgasm the likes of which
she'd never experienced before.

And just when she thought she couldn't possibly take
any more, couldn't stand on her feet a second longer, she
suddenly felt herself scooped into strong arms.

"Wait, I'm too heavy."

"No, you're not," he said, gathering her up.

She buried her face in the warm, muscular texture of
his chest and felt them moving. She wasn't sure where
he was taking her and at the moment she didn't care.

But when she felt the softness of the mattress against
her back, she knew. She opened her eyes and watched
as he went about removing her shoes and socks and
tossing them aside before tugging her jeans and panties completely off.

He gazed down at her naked body with heated desire
before leaning over and kissing her lips in a slow, thorough exchange. Moments later he drew back from the
kiss and in a surprise move pulled the covers over her,
then tucked her in tenderly, as if seeing to her comfort.
He then leaned over and kissed her again, and this time
when he withdrew, he held her gaze and whispered,
"Good night, Patrina. Sleep well."

She felt too weak to respond, so she said nothing.
She lay there and watched as he crossed the room to
the door, opened it and eased out, gently closing it behind him.

The moment Cole stepped into the hall he leaned
against the nearest wall and drew in a sharp breath. It

had taken all the control he could muster not to crawl into bed with Patrina, especially when her eyes had looked so inviting. Never had he wanted a woman more, and with his history, that said a lot.

There was something about her that brought out his primal instincts, instincts that he always thought he could control. But with her he couldn't. It was as if after their first kiss he had become nearly obsessed with kissing her every chance he got, consumed with the taste of her and wanting to discover and explore all the different facets of that taste.

Tonight he had.

He had tasted her lips, her breasts and the very essence of her femininity, everything that made her the beautiful and desirable woman she was. If he had lingered in that bedroom with her a minute longer, he would have been tempted to strip off his boxers and join her in bed to find the heaven he knew awaited him between her lush thighs. She stirred a need within him that even now had him weak in the knees.

He lifted his hand to touch his mouth and couldn't help but smile. There was no way his mouth and tongue hadn't gotten addicted to her taste. Everything about her was perfect—the shape of her breasts, the flare of her thighs, the shape of her mouth, lips—everything.

Knowing if he didn't move well away from her bedroom door he would be tempted to go back into the room, he forced himself to walk toward the kitchen, needing some of the coffee she had made earlier.

A few moments later he was standing back at the window gazing out and holding a cup of coffee in his hand. What he'd told Patrina earlier about the full moon was true. He'd always had an interest in astronomy himself, but had never taken the time to develop that interest and had been surprised when he'd discovered he had a cousin who had.

He couldn't help but smile when he thought about his eleven male cousins and how he and Clint had been able to bond with them in a way that made it seem they had known each other all their lives and not just a few years. Quade had been the first one they had met, and only because he had shown up in Austin wanting to know why they were having his uncle investigated, and had been more than mildly surprised when they'd told him that the uncle he knew was their biological father—a father who didn't know they existed. Durango and Stone had been next, since they'd been in Montana when he and Clint had arrived to meet Corey.

He then thought about what he'd told Patrina earlier about not letting anyone know he'd been stranded here with her. He knew how some small towns operated. Patrina was a highly respected doctor and he wouldn't do anything to tarnish that. Although she was a widow, old enough to do whatever she wanted, some wouldn't see it that way. Besides, what they did was nobody's business but theirs.

Moving away from the window, Cole walked over to the counter to pour another cup of coffee. Although he wished otherwise, he was too keyed up to sleep. A cold shower would probably do him justice. Just the thought that Patrina would be sleeping in the room across the hall from him gave him a sexual ache that wouldn't go away, an erection that refused to go down.

For as long as he lived, he would never forget the look on her face when her orgasm had struck. It had been simply priceless and one he would love seeing again. The intensity of it had him wondering if she'd ever had one of that magnitude before.

He turned when he heard a sound and looked up to find Patrina standing in the doorway. Her hair was flowing around her shoulders and her features glowed with that womanly look—the one he enjoyed seeing on her. She was wearing a beautiful blue silk robe and the way it was draped around her curves showed what a shapely body she had. It was his opinion that she looked sexy as hell.

"I couldn't sleep," she said softly, her eyes locked with his.

He crossed the room to come to a stop directly in front of her, being careful not to get too close. He would definitely lose control if he touched her. Just inhaling her scent was doing a number on him already. "Would you like a cup of coffee?" he heard himself asking.

He watched as she shook her head. "No, coffee isn't what I need."

He drew in a tight breath, almost too afraid to ask, but knew he had to do so, anyway. "What is it that you need?"

The dark eyes that gazed back at him were filled with an expression she wasn't trying to hide, a sexual allure he could actually feel all the way to the bone. A fierce abundance of desire rammed through him when she responded in a soft and sexy voice, "You. I need you, Cole."

Chapter 7

Patrina stood and watched Cole as he stood staring at her. She wondered what he was thinking and was certain he'd heard what she said. Saying it hadn't been easy, probably a few of the hardest words she'd ever spoken. But she had lain in bed, totally satisfied and remembering what he'd done to her right here in the kitchen, first while sitting on the windowledge and then on his knees. She wanted more. She *needed* more.

He'd always told her to feel the passion, but tonight he had taken those feelings to another level, and thanks to him she had done more than just felt the passion. She had experienced it in a way she never had before. That was in no way taking anything from Perry. It was just giving Cole his due. He was experienced when it came to pleasing women; he had a skill you didn't have to wonder how it had been acquired. The man was totally awesome and had a mouth that was undeniably lethal.

"Do you fully understand what you're saying?"

He'd asked her a similar question earlier tonight in this kitchen when he had wanted to kiss her. At the time she had said she understood because she'd been more than certain that she had. It hadn't taken long to discover that she hadn't understood the full extent of anything.

She definitely hadn't understood or known the degree of her passion. But Cole had. Somehow he had sensed it, had homed in on it from the first and immediately set out to taste it.

And tonight he'd gotten more than a taste. He'd gotten a huge whopping sample. But so had she. While he had taken control of her body, soul and mind, she had been driven to a need of gigantic proportion. And just to think she hadn't indulged in the full scope of what was possible. And more than anything she wanted to. Tomorrow he would be leaving and that would be it. The finale. But a part of her didn't want their time together to end.

"Yes, I fully understand," she finally said while holding his gaze and hoping he saw what was in her eyes— her determination, her heartfelt desire and now…her impatience.

She moved, took a step closer to him at the same time that he came forward, and suddenly she was in his arms. The fire they had ignited earlier was now a blaze and when he captured her mouth in his, the only thing she could think of was that this was where she belonged.

No man had ever possessed her this way. His hands seemed to be everywhere, all over her. The robe was stripped from her body, leaving her completely naked, but things didn't stop there. It seemed they were just beginning. He backed her out of the kitchen into the living room. Once there he stripped out of his boxers and the size of his erection had her blinking to make sure her eyes weren't playing tricks on her. He was huge. She should not have been surprised, but seeing him in the flesh was sending shivers down her body.

"You sure about this?"

She glanced up at him. Even now, with them standing facing each other as naked as two people could be, he was giving her a chance to change her mind.

Seeing the size of him was enough reason to consider doing so. But she wanted this. She needed this and she had to assure him. "Yes, I'm sure about this as long as you realize I don't come close to the level of experience or expertise that you're probably used to."

Cole nodded. A smile touched his lips. "I'm glad you don't."

And then he was pulling her into his arms, and when flesh melded into flesh, he kissed her with a longing she felt all the way to her toes. Her mouth opened fully to his, as far as it could stretch, and their tongues entwined, mingled, and their breathing combined, enticing her to feel things she could only experience with him. And then she found herself swept into strong arms. But the kissing continued. In fact, he picked up the pace, going deeper, making it hotter and more urgent.

He lifted his head and his gaze burned down into

hers. It took her several seconds to catch her breath…
as well as realize they were moving and that Cole was
walking with her in his arms from the living room toward the bedroom he'd occupied for the past two days.

When they reached their destination he placed her
on her feet beside the bed and she knew once again he
was making sure this was what she wanted. She would
have to get into his bed on her own accord. She looked
at the neatly made bed, a representation of his handiwork, and marveled at how tidy a job he'd done. It was
nothing like the haphazard-looking made-up beds she
was used to whenever Dale came to visit.

Knowing he was watching her intently, she took a
step closer to the bed and turned down the covers, and
without saying anything she slid between the sheets and
then looked at him expectantly. She felt totally aroused
to see him standing there, naked with a huge erection
and a tantalizing smile tugging at the corners of his
mouth.

She was no longer angry with herself for being weak
where Cole was concerned. Instead, she had accepted
the fact that she was a woman with needs—needs she
had tried ignoring for more than three years. And they
would be needs she would once again ignore once Cole
left. What she was taking with him was some *me* time.
For once she would think of no one but herself and do
something that would make her happy and satisfied.

"We're sleeping in tomorrow," Cole said in a voice
so sexy it made her breath lock in her throat, and she
scooted over when he joined her in the bed. It was
queen-size, and a good fit for the two of them. The

size of the bed vanished from her mind the moment he shifted and pulled her into his arms, claiming her lips in the process.

The kiss was everything she had gotten used to, had come to expect. His tongue was driving her crazy, stirring up her passion and sending shivers all through her body. It was the same body that his hands were all over, becoming reacquainted with all her intimate places. He was making it obvious that his focus was on pleasing her. She was touched by the gesture and decided to follow his lead. However, her focus would be on pleasing him.

She felt one of his hands slide between her legs, touching what she now considered her hot spot. His fingers began exploring at will, familiar territory to them now. She felt an instinctive need to touch him, as well, and slightly shifting her body, she reached down and took him into her hands. He released her mouth to pull in a sharp breath the moment he felt her touch.

He felt hard and smooth both at the same time, warm to the touch, huge in her hand. Then she began moving her hand, stroking him with an ease that surprised her. She became fascinated by what she was doing, totally enthralled with the way her fingers glided softly back and forth across the silken tip. And when she glanced up at Cole and met his gaze, what she saw in the dark depths took her breath away, made her aware of just how affected he was by her intimate touch.

Without saying anything he lowered his head and that same mouth he had used just moments earlier on hers now targeted her breasts. He drew between his lips an aroused peak and began sucking on it in a way that made her cry out his name.

She pulled her hand off him when he shifted their positions to place himself over her and used his knee to farther nudge her legs apart. He gazed down at her, giving her one last chance to stop him from going further. Instead she took the hand that had stroked him earlier and skimmed his chin and whispered, "I want this, Cole. I want you."

On a deep guttural groan he entered her and her body automatically arched, then proceeded to stretch to accommodate him. She felt all her inner muscles grab hold of him, begin clenching him as every nerve between her legs became sensitive to the invasion. She inhaled the masculine scent of him, the musky scent of sex, when he began moving, with quick, even strokes that sent her nearly over the edge with each hard thrust.

And then when she thought she couldn't possibly take any more, felt her body almost splintering in two, he gave one last hard thrust that triggered his release at the same time her body shattered into a thousand pieces. Too late it hit her that they had forgotten something, but there was nothing they could do about it now. Tremors were rocking her body to the core, and the only thing that registered on her mind was how he was making her feel at this very moment. And when he leaned down, enveloped her more deeply in his arms and captured her mouth with his, she felt herself tumbling once again into a sea of desire.

Cole came awake, not sure how long he'd been asleep. He glanced at the woman securely tucked in his arms and licked his lips. His mouth still tasted of her, her scent was all over his skin, just as he was certain his scent was all over hers. He recalled the exact moment she had come apart, triggering his body to do likewise. It had been one hell of a joining. Filled with fire, passion… He thought further, closing his eyes when realization hit—one that had been unprotected.

He let out a frustrated moan. How could he have been so careless? Condoms were tucked away in his wallet. It wasn't like he didn't have any. He just hadn't thought of using one. It would be the first time he'd ever made love with a woman without protection.

He again glanced at Patrina. She was sleeping with a satisfied look on her face. And rightly so. Their joining had been nothing short of magnificent. It had left them so drained they'd drifted off to sleep in each others' arms.

They had to talk and it was a discussion that couldn't wait until morning. She needed to know what he hadn't done—or more precisely what he might have carelessly done. He hated rousing her from sleep but leaned over close to her ear and whispered, "Patrina."

He said her name several times before she finally forced her eyes open to look at him. Before he could fix his mouth to say anything, she reached up and looped her arms around his neck, and on a soft groan she pulled his mouth down to hers.

Sensations skyrocketed through him and he returned her kiss with a passion that went all the way to the bone and instinctively, once again, he moved and positioned his body over hers. And when her thighs parted for him, he pressed down, entered her, filling her completely. And then their bodies began mating once again and every time he surged forward into her aroused flesh, he felt his own body trembling, blatant testimony to his own ardent desire.

And when she wrapped her legs tightly around him, as if to hold him inside, he was filled with a sense of possession that until now had been foreign to him. He ached for her and would always ache for her. And she would be the only one who could satisfy that ache, as she was doing now.

And when her body began quivering uncontrollably just moments before she released his mouth to scream his name, he knew her power over him was undeniable and absolute. Just like he'd known he would, he helplessly followed her over the edge and into the grips of an orgasm so mind-blowingly strong that he felt his every nerve ending leap to life. He also knew she had become an addiction that would be hard as hell for him to kick.

"It's stopped snowing."

Cole's statement filtered through Patrina's mind as she glanced out the window. Not only had it stopped snowing, but a semblance of sun was forcing its way through the Montana clouds. She couldn't say anything because she knew what that meant. He would be leaving.

As if he read her thoughts, he said, "I plan on being here for a while, Patrina. I need to call the car-rental agency and let them know about the car so they can go get it and bring me another one here."

He pulled her deeper into his arms and then said, "And I meant what I said yesterday. None of my family knew I was coming this early, so they aren't going to be worried and wondering where I am. I want my being here with you these past two days to be our secret."

She knew he wanted that to protect her reputation and she appreciated it, but it wasn't necessary. She opened her mouth to tell him so, but then he kissed her and she could no longer think. She could only feel.

After they had made love that first time, they had fallen asleep and had awakened to make love again, and again, into the wee hours of the morning. If she never made love to another man again, she would be satisfied. But then, she couldn't imagine ever being in another man's arms this way, sharing his bed. In the space of forty-eight hours she had gone from being tucked away safely on a shelf to having been brought down and placed on a counter where she had experienced things she never thought could happen between a man and woman.

Cole released her mouth and said in a strained voice, "I didn't use protection, Patrina. Not that first time or any of the other times. I'm sorry for being so careless. That's not the way I operate. If anything develops from it, I will take full responsibility. You and my child won't want for anything."

She met his gaze, was touched by what he said but felt that this, too, wasn't necessary, although she wished she could say the words that would assure him that it wasn't the right time for her to get pregnant. She didn't want to think of how many babies she'd delivered whose mothers had thought it hadn't been the right time.

"You don't have to worry about that, Cole. If I am pregnant, I can certainly manage to take care of my baby."

He reached out and stroked the side of her face. "Our baby. You would not have gotten pregnant by yourself. Promise me that if you discover you are, you will contact me in Texas."

She nodded. She would contact him only to let him know he would be a father because he had a right to know—if it came to that. But she would not let him fill his mind with any thoughts of obligations toward her. He hadn't forced himself on her. She had come willingly. Had gotten into his bed herself. And she had been in her right mind.

"I'll be back."

He whispered the words in her ear just before easing away from her side. She figured he was going to the bathroom and was already missing his warmth. She glanced over at the clock. It was 10 a.m. It seemed later than that. She settled under the thickness of the covers as images played across her mind of them making love. Even the thought of an unplanned pregnancy didn't bother her like it probably should. She'd delivered countless babies to other women and had always yearned for a child of her own. It was a secret desire.

She felt the dip in the bed and without looking over her shoulder she knew that Cole had returned. She could feel his heat again, and as he snuggled closer and pulled her into his arms…she felt something else. His huge erection. She flipped on her back and stared up at him.

"I went and got a condom out of my wallet and put it on. You'll be protected this time."

And then he was kissing her. A part of her wanted to pull her mouth free and tell him it was okay. He didn't have to protect her. To have his baby wouldn't be so bad…

But when he deepened the kiss, she ceased thinking at all. And when he shifted positions and slid into her, she instinctively wrapped her legs around him as erotic sensations swept through her, intensified with every stroke he made. She exulted in the feel of him inside her. It was as if this was where he was supposed to be. And moments later when her body exploded in a fire of sensual pleasure, she moaned his name over and over as waves rippled through her body.

Afterward, he pulled her close against him, held her tight in his arms and kissed her temple. For the first time in more than three years she felt total contentment.

Cole loaded the last of his luggage into the rental car the agency had brought him. The sky was clear and it was time to leave, but he would always have memories of the two days he had spent here with Patrina.

He turned around. She was standing in the doorway in her bathrobe. He had asked her not to get dressed. He wanted to remember her that way. When he saw her at his father's birthday party in a few weeks and fully clothed, that would be soon enough to stop thinking of her with only a bathrobe covering her nakedness. But he would never stop thinking of how many times they had made love, how his tongue had tasted her all over, or the moans that would pass from between her lips each and every time she came.

Inhaling deeply, he closed the trunk and walked back toward the porch. A part of him wasn't ready to go, but he knew it was something he had to do. Taking the steps slowly, he walked over to her and without saying a word he pulled her into his arms and kissed her like a soldier about to leave behind his woman before being carted off to war. She returned his kiss with a degree of passion he was getting used to. He would miss her. He would miss this.

He reluctantly pulled his mouth from hers and whispered against her moist lips. "Time for me to go."

"Will you drive more carefully this time?"

A smile touched his mouth. "Will you come to my rescue again if I don't?"

She chuckled and he felt the depth of it in his gut. "Yes. I would come to your rescue anytime, Cole Westmoreland."

She wasn't making leaving easy. He didn't say anything for a moment and then asked. "Was I a good houseguest?"

"The best. Was I a good doctor?"

"Off the charts."

He paused a moment, then added. "But I think you were an even better bedmate. It's going to be hard, the next time I see you, to not want to strip you naked. Just like it's hard as hell for me to leave now without taking you in that bedroom and making love to you one last time."

"What's stopping you?"

Patrina's question aroused him, tempted him sorely. "Because one more time won't be enough. I'd want to go on and on and on. I'd never want to leave."

Cole sighed heavily. That admission had been hard to make, but it was true. Then, feeling as if he might have said too much, true or not, he took a step back.

"Remember me," he said fiercely, fighting the urge to pull her back into his arms. Instead, he took her hand and gave it a gentle squeeze. "You're off the shelf now, Patrina. Don't go and put yourself back up there. You're too sensual a woman for that."

He turned and headed for the car and refused to look back. At least he didn't until he was pulling into the long driveway that would take him to the main road. And when he saw her in his rearview mirror, she was still standing there. The most passionate woman he'd ever had the pleasure of meeting.

Chapter 8

"**Y**ou're definitely a welcome surprise," Casey Westmoreland Quinn said. She grinned across the dinner table at her brother, who had shown up unexpectedly a few hours before.

"And you made perfect time," she added. "Had you arrived in Bozeman a few days ago you would have been met with one nasty snowstorm. Everyone's been stranded in their homes for the past couple of days."

"That couldn't have been much fun," Cole replied, trying to keep a straight face.

"We had no complaints," McKinnon Quinn said, smiling at Casey before taking a sip of his coffee.

Cole chuckled. He could read between the lines and couldn't help but be happy for his sister and the man she'd chosen to spend the rest of her life with. It was so obvious that they were in love. Casey had always been a person who believed in love, romance and all that happily-ever-after stuff, but she had become disillusioned after discovering that the storybook love story their mother had weaved for them concerning their father all those years had been a lie. Cole was glad to see that things had worked out for Casey, after all, and thanks to McKinnon, she believed in love again.

He then thought about Clint and his recent marriage to Alyssa. That, too, he thought, was definitely a love match and Cole was happy for them, as well. But while falling in love and getting married were good for some people, he had decided a long time ago he wasn't one of them.

He figured he would probably be like his uncle Sid and remain a bachelor forever. Some people did better by themselves. He liked the single life, the freedom to come and go as he pleased and not be responsible for anyone but himself. He had no problem with seeking out female companionship those times when a woman became necessary.

His thoughts shifted to Patrina and the time they had spent together. She had definitely been necessary and he was glad he'd made the decision not to mention to anyone that he'd spent the past couple of days stranded at her place. But there was the possibility she could be pregnant. He decided not to worry about anything just yet.

In the meantime, the time he had spent at her place was their secret, one he preferred not sharing with anyone, least of all his sister. The last thing he needed was for Casey—who had such a romantic heart—to get any ideas about his relationship with Patrina. Besides, given his reputation with the ladies, one his sister knew well, he didn't want her to wonder what might or might not have happened at Patrina's place.

And a lot had happened. Even now he had a tough time not remembering every single detail. He bet if he were to close his eyes he could probably still breathe in her scent.

"You want more coffee, Cole?"

Casey's question broke into his thoughts and he figured from where his thoughts were headed, it was a good thing. "No, thanks, and dinner was good."

"Thanks."

"So, how are the plans for the birthday party coming along?" he asked.

Casey smiled. "Fine. And as far as it being a surprise, Abby and I decided why bother, since Dad isn't a man you can easily pull anything over on. I can't wait to call to let him know you're here. He's going to be happy to see you."

Cole knew what she said was true. Ever since finding out he was the father of triplets, Corey had done everything within his power to forge a strong relationship with his offspring.

"There's something McKinnon and I want to tell you. We told Dad and Abby, as well as McKinnon's parents last week. I was waiting to tell you and Clint at the party."

Cole raised a curious brow. "What?"

Casey and McKinnon exchanged smiles and again

Cole felt the love flowing between them. Casey looked back at Cole and said, "We're adopting a baby."

Cole couldn't help the grin that shone on his face. "That's wonderful news," he said. "Congratulations." He knew how much the two of them wanted to become parents. He also knew that, due to a medical condition McKinnon had, they could not have children the natural way.

"Thanks." Casey beamed. "And we have Dr. Patrina Foreman to thank for this wonderful news."

Cole forced his features to remain neutral when he said, "Dr. Foreman?"

"Yes, she's the doctor who delivered little Sarah. She runs a women's clinic in town, one she helped found when she saw a need. One of her patients at the clinic, an eighteen-year-old girl, wants to give up her child as soon as it's born, but wanted to make sure the baby went to good parents. Patrina called me and McKinnon, we met with the young woman and everything has been arranged, all the legal matters taken care of. We'll be given the baby within hours of its birth."

"And when is the baby due?"

"Next month."

Cole smiled. "That's wonderful. Yes, it seems that you do owe a lot to Dr. Foreman."

"She's such a nice person," his sister went on. "I'm surprised you didn't meet her either at the party that was given for me last year or my wedding, since she was at both. She's been nominated for the Eve Award here in town. The winner will be announced later this year at a special ceremony."

"The Eve Award?" Cole asked.

"Yes, each year women are nominated and judged on their accomplishments in their community. The accomplishments must have helped improve the quality of life in the community, and with all the volunteer work she does at the clinic, Patrina has certainly done that. Her husband was sheriff here and was killed in the line of duty. I think she puts in a lot of community hours because she has a genuine desire to help people, but then I'm sure it's probably rather lonely living at that ranch by herself. She spends a lot of her free time in town at the clinic."

Cole didn't say anything as he took a sip of his coffee. He didn't want to think about how lonely Patrina was or how much spending those two days with her had meant to him. Nor did he want to recall the satisfied look on her face, after spending almost an entire night and day in bed with him.

He gave a deep sigh and decided now was the time to share his good news. It was something he hadn't told Patrina and she'd become involved with him, anyway— but only because she'd known it was an involvement that would lead nowhere. He was not looking for a serious relationship with anyone, but then, neither was she.

"I have some good news," he said. "I'm no longer a ranger. I followed Clint's lead and took an early retirement." He could tell from Casey's expression that she was surprised. She of all people knew what a dedicated ranger he'd been.

"That's wonderful, Cole," Casey said, smiling brightly at him. "What on earth will you do with all that time you're going to have on your hands?" He wasn't surprised by her question. She knew he was someone who had to stay busy or else he would get restless and ornery.

"I invested a lot of the money I made when I sold my third of the ranch to Clint. They were investments that paid off. I'm meeting with Serena Preston next week. I understand she's looking for a buyer for her helicopter business. Quade's also going to join me while I'm here. He and I are working on a business deal that involves opening several security companies around the country. We've even talked to Rico Claiborne about joining us as a partner."

Rico was a topnotch private investigator who owned a successful agency. His sister, Jessica, was married to Cole's cousin, Chase, and Rico's other sister, Savannah, was married to Durango. With the family connections, the Westmorelands considered Rico one of their own.

"Sounds like you're going to be busy."

"I plan to be," he said, and decided not to add that staying busy would be a surefire way to keep Patrina Foreman off his mind. He swallowed against the heavy lump he felt in his throat. Damn, he was missing the woman already.

He leaned back in his chair remembering how she had stood on the porch watching him drive off. She had looked beautiful with the sun slanting down on her features, emphasizing that womanly glow he had left her with. Heat fired through his veins just thinking about it, as well as remembering all they had shared. He sighed deeply. Those kinds of thoughts could land him knee-deep in trouble if he wasn't careful.

Casey interrupted his thoughts. "So how long will you be staying with McKinnon and me before you head up the mountain to see Dad?"

Cole tried not to think how far away from Patrina being on Corey's Mountain would put him. But then, he hadn't planned on seeing her again anytime soon, anyway. He figured he wouldn't be seeing her before Corey's birthday party.

"I'm not sure," he finally said. "Probably in a couple of days. I hope the two of you don't mind the company."

McKinnon chuckled. "Not at all. Besides, I want to show you all the new horses Clint sent. They're beauties."

Later that night, Cole lay on his back with his head sunk in the thick pillow, thoughts of Patrina on his mind. He glanced over at the clock. It wasn't quite nine o'clock and it didn't take much to recall what he'd been doing around this time the previous night.

He couldn't fight the memories any longer so he closed his eyes to let them take over his mind. Images of kissing her, making love to her through the wee hours of the morning gripped him, made him hard, made him long for more of the same. But then by an unspoken agreement, what they'd shared was all there ever would be. Their paths were not to cross that way again. It had just been a moment in time.

If that was the case, why did he still desire her in every sense of the word? Even now, when he didn't want to think about her, when he didn't want to remember, he couldn't stop himself from doing so. Maybe going up on Corey's Mountain and putting distance between him and temptation was for the best.

He turned his head when he heard his cell phone. He quickly reached for it on the nightstand and flipped it open. "Hello."

"Cole, this is Quade. Have you made it to Montana yet?"

"Yes, I arrived at McKinnon and Casey's place earlier today," which in essence wasn't a lie, Cole quickly thought.

"I'm flying out of D.C. the end of the week to head that way. Have you heard from Rico?"

"No, but McKinnon mentioned he's here visiting with Durango and Savannah. A bad snowstorm has kept everyone stranded for the past couple of days. The natives are just beginning to thaw out and venture outside."

He heard Quade's chuckle. "Maybe we ought to have our heads examined for thinking about purchasing that copter service. In bad weather we'll be grounded."

"Yes, but think of all the money we'll make those days when we're in the air." Cole had done his research and had no apprehensions about the helicopter business being profitable. And with all the expansions they planned to make, he saw it as a very lucrative investment.

"I'll remind you of those words when it's thirty below zero and we're inside sitting around a roaring fire waiting for the copter's blades to defrost."

He and Quade spoke for several more minutes and Cole welcomed the conversation. It kept Patrina from intruding on his mind. But the moment the call ended, the memories were back, hitting him smack in the face, and he couldn't help wondering how much sleep he would be getting tonight.

Restless and knowing a good night's sleep was out of the question, Patrina sat up in bed and glanced at the clock. It was still fairly early, not even eleven. However, considering all the chores she'd done after Cole had left to stay busy and to keep her mind occupied, she should be sleeping like a log. But that wasn't the case. Her body felt edgy, achy with a hunger only one man could satisfy.

Cole.

Each and every time she closed her eyes he was there in her thoughts, taking over her mind and reminding her of things so intimate that she was filled with intense longing. It was recapturing all the moments she had spent with him, all the kisses they had shared, but especially when she had given her body to him....

Getting out of bed, she crossed to the window and glanced out at the full moon. She recalled what Cole had said that meant. *A full moon in April is the Seed Moon. It's the time to physically plant your seeds of desire in Mother Earth.*

Her hands immediately went to her stomach when she recalled their unprotected lovemaking. Her gaze stayed firmly locked on the full moon while she considered the possible meaning of the words Cole had spoken that night. Had it been their fate to make a baby? If she was pregnant, Cole had planted seeds of desire in her, since they definitely hadn't been seeds of love. She was smart enough to know that love had not governed their behavior for the past two days. Lust had.

Her eyes shimmered with unshed tears when she recalled the months following Perry's death when she had felt so alone. It was during those months she had regretted their decision to wait before starting a family. A child would have been something of his that would have been a part of her forever.

Patrina closed her eyes and the face she saw was no longer Perry's but Cole's. She bit her lip to stop it from trembling when she was reminded of the vow she'd made never to give her heart to another lawman. It was a vow she intended to keep. She couldn't handle the pain if anything were to happen to Cole like it had Perry.

She opened her eyes. No matter what, she would never let Cole Westmoreland have possession of her heart.

Chapter 9

A week later

Cole glanced at the scrap of paper he held in his hand and then back at the man by his side. "How in hell did we get roped into doing this, Quade?" he asked his cousin as they got out of the truck to enter the grocery superstore.

Quade chuckled. "Mainly because this is Henrietta's day off and we weren't smart enough to get lost like McKinnon did. Hey, look at it this way—the list could have been longer. And besides, Casey's *your* sister. If anything, you should have known she was bound to put us to work sooner or later."

Cole's eyebrows drew together in a frown. "Yeah, I guess you're right, but that doesn't mean I have to like it." He grabbed a buggy and went about maneuvering it down the first aisle while glancing at the list.

"Hey, isn't that Patrina Foreman over there in the frozen-food section?"

Cole's head whipped up. Yes, that was Patrina, all right. He didn't need for her to turn all the way around to make a concrete identification. His body was already responding to the sight of her. It had been a week, but it seemed like yesterday when he had made love to her, mainly because he replayed each and every detail in his nightly dreams. He couldn't close his eyes at night without reliving the time his body had been connected to hers, thrusting in and out of her and—

"Hey, Cole. You all right?"

His gaze swiftly switched to Quade. "What makes you think I'm not?" he asked, the question coming out a little gruffer than he'd intended.

He didn't miss the way Quade's mouth quirked in a teasing smile when he said, "Mainly because I asked to see that list three times, but you were so busy staring at Patrina, you didn't hear me." Quade paused for a minute, lifted a brow and asked, "Hmm, do I detect some interest there?"

Cole's chin shot up as he shoved the list at Quade. "No."

Quade chuckled. "You spoke too soon and that was a dead giveaway."

Cole quietly cursed, refusing to let Quade bait him. But it really didn't matter when he found himself steering the buggy in Patrina's direction.

"I don't see any frozen foods on Casey's list," he heard Quade say.

Cole rolled his eyes and in doing so, barely missed knocking over a display of pastries in the middle of the aisle.

"Don't you think you need to watch where you're going?" Quade said, laughing.

Cole was about to shoot some smart remark over his shoulder to Quade when suddenly Patrina turned and her widened eyes stared straight at him. "Hello, Patrina."

From the expression on her face he could tell she was surprised to see him and he couldn't help wondering if that was good or bad. He also couldn't help wondering if her nights had been as tortured as his. He was less than five feet away and had already picked up her scent, something he knew he would never forget. She was wearing a long, white lab coat over a pair of navy slacks. She looked totally professional, but he knew firsthand that underneath her medical garb she was totally female.

"Hello, Cole." She looked past him. "Hello, Quade."

A smiling Quade came to stand by Cole's side. "Hey, Trina, how's it going?" Then without missing a beat, Quade looked at Cole and then back at her. His smile widened when he said, "I didn't know the two of you knew each other."

Cole threw Quade a sharp glance. "Patrina and I met last year at Casey's party."

"Oh, I see."

As far as Cole was concerned, his cousin saw too

damn much. "Don't you want to take the buggy and finish getting the stuff on Casey's list, Quade?"

His cousin glanced at Cole and said smoothly, "Sure, why not?" Then he looked at Patrina. "You're coming to Uncle Corey's party next weekend, aren't you?"

A small smile touched her lips. "Yes, I plan to."

"Good. Then we can talk more later. I'll be seeing you."

"Goodbye, Quade."

At exactly the moment Quade and the buggy rounded the corner, Cole found himself taking a step forward. There were others around and he didn't want anyone else privy to their conversation. He glanced sideways and caught a glimpse of his reflection in the freezer's glass door. He caught a glimpse of Patrina's reflection, as well. She'd taken her tongue and given her lips a moist sweep, a gesture that always turned him on. Today was no exception. He felt it, the sexual chemistry, the charged air and electrical currents that always consumed them whenever they were in close range of each other.

"I ran into Casey last week and she told me you were here but had gone to spend a few days up on Corey's Mountain," she said.

He shifted his gaze from the glass door to her. "I was on the mountain for only a couple of days."

"Oh."

"And how have you been, Patrina?"

She met his gaze. "Fine."

"Do you have anything in particular that you want to tell me?"

He could tell from her expression that she knew what he was asking. "No," she said quickly.

He couldn't help wondering if she meant, no, she didn't have anything to tell him because it was too early to know anything or, no, she didn't have anything to tell him because she knew for certain she wasn't pregnant.

"And how have you been, Cole?"

He met her gaze and held it. "Do you want to know the truth?" he asked, his voice going low and sounding husky even to his own ears.

She evidently had an idea what he might say and nervously glanced around. "No. Not here."

"Fair enough," he conceded. "Then where? Tell me where, Patrina."

Cole watched as she licked her lips again and he felt his guts clench. The need to kiss her, take hold of that tongue with his own, was a temptation he was fighting to ignore. If she had any idea what effect seeing her lick her lips had on him, she would keep her tongue inside her mouth.

She met his gaze and he knew she had to see the desire in his eyes he wasn't trying to hide—at least not from her. He wasn't sure if Quade had seen it or not. But at the moment he didn't care.

When it seemed she didn't intend to give him an answer, he opened the glass freezer door and pretended to take something out so he could get close enough to her to whisper. "I want you."

He saw her shiver. He knew his words had been the cause. Anyone else would assume it had been the result of the blast of cold air from the freezer.

"You've had me," she finally responded.

He looked at her reflection in the freezer door, imprisoned her gaze with his own. "I want you again." And to make sure she hadn't misunderstood him, he closed the door and turned to her. He held her gaze and repeated, "I want you, again, Patrina."

The stark determination she saw in Cole's eyes sent another shiver up Patrina's spine. She inhaled deeply, fought for control with all the strength she could muster. She wanted him, too, but if she was going to stick to her resolve, she knew what she had to do.

It wasn't that she regretted anything they'd done when he'd been stranded at her place, but a repeat performance would serve no purpose and in fact, only make matters worse. She could barely sleep at night as it was. If she took him up on his offer, what would happen to her when he left Bozeman? With some people, usually men, it was easy to replace one lover with another, but that wasn't the case with her. Cole was the man her body wanted. The only man it wanted. And she refused to become addicted to something she couldn't have.

"Patrina?"

She forced even breaths past her lips, while fighting the sexual pull between them. She had to stand firm. She had to stay strong. She had to ignore that telltale ache between her legs, and the tingle in her breasts.

"No, I don't think that's a good idea," she finally said softly, making sure the words were for his ears only.

Then, simultaneously taking a deep breath and tak-

324 Cole's Red-Hot Pursuit

ing a step back, she glanced at her watch and said in a normal tone, "I didn't know how late it is. I have to go. It was good seeing you, Cole. Tell Casey and McKinnon I said hello."

Then she quickly swept her buggy past him, ignoring the determined glint in his dark gaze. She could still feel the heat of that gaze on her back when she steered her buggy toward the checkout line. She was tempted to stop, turn and look him in the eye and invite him over tonight, but to do so would be foolish.

She had gotten her purchases paid for and bagged when she finally looked back. Cole was nowhere in sight, but she had a feeling she hadn't seen the last of him. She of all people knew he was a man who eventually got whatever he wanted.

"Okay, what's going on with you and Patrina?"

Cole shrugged, then turned the key in the truck's ignition and pulled out of the store's parking lot. "What makes you think there's something going on?"

Quade rolled his eyes heavenward. "Have you forgotten I'm considered one of the president's men? For years my job has been to notice things others might find irrelevant. And to pick up on things some might overlook." He smiled. "Besides, the heat between you two was so hot I was worried about the food in the freezer thawing."

"You're imagining things."

"I'd rather you told me it's none of my business than insult my intelligence."

Cole brought the truck to a stop at a traffic light and

glanced at his cousin. Quade, at thirty-four a couple of years older, was the first of the Westmorelands he and Clint had met on their quest to find their father. Quade had shown up in Austin, demanding to know why they were having his uncle, Corey Westmoreland, investigated. And then, after they had given him their reasons, he had been the first one to welcome them to the Westmoreland family and the one who'd brought them to Montana to meet face-to-face the father they'd thought was dead. For that reason, the two of them shared a special bond that went beyond family relations.

He knew he couldn't tell Quade everything, but he would tell him enough, especially since he'd picked up on the vibes, anyway. Cole returned his gaze to the road when the traffic light changed and the truck began moving again. "Patrina and I are attracted to each other. Have been since that night we met last year at Casey's party."

"I picked up on that much," Quade said, shaking his head. "Tell me something I don't know."

Cole chuckled. Quade wasn't the easiest of men at times. "She prefers not getting involved with anyone in law enforcement."

"Um, last time Trina and I talked she wasn't interested in getting involved with anyone, period, lawman or otherwise."

Cole snapped his head around and gave Quade a stony look. Quade grinned. "Please keep your eyes on the road, cousin, and take off the boxing gloves. It's not that way with me and Trina. We're nothing but good friends and always have been. I've known her since she was knee-high and would see her every summer when all of us came to spend time with Uncle Corey on his mountain. She, her brother, Dale, along with McKinnon, were my playmates."

Cole nodded. He'd heard about those summers. They were times he, Clint and Casey had missed out on because his mother hadn't told them the truth.

"Why haven't you told her you're no longer a ranger?" Quade asked, breaking into his thoughts.

"Because what I do for a living shouldn't matter."

"It does and you know why. Trina and Perry had been together for years and she took his death hard. I can understand her feeling that way."

"Well, I can't. It's been more than three years and at some point she needs to get on with her life. She has a lot to offer a man. She's special. I picked up on that the night we met. I also picked up that she was standoffish where men were concerned."

"And why does that bother you so much, Cole? Could it be more than just a physical attraction you feel for her?"

Cole didn't like where Quade was going, especially when he didn't know the whole picture. Cole would be the first to admit that when they'd made love, he'd had feelings for her he'd never had with any woman before. He would go even further and admit that since that time she had become lodged in his mind and he couldn't get her out, and that although he'd told her today that he wanted her, she didn't have a clue about just how *much* he wanted her. She'd become an ache he couldn't get rid of and he didn't like it.

"Cole?"

It then occurred to him that he hadn't answered Quade's question. "It's nothing more than a physical attraction. No big deal. I'm not looking for serious involvement and I don't do well with long-distance romances. Besides, I'm a loner. I don't ever plan to get serious with a woman and marry."

"Same here. Unless…"

Cole glanced at Quade when they stopped at another traffic light. "Unless what?" he couldn't help asking.

Quade met his gaze. "Unless my path crosses again with that woman I met in Egypt a few months ago. I went over there to scope things out before the president's visit, and late one night when I couldn't sleep, I went walking on the beach. She was out walking on the beach, too."

"An Egyptian girl?"

"No, American."

Quade didn't say anything for a moment, but Cole could read between the lines. Quade and the woman had ended up spending the night together. "So…" Cole said slowly, "did you get her phone number so the two of you could stay in touch?"

Quade shook his head. "No. When I woke up the next morning she was gone. The president arrived that day so I didn't get a chance to go look for her. But believe me when I tell you that she is one woman I will never forget."

Cole nodded. He knew that no matter where *he* went in life, Patrina was the one woman he wouldn't forget, either. He also knew he would seek her out for a definitive answer to his question about her possible pregnancy. If it was too early to tell, fine, he would wait it out. But he figured that with her being a gynecologist, she had the ability to find out way ahead of most people.

He made up his mind to pay her a late-night visit. She had avoided him in the store but he wouldn't let her avoid him tonight.

When her car came to a stop at the last traffic light she would see for a while, now that she was on the outskirts of town, Patrina rubbed the back of her neck, feeling totally exhausted.

Today she had done a double duty. First she had worked eight hours at her office, and then she'd gone to the clinic where she had worked an additional eight. She hadn't intended to stay that long at the clinic, but it had been short staffed. Several women had delivered and a few other women, who had sought shelter from the blizzard, had received treatment for a few common gynecological concerns. The clinic needed money for new equipment, and she hoped the kickoff to their fund-raising drive would send some generous donors their way.

Without work to keep her mind occupied now, she couldn't help but remember running into Cole today at the store. She had volunteered to do grocery-shopping for Lila Charles during her lunch hour. Ms. Charles, who was close to eighty and lived alone, had been one of her grandmother's dearest friends. Whenever Patrina got the chance, she would stop by to check on the elderly woman and go pick up whatever items she needed from the grocery store. Cole Westmoreland had been the last person she had expected to run into there.

But she had, and it had taken everything within her to keep a level head, especially since her body had responded to him immediately. He had looked so good, but then Cole never looked anything but. He wore jeans like they'd been made exclusively for him, and a shirt that fit perfectly over the muscles of his chest.

She'd understood what he'd wanted to know. But she didn't have an answer for him yet. It would be another week or so before she did, and so far she hadn't felt any changes in her body. But it was too soon to tell.

She reached toward the car's console and pushed the CD button, deciding to listen to some music to soothe her rattled mind. She had another ten or so miles to go and decided she would let Miles Jaye, his red violin and his sexy voice relax her a bit. A short while later, she decided Miles was relaxing her too much with such romantic and heart-throbbing sounds. And the songs reminded her of cold nights wrapped up in the heated embrace of a man. Although she had listened to these songs countless times, she hadn't been able to relate to them so intensely until now. She was reminded of the time spent making love with Cole.

Even with her eyes fully opened, she could vividly recall every moment of the night and day they had spent in each other's arms. A heated shiver went up her spine when she thought of the look in his eyes just seconds before his body slid into hers and how she had stretched to receive him and the way her thighs had tightened around him and how her hips had cradled him while he moved in and out of her at such a luscious, mind-blowing rhythm and pace.

Preoccupied with those lustful memories, once she made the turn into her driveway off the main road, it took her several moments to register that a car was parked in front of her house. Once her lights shone on the vehicle, she recognized it immediately as the rental that had been delivered to Cole. Her heart skipped a beat. It was close to midnight. What was he doing here? What did he want?

Then it dawned on her just what he wanted when his words of earlier that day came back to her, and stroked her skin like a sensual caress. *I want you again, Patrina.*

She sucked in a deep breath when she brought her car to a stop. She unbuckled her seat belt and watched as Cole opened his car door and eased out of the vehicle, closed the door and then leaned against it. Waiting.

She knew she couldn't sit in her car forever; besides, she was tired, annoyed…and edgy. Boy, was she edgy. The insistent, aching throb between her legs that had been there all week just wouldn't go away.

She pulled the key from the ignition, placed her purse around her shoulder and opened the car door. The moment she did so, Cole moved toward her, forever the gentleman, and offered her his hand. She decided not to take it just yet. She watched him study her features and figured she must look a total mess, but then, who wouldn't after working sixteen hours straight?

"What are you doing here, Cole?" she asked, his height making it necessary to tilt her head back to meet his gaze.

"I didn't think we had much privacy earlier today and felt we still needed to talk."

"Well, you thought wrong. I've been at work since six this morning and—"

"Why?"

She lifted a brow. "Why what?"

"Why are you just coming home now?" he asked, his features hard.

Patrina's temper flared. "Not that it's any of your business, but I worked at my office seeing patients and then I left there and put in another eight hours at the clinic. When you saw me today at the store I was there picking up a few items for Lila Charles, an elderly woman who was a good friend of my grandmother's. She doesn't have any family."

Thinking she'd said enough, more than he really needed to know, she sighed deeply and saw his hand was still stretched out to help her out of the car. Convinced she was only accepting his act of kindness because she was too tired to do otherwise, she took his hand.

The moment their hands touched, it happened. A shiver raced through every part of her body and she glanced up at him, hoping he hadn't felt it, too. But from the darkness of his eyes, the heated gaze, she knew that he had. Her heart skipped a beat. Then another. And another.

All sense of time was suspended as they stared at each other and finally she knew she had to say something. So she said just what she felt. "I'm tired."

She saw a softening around the edges of his gorgeous mouth and then he said in a low, throaty voice, "Of course you are, sweetheart."

She didn't have time to react to his term of endearment when, still holding her hand, he leaned down, pushed her hair aside with his other hand, then cupped the back of her neck and drew her mouth to his. She closed her eyes the moment their mouths made contact and forgot how tired she was. Instead, she felt only the way his lips were gliding over hers, the way his tongue went inside her mouth when she released a breathless sigh and the gentle way it was mating with hers. She felt her entire body respond, felt the nipples of her breasts throb with an urgency to have him touch them, take them in his mouth and taste them.

And then, without warning, she felt herself being gently pulled from the car and lifted up into his arms. As he closed the car door with his hip, she pulled her mouth away from his. "Cole, put me down. I'm too heavy."

"And I've told you before, you're not."

She sighed deeply, too exhausted from work, as well as from the effects of his kiss, to argue. Instead, she buried her face in his chest, inhaling the manly scent of him.

"Open the door, Patrina."

While still cradled in his arms, she managed to work her door key into the lock and felt the warmth of the interior of her home when he stepped over the threshold and closed the door behind them. She thought he would put her on her feet, but instead, he moved down the hall toward her bedroom.

"Now wait just a minute, Cole. How dare you assume that you can show up here tonight and think I'll sleep with you again?"

He placed her on the bed and gazed down at her. "That's not why I'm here, Patrina. I came to talk, but you're too tired. There's something else I can do, though."

He left the room and walked into the adjoining bathroom. Then, seconds after she heard the sound of water running, he reappeared in the doorway. "Your bath will be ready in a minute, so start taking off your clothes. I'll give you five minutes and if you haven't stripped down by then, I'll be more than tempted to do the honors myself." And then he disappeared again into the bathroom.

She glared at the closed bathroom door, but then thought, *Wow!* She'd never had a man run a bath for her and God knew she could use a good soak tonight. Deciding to move as quickly as she could before he made good on his threat and came back, she stripped off her clothes and slipped into her bathrobe, then pulled a short nightgown out of the dresser drawer. All in five minutes.

She turned when he opened the door again. He lifted a brow as he looked her up and down and then glanced at the pile of clothes in the middle of the floor. As if satisfied, he returned his gaze to her. "Ready?"

She nodded. "Yes."

And then he moved toward her and in one easy swoop, picked her up in his arms and headed for the bathroom. "You're going to hurt yourself if you keep doing this," she said.

"No, I'm not."

She didn't have time to argue when she felt him lowering her into the warm, sudsy water, removing her robe in the process. Part of her robe got wet, anyway, but she didn't care. He had used an ample amount of her favorite bubble bath, more than she would have, but she didn't care about that, either. At the moment she didn't want to care or worry about anything and she settled back against the tub, closed her eyes and let out an appreciative moan. The warm, sudsy water felt heavenly.

"Let me know when you're ready to get out."

She opened her eyes and looked up at Cole. He was standing at the foot of the tub. "I can get out myself."

He nodded. "I know you can, but I want you to let me know when you're ready to get out so I can help you."

She frowned and decided to take advantage of the wonderful bath he'd prepared for only a few minutes longer and get out of the tub on her own before he came back. She closed her eyes again and that was the last thing she remembered.

Cole glanced at his watch after neatly placing Patrina's clothes across the back of the chair. Her lush feminine scent was all in them, especially her undies. He forced the thought from his mind as he made his way back into the bathroom. He had expected her to call him by now, and when he eased open the door and saw her in the tub asleep, he wasn't surprised.

Taking the huge velour towel off the rack, he reached down and pulled her up into his arms. She came wide awake in that instant. "No, Cole, I can dry myself. You don't need to do this."

"Yes, I do, baby. Let me take care of you, okay," he said softly, politely.

Something in his voice must have calmed her, he thought, made her give up the protest, or it could be as he assumed. She was just plain tuckered out. He wondered how often she worked like this, pulling double hours. He then recalled what Casey had said about Patrina being up for some award for her dedicated service to the community. Now he understood why. The blasted woman needed someone to take care of her or she would work herself to death.

He went about wrapping a dripping wet Patrina up in the large towel and, after placing her on her feet, he made an attempt to dry her off. When she reached her hands down to cover her feminine mound from his view, he smiled and said, "There's no need to do that. I've seen it all before, remember?"

She removed her hands. Going down on his knees, with painstaking gentleness he began drying her, every inch of her body, and as he'd told her, every place the towel touched he had seen before. But it didn't stop him from fighting the urge to replace the towel with his hands and touch her all over, fondle her in those areas he remembered so well, those he loved caressing. And that would be every single place on her body—skin to skin, flesh to flesh. Especially those full-figure curves, voluptuous thighs and childbearing hips.

Childbearing hips.

That immediately reminded him of the reason he had sought her out tonight. Instinctively, his hand went to her stomach and his palm gently flattened against it. Something primal, possessive and elementally male clicked inside him at the thought that even now, his child could be right here inside her.

Amazing.

Leaning forward, he removed his hand and placed a kiss right there, just below her navel. It didn't matter to him if she was pregnant or not, what mattered was the possibility and the fact that he had given her a part of him no other woman could claim—his seed. Whether it hit fertile soil, only time would tell. Unless…

He glanced upward and she shook her head and said softly, "It's too early to tell, Cole. I promise that you will be the first to know."

He nodded. Satisfied.

Tossing the towel aside, he grabbed her nightgown from the vanity. "Raise your hands, Patrina," he said, trying to ignore her nakedness, especially those breasts that moved upward when she lifted her arms. They were breasts that he enjoyed putting his mouth on. He pulled down the nightie, which barely covered her hips. He immediately thought of one word to describe how she looked in it. Sexy.

He then swept her up into his arms and carried her from the bathroom into the bedroom, where he settled her on her feet. "Did you enjoy your bath?" he asked as he turned back the covers of the bed,

"Yes, and thank you."

"You're welcome."

He moved aside. "Come on, let me tuck you in."

She slid between the sheets and he pulled the blanket and spread up to cover her. "Is there anything else I can do for you?" he asked.

"No. You've done more than enough."

He grabbed the book she had placed on her night-stand and settled in the chair beside her bed. The book was the same one she had finished reading last week, the one his cousin Stone had written. "You aren't going to leave?" she asked him.

"Not until you've fallen asleep."

She nodded. "Where does your sister think you are this time of night? It's almost one in the morning."

He smiled. "She thinks I'm over at Durango's play-ing cards with him and Quade."

"What if she—"

"Relax, she won't." He met and held her gaze. "And if she does, will it bother you?"

She didn't hesitate. "No." Then a few seconds later, she added, "To keep it a secret was your idea, not mine. Besides, if I'm pregnant everyone is going to wonder how it happened."

His mind was suddenly filled with the memory of how it happened, all the times they'd made love. He began to get aroused. Thinking it best to steer his thoughts in another direction, he said, "Don't worry about it. I have everything under control."

A smile touched her lips before she shifted her body to a more comfortable position and closed her eyes. He sat there for a long time just staring at her, tempted to reach out and push a stray lock of hair from her face. He was tempted even further to lean over and kiss her, slide into bed with her and hold her during the night.

And like before, his feelings were intense. Feelings he'd never had for any other woman. Damn, he thought, what was happening? Those feelings shouldn't be possible for him.

He pinched the bridge of his nose and sighed deeply. He glanced over at the bed, saw the steady rise and fall of her chest and knew she had lapsed into a deep sleep.

It was time for him to leave, but he couldn't seem to force his body from the chair. So he decided to stay and watch over her for a little while longer. And the longer he sat there, the more he knew that Patrina Foreman was digging her way under his skin. He didn't like it.

Chapter 10

"Good morning, Dr. Foreman."

Patrina glanced at her receptionist when she entered the office. Tammie Rhodes was a perky twenty-year-old who worked for her full-time while taking night classes at the university. "Good morning, Tammie. How are you this morning?"

"Great. You have a full schedule today and Ellen Cranston's husband called, claiming she's having labor pains again."

Patrina smiled as she slipped on her lab coat. "Are they real labor pains this time?" she asked, thinking of the woman who wasn't due for another two months. Last time what Ellen and her husband, Mark, thought were labor pains were nothing but a severe case of an overactive child.

Tammie grinned. "I told him it would be okay if he brought her in so we could check to make sure."

Patrina nodded as she headed toward her office. Her first patient was due in an hour. That would give her an opportunity to sit down with a cup of coffee in the privacy of her office and relive everything that happened last night with Cole. She still found it hard to believe he had been there waiting for her when she'd gotten home and then gone so far as to run a bath for her, dry her off and then tenderly tuck her into bed.

She had slept like a baby and had awakened this morning to find him gone. She'd have sworn she'd dreamed the whole thing if it hadn't been for the note he had scribbled and left on her kitchen table that read, "I'll see you later." Did that mean he would be parked outside her house when she came home again tonight?

"Oh, and you got another call, Dr. Foreman. This one personal."

Patrina turned around just seconds before entering her office and lifted a brow. "From who?"

"Cole Westmoreland."

She didn't miss the look of interest in Tammie's eyes. "Did he leave a message?"

Tammie smiled. "Yes. He told me to tell you he was taking you to lunch."

Patrina frowned. "I don't do lunch."

Tammie chuckled. "That's what I told him."

"And?"

"He said you would today."

Patrina tried to keep a straight face but wondered where Cole came off saying what she would do.

"Isn't he Durango Westmoreland's cousin? One of Corey Westmoreland's triplets?"

Tammie's question broke into Patrina's thoughts. "Yes."

Both Durango and Corey were popular around these parts, but for different reasons. Before his marriage to Savannah, Durango had been well-known among the single ladies, and Corey was a highly respected citizen of the town. Everyone knew about his mountain. And everyone knew when he'd discovered he had triplets born more than thirty years ago.

"I heard that Cole Westmoreland is good-looking," Tammie said, again breaking into Patrina's thoughts.

"Excuse me?"

Tammie's smile widened. "I said I heard that he and his brother are extremely handsome."

That was something Patrina could certainly agree with. "They are."

She studied her receptionist. "Aren't they way too old for you, not to mention that Clint is now a married man?"

Tammie laughed. "I overheard my oldest sister, Gloria, tell that to one of her girlfriends. She was working at the tuxedo-rental shop and saw them last year when they came in to get fitted for tuxes to wear at their sister's wedding."

Patrina nodded. "Well, if Cole Westmoreland calls again, please tell him I'll be too busy today to go to lunch."

"He won't be calling back. He said he wouldn't. Told me to tell you to be ready to go exactly at noon."

Patrina frowned. Cole's bossiness completely erased all his kindness of last night. Instead of saying anything else about Cole, especially to Tammie, she opened the door to her office and went inside, dismissing Cole from her mind. Or rather, she tried to, but found that she couldn't.

"Let me know the next time you decide to use me as an alibi," Durango said to his cousin as they were horseback riding on the open range. Quade had left early that morning to trek up the mountain to visit with Corey.

Cole lifted a brow. "What happened?"

"Casey showed up early this morning to visit with Savannah and made a remark that it must have been some poker game last night since you didn't get in until almost three this morning."

Durango, who was three years older than Cole, shook his head and added, "Lucky for you, Savannah went to bed early, leaving me and Quade up talking, so she had no idea whether you dropped by last night or not. So rest assured, Quade and I ended up covering your ass."

Cole smiled. "Thanks."

Durango stared at his cousin. "Any reason we needed to? Quade said he had an idea where you were but he wasn't talking."

"I appreciate that and for the moment there is a reason my ass needs covering, but how much longer that need will last, only time will tell."

Durango shook his head. "Sounds like it involves a woman. I just hope she's not married."

"She's not."

"Good."

Cole couldn't help but laugh. "Look who's talking. Everybody knows your and McKinnon's history." Durango, Quade's brother, had been the second Westmoreland that Cole and Clint had met. Upon arriving in Montana, it had been Durango who had picked up him, Clint and Quade at the airport. After spending the night at Durango's ranch, the four had made the trip up to Corey's Mountain. Once there, he and Clint had come face-to-face with the man who had fathered them, as well as another cousin, Stone, and the young woman Stone would later marry, Madison. That particular day they'd also met Madison's mother, Abby, who had just reentered Corey's life a month before. Abby was the woman who had been Corey's true love for thirty-plus years.

"According to Casey, things are falling into place for Dad's party," Cole said, as a way to change the subject.

Durango chuckled, knowing exactly what he was doing. "Yes, and it will be a pretty classy event if Abby has anything to do with it. Savannah's excited about all the Westmorelands who will start arriving next week. All of us haven't been together since Casey's wedding. Everyone couldn't make it to Clint's wedding." He shook his head. "I still can't believe he got married."

"Believe it and trust me when I say he's an extremely happy man," Cole responded.

"Hey, I know the feeling."

Cole studied his cousin and believed he really did know the feeling. All it took was a few minutes around Durango and Savannah to see just how happy they were together. Marriage definitely agreed with some people.

"McKinnon and I are meeting today for lunch at the Watering Hole. You want to join us?" Durango asked him.

Cole met his cousin's gaze and smiled. "Nope. Thanks for asking, but I've made prior lunch arrangements."

Patrina smiled while studying the new set of ultrasounds she had ordered on Ellen Cranston. Ellen and her husband had come in after Ellen had endured another sleepless night of stomach pains. Tammie had made an appointment with them to arrest their fears that Ellen was having labor pains.

Patrina had ordered a new set of ultrasounds after examining Ellen's stomach. She hadn't wanted to get the couple's hopes up regarding her suspicions until she was absolutely sure. Now she was. The Cranstons, who'd been trying to have a baby for more than five years, were having twins, something their first ultrasound hadn't shown because the little boy had been hidden behind his sister. A boy and a girl. She knew how pleased the Cranstons would be and couldn't wait to tell them the news. She reached for the phone to make the call.

Ten minutes later Patrina leaned back in her chair very pleased with her conversation with the Cranstons. Ellen and Mark had been so happy they had started crying on the phone and Patrina couldn't help but be happy for them. She then unconsciously reached down and touched her own stomach. What if *she* was pregnant? If she was, she knew her heart would know the same joy that the Cranstons were experiencing right now.

There were over-the-counter ways she could find out now, but she didn't want to find out that way. Having a missed period would be sign enough, which meant she would probably know something sometime next week.

"Dr. Foreman, your noon appointment has arrived."

Patrina lifted a brow at the sound of Tammie's excited voice over the intercom. In other words, Cole was out front.

Patrina stood. "Please send him in."

No sooner had the words left her mouth than her office door opened, and Cole, looking larger than life, boldly walked in and closed the door behind him. He smiled at her and said in the sexy voice that had undone her several times, "I'm here."

Cole leaned against the closed door and stared at Patrina, and the first thought that ran through his mind was how beautiful she looked today. And when she nervously swiped her lips with her tongue, the second thought was how much he wanted to taste her. Hell, from the deep inner throb in his body, he wanted to do a lot more than that, but tasting her mouth would suffice for now.

"Hello, Cole."

"Hello, Patrina."

He moved away from the door and walked over to where she was standing beside her desk. "Did you get a good night's sleep?"

"Yes, thanks for asking, and thanks for all you did to assure that I did."

He reached out and placed his hands at her waist and met her gaze. "Thank me this way."

And then he leaned forward and captured her mouth with his. The moment his tongue mingled with hers, he heard the deep moan that came from her throat and combined with the deep groan from his own. This was more than he wanted, he thought. This was what he needed—now—in a bad way. And when she arched her body and looped her arms around his neck, he shifted his hands from her waist and placed them on the thickness of her rump to urge her even closer to the fit of him, needing for her to feel him so she would know just how aroused he was. How quickly she could turn him on.

Reluctantly, torturously, he pulled back from her mouth, but not before giving it one final, thorough sweep. "I needed that," he whispered against her moist lips.

"So did I."

He pulled back, tilted his head and gazed at her, surprised by her throaty admission. He could tell from her expression that she'd even surprised herself in making it. "Will you be going to the clinic when you leave here today?" he asked her.

She nodded. "I go to the clinic every day. I'm needed there."

It was on the tip of Cole's tongue to tell her that she was needed here where she was now, right in his arms. Instead, he said, "How late will you be staying?"

She shrugged. "Until I'm no longer needed."

"Not a good answer. I'm coming to the clinic to

pick you up at eight. You can give me the address over lunch."

She lifted a brow. "Excuse me?"

He smiled. "You're excused. You're also beautiful." He then leaned in to kiss whatever words she was about to say off her lips.

Patrina glanced at the clock. It was a little past seven and the clinic wasn't nearly as busy as it had been the night before, which was a good thing since Cole had been adamant about picking her up at eight. One of the other doctors had gone home, which left only her and a staff person, which was fine.

She grabbed a cup of coffee and decided that although she would be leaving work in less than an hour, she deserved a break. Earlier, things had gotten pretty hectic but now all was calm.

Pausing at the front desk to let Julia, the night clerk, know where she'd be if things got hectic again, she strolled down the corridor that would take her to the outside patio. Upon opening the door, she pulled her jacket around her to ward off the cool breeze and recalled that this time last week the entire area had been covered in snow. Like everyone else, she hoped it was the last snowfall of the season.

She stood at the rail and looked out over the lake, remembering her lunch with Cole. He had taken her to a popular café not far from the hospital and she had to admit that she had enjoyed his company. He'd told her how the plans for his father's birthday party were coming along, and that all his cousins—most of them she knew—planned to attend. Even Delaney and Jamal would be flying in from the Middle East. They had laughed together when Cole had told her about the baby bed Thorn had built for his firstborn. It was in the shape of a motorcycle, with wheels and everything.

Then things had gotten somewhat serious when she'd asked him to tell her about his mom. She had heard the story of how his mother hadn't told them until she'd been on her deathbed that their father was still alive. Patrina admired Cole for saying that although he wished he could have gotten to know his father a lot sooner than he had and regretted the things he'd missed out on—like the summers with everyone on Corey's Mountain—he was not angry at his mother for doing what she did. It had been her decision and he respected that.

Just from hearing him talk, Patrina knew he had been close to his mother and had loved her dearly. Cole knew how it felt to lose someone, and he also knew how it was to move on, something she hadn't been able to do—until now. But still, there was something she couldn't get past and that was the fact that Cole was a lawman. While he was on duty, upholding the law, at any time some crazy person could end his life.

For the first time since losing Perry she could admit to something she thought would never happen to her again. She had fallen in love with another man. Cole.

She knew Perry would be happy for her, for find-ing someone else to love and moving on with her life, but knowing what Cole did for a living, she wasn't sure if she could get on with her life with him. She would always worry about the risks he might take, and she couldn't go through that again.

Anyway, the problem was academic. Cole was not in love with her. All she was to him was a challenge.

Deciding her break time was up, Patrina headed back inside. When she reached the area where Julia was working, she smiled at the woman. Julia had a very odd look on her face and had sunk back in her chair. She regarded Patrina silently when she neared.

"Julia? Is anything wrong?"

Before Julia could answer, Patrina felt something cold and hard at the middle of her back.

"No, nothing's wrong, Doc, now that you're here," a deep male voice said close to her ear. "I need the key to your medicine cabinet."

Patrina swallowed, tried to keep her cool and slowly turned to look into the hard eyes of a young man who couldn't have been more than twenty. He was holding a gun on her. "Why do you want the key?" she asked in an even voice.

The man sneered. "Don't act stupid. You know why. I want all your drugs."

Cole was just about to round the corner to see what was keeping Patrina when he heard the man and stopped dead in his tracks. He eased back against the wall, then leaned forward and peeped around the corner. The man was holding a gun on Patrina and another woman. Intense anger, combined with stark fear, crept up Cole's spine, but he knew he had to keep a level head.

He glanced around, noticed the high ceiling, the windows whose blinds were drawn and the long hallway that led to several rooms. Given a choice, he would have preferred knowing the layout of the clinic, but he didn't have a choice. The only thing he knew was that some lunatic was holding a gun on Patrina.

He then heard the man's voice raised when Patrina tried to convince him she didn't have a key. Deciding he had to do something and quickly, he backed up and came to a closet, looked inside, grabbed a lab coat and put it on. Knowing the element of surprise was definitely not a good idea in this case, he began whistling to let everyone know he was coming and hoped and prayed that neither Patrina nor the other woman gave anything away.

Taking a deep breath, he rounded the corner and saw both Patrina and the other's woman eyes widen when they saw him. He saw the look of nervousness in the man's eyes and Cole knew more than anything he had to convince the man that he was not only a doctor, but that he was the doctor with the key.

"Oh, we have another patient," Cole said, approaching the three with a cheery smile on his face. He pretended to see the gun for the first time when the man turned toward him.

"Get over here with the others, Doc," he snapped, "and one of you has less than a minute to produce the key to the medicine cabinet."

Cole, seemingly at ease, widened his smile and said, "Oh, is that what you want? I'm the one who has it."

"Then give it to me," the man said, his attention now on Cole.

"Sure. I know not to argue with man with a gun," Cole said, retaining his smile as he slowly reached into his back pocket to pull out a set of keys.

He handed them to the man, who gave them a quick glance and frowned. He then looked back at Cole. "Hey, this is a set of car keys."

Cole shook his head. "No, they're not. Look again."

The moment the man glanced down to study the keys, Cole kicked the man in the knee at the same time as he knocked the gun from his hand. Cole was about to give him a right hook, but Patrina beat him to it. Cole finished him off by hitting him hard behind the neck, which sent him crumbling to the floor, unconscious.

"Call the police," he told the other woman who'd had the sense to keep her cool through it all. He kicked the gun farther away as he glanced down at the unconscious man. He then looked at Patrina, who was rubbing her knuckles. "Who in hell taught you to hit like that?"

"Dale. After Perry died he figured I needed to know a few moves to protect myself, since I would be living alone."

Cole nodded, grateful that her brother had had the insight to do that. "You okay?" he asked softly, crossing the room to take a look at her knuckles.

"Yes, I'm okay." Then she said in quiet tone. "You could have been killed."

He lifted his gaze and looked into her eyes. "Yeah, but then so could you," he countered.

They both glanced around when they heard Julia return. "The police are on their way," she said in an excited tone.

"Thanks," Cole said, releasing Patrina's hand to glance around. He turned back to Patrina. "Where the hell is security?"

"We haven't had security in months," the other woman answered. "Couldn't afford it. The clinic's on a tight budget."

Cole switched his gaze from Patrina to stare at the woman, not wanting to believe what she'd said. *No security?* He was about to say something and decided not to. There was one way to remedy the problem, and he knew that after today, there would always be security protecting the clinic.

It was hours later before they were finally able to leave the clinic. That was only after law enforcement had asked questions, taken statements and made an arrest.

By the time Julia had finished telling her side of the story to the authorities and news media, Cole had become a hero and made the ten o'clock news. He received calls from Casey, Durango and his father wanting to make sure he was okay. Only Casey had a hundred questions for him since the television reporter indicated the reason he had shown up at the clinic in the first place was to pick up Dr. Patrina Foreman. So much for keeping his relationship with Patrina a secret. Now the entire town knew he was seeing her.

He glanced at Patrina and was glad they were finally on the road to her house. She hadn't said much and he couldn't help wondering what she was thinking, especially when during the police officers' questioning it came out that he was a *former* Texas Ranger. He would never forget how her eyes had met his for several pulsing moments before looking away.

He figured they needed to talk about it since she'd figured, and rightly so, that he had deliberately not told her. "Let's talk, Patrina."

She met his gaze. She gave her head a little toss and her shoulder a shrug before saying, "What about?"

"Whatever you want to talk about. Let's do it now because when we get to your place and I get you inside, talking will be the last thing on my mind."

Just like he'd known it would, intense anger appeared in her face and her eyes looked to be shooting darts. He had gotten more than a rise out of her. Now she was fighting mad. He figured if he hadn't been the one at the wheel she would probably haul off and punch him the way she'd punched the intruder.

"You arrogant ass. How dare you think when you get me home, you will do anything to me? You haven't even been honest with me. Not once did you tell me that you were no longer a ranger. You had me thinking you were still in law enforcement. Why didn't you tell me?"

"Was I supposed to?" He pulled the car off the main road and into her driveway, then parked in front of her house and turned off the ignition. Good. They would have it out now, because like he said, when they got inside they would make love, not war. He turned to face her.

"You knew how I felt," she said angrily.

"How you felt about what you *thought* was my job didn't matter to me, because sleeping with you, becoming involved with you, had nothing to do with what I did for a living. You assumed I was a Texas Ranger, yet you slept with me, anyway. Your mouth was saying one thing, but your body was saying another, Patrina. I decided to pay closer attention to what your body was saying because it truly knew what you wanted."

She stared at him and then said quietly, "You could have gotten killed tonight, Cole."

"Hey, he was holding that gun on you first, Doc. You could have lost your life just as easily." The thought of that made his gut twist. He had come close to knocking the damn man unconscious again after the police brought him around to make an arrest.

Then in a softer voice, he said, "I could have lost you."

Releasing his seat belt, he leaned toward her. "And that's something I could not let happen."

Patrina stared deep into Cole's eyes, and then shifted her gaze to stare at his mouth. What was there about the shape and texture of it that made her want to run the tip of her tongue all over it, kiss it, get lost in it?

She tried keeping her mind on track, taking in what he'd said, noting the heartfelt way he'd said it. They were involved, at least for the moment. In another week or so he would be leaving Montana to return to Texas. Things between them would come to an end. And if she was pregnant, she would become a single parent.

One of the reasons she had made love with him was because she'd known, regardless of him being a Texas Ranger, she was only capturing a moment in time, seizing an opportunity. She hadn't been looking for anything more than that, definitely not anything lasting. He hadn't promised her that and she hadn't expected it. What they had shared had been about wants and needs, fulfilling desires, experiencing satisfaction of the most potent kind.

It was about him taking her off the shelf to live a vibrant and rewarding life, reminding her of the woman she was, of the passion she had tried so hard to ignore and hide.

"I'm going to kiss you, Patrina."

His words penetrated her mind and she met his gaze. He'd spoken with amazing calmness, deep-rooted determination and ingrained authority. He was a take-charge kind of guy. If she had any doubt about that characteristic before, she didn't now, especially after seeing how he'd handled the would-be robber.

"But that's not all I'm going to do to you," he added, inching his face even closer to hers. "We can do it out here or we can take it inside." His mouth curved into a warm smile.

His smile would be the death of her yet. It had become her weakness. She felt desire being stirred inside her. She inhaled deeply. He was making her crazy. She hadn't slept with a man in over three years and then Cole showed up, taking over her mind in red-hot pursuit. Even now she could feel her common sense tumbling.

"Patrina?"

She shifted her gaze from his mouth back to his eyes, thought for a second, then threw caution to the wind. "Let's take it inside."

Chapter 11

So they took it inside.

The moment they were across the threshold, Cole closed and locked the door behind them. She turned and he was right there, pulling her into his arms and taking her mouth with a hunger he knew was possible only with her. There was an instinctive need to mate with her the way a man mated with a woman he claimed as his.

Claimed as his.

Something jolted through Cole. He really didn't like the thought of that. He had never considered any woman as his. There might have been a passing fancy for one, but that was all there had ever been. However, he would be the first to admit that something with Patrina was different. He couldn't put his finger on what, but there was a difference. He didn't particularly care to know a difference existed, but at the moment, he would go with the flow. Especially when she brought some pretty hot dreams his way every night and given the fact that whenever he saw her, he immediately thought of sex, sex and more sex.

Like he was doing now.

And then there was the possibility that she could be pregnant with his child, which put a whole new spin on things. But he would concern himself with that when the time came. Something else that troubled him was the realization that it wouldn't bother him in the least if she was pregnant. Just *when* his thought process got shot to hell on an issue that monumental, he really didn't know.

The only thing he did know was that for the last seven days, he had been thinking about her nonstop. Had craved her constantly and needed intimate contact with her as much as he needed to breathe. And the urgency of his kiss, the hungry way his tongue was devouring the cavern of her mouth, was making him realize just how over the edge he was and just how uncontrollable he'd become around her.

He broke mouth contact thinking this had to stop. He immediately took possession of it again, deciding hell, no, it didn't. And this kiss was deeper than and just as thorough as the one before. And then moments later, it was she who pulled her mouth away, mainly to inhale air into her lungs. The pause gave him a chance to step back to see his handiwork. He saw how moist her lips were, how swollen, how thoroughly kissed. Seeing them touched him deeply. Just as deeply as seeing her standing there staring at him through the veil of lashes, with the dark mane of hair in disarray around her face. She looked sexier than any one woman had a right to look.

And he wanted her.

Desire, thick as anything he'd ever felt, surged through him, nipped at every vital part of his body, making him as aroused as a man could possibly get. If he didn't get out of his jeans fast, there was a chance he might damage himself in a way he didn't want to think about.

But he wanted to see Patrina naked first. "Come here, baby."

He watched her take a step closer to him, and despite her outward calm appearance, he saw the shiver that went through her body. When she came to stand directly in front of him, he whispered, "Closer."

When she took the step that made their bodies touch, he reached for the side zipper of her skirt and with the flick of his wrist he stepped back to watch it glide down her hips, leaving her clad in a full slip, bra and panties.

"I want it all off you, Patrina," he said in a low voice, reaching out and tracing his finger along the lace-trimmed V neckline of her slip and hearing the tiny catch of breath in her throat at his touch.

She took a step back and began removing every stitch covering her body. It took all the control he had not to help her, but he wanted to see her strip for him. And what he saw escalated his pulse, burgeoned his awareness of just what a beautiful, full-figured woman she was. The power of her feminine sexiness could literally bring a man to his knees. When she eased out of her panties, he groaned and his heart began racing a mile a minute. He felt himself get even harder.

"Now remove yours," she said.

Her words floated across to him like a gentle caress and she didn't have to say them twice. He unbuttoned his shirt, pulled it off his shoulders and sent it flying across the room. Then he kicked off his shoes, leaned over and pulled off his stocks. Straightening his tall frame, he pulled a condom packet out his back pocket and held it between his teeth while his hands went to the zipper of his jeans.

His gaze never left hers and with excruciating care, he eased his jeans, along with his boxer shorts, down his legs. He stepped out of them and, taking the packet from his mouth, he reached out to sweep Patrina off her feet and into his arms, kissing her like a man starved for the taste of her.

And then he was moving toward her bedroom. After placing her on the huge bed, he stood back to put on the condom, knowing she was watching him attentively the entire time. Being aware that her eyes were on him, especially that part of him, made him even more aroused, making it difficult to sheath himself in latex.

"Need my help?"

He glanced up at Patrina and couldn't help but smile at her serious expression. "Thanks, Doc, but if you were to touch me now, I might embarrass myself. I want you that much."

"Oh."

He shook his head. Sometimes he found it hard to believe that she didn't have a clue how sexy she was.

"Okay, that does it," he said, finishing up and moving toward the bed. A smile tugged at the corners of his mouth. He would take pleasure in showing her once again the degree of his desire for her.

Patrina scooted to the edge of the bed, intent on showing Cole the degree of *her* desire for *him,* and was surprised that she could be so bold. But while she'd watched him put on the condom and seen his growing arousal as he did so, something deep inside her had been triggered. A desire to know him in a way she had never known any man, including Perry.

She reached out and looped her arms around Cole's neck and he pulled her closer to him. So close that she felt the tips of her breasts pressed against his hard, muscular chest. She felt secure in his arms. She felt like she was in a very special place, a place where she belonged.

She moved her hands to his shoulders and thought he felt rather tense. "Relax," she whispered softly.

"Uh, that's easy for you to say, baby. You're not the one about to come unglued."

"Wanna bet?"

And then she pushed him sideways and he tumbled on the bed with her straddling him. Cole was a take-charge man, but for once, she wanted to be in control. She gazed down at him.

"This position is different," he said, and before she could respond, he lifted his head from the pillow and captured a breast with his mouth.

The moment his mouth captured the nipple between his moist lips, she threw her head back and moaned.

The man definitely had a way with his tongue. He also had a way with something else, and it was something she wanted.

But first…

She pulled back and he had no choice but to release her breast. She scooted back some to lean back on her haunches and look at him, getting a good view of him from the knees up. He evidently saw the determined glint in her eyes, saw where her attention lay while she licked her lips, and he said huskily. "I hope you're not about to do what I'm thinking."

A sweet smile touched her lips. "I don't know what you're thinking," she said, reaching out and running her hand up his inner thigh, marveling at how firm the muscles were there.

"You're trying to kill me, aren't you," he said, and she could tell the words had been forced through clenched teeth.

"No. I want to pleasure you the way you've pleasured me," she said, watching how he got even more aroused before her eyes. She suddenly felt downright giddy at the thought that she had the power to make him do that.

Her fingers began moving again, easing closer to his aroused shaft, and she could hear his sharp intake of breath the closer she got. And then she had him in her hands, and deciding she wanted to taste him and not latex, she slowly rolled the condom off him.

"Do you know how hard it was to put that damn thing on?" she heard him ask in a near growl.

"Yes, I watched you the entire time. And watching you is why I want to do this," she said, bending forward to take him into her mouth. His body jerked at the intimate contact, and she took her hands to hold down his thighs, deciding he wasn't going anywhere except where he was right now.

She tasted him the way he had done her several times that night they'd been stranded together, and felt the size of him fill her mouth. And with each circular motion she made with her tongue, with each tiny suction of her lips, she felt him gasp, felt the flat plane of his stomach tighten. She was aware of the exact moment he reached for her hair and began methodically massaging her scalp while uttering her name over and over again. She hadn't known until now how much pleasure she could bring him this way.

And then she felt his body jolt, felt his hand tugging hard, trying to pull her mouth away, but she held firm, showing him just how much staying power she had. He was left with no other choice but to shudder through it, and he cried her name, a loud piercing sound, as his body quivered uncontrollably.

After one final hard jerk of his body, she slowly released him and watched as he lay there trying to discover how to breathe again. She reached into the nightstand next to the bed and retrieved a new condom packet. Ripping it open with her teeth, she began putting it on him. He opened his eyes and met her gaze.

She shrugged and said softly, "After the last time we did this, I decided to be prepared, since I wasn't sure when you might come back."

"But you knew I would." He issued it as a statement and not a question.

"I was hoping you wouldn't. We took chances. You made me feel things I've never felt before. You made me appreciate being a woman."

"And was that a bad thing?" he asked quietly.

"No, but I hadn't wanted to feel that way again, at least not to the extent that you were forcing me to."

He didn't say anything for a few moments and then asked in a low, throaty voice, "And now?"

A smile touched her lips and she moistened those lips with her tongue. "And now I want to make love to you all night and worry about what I should or should not do tomorrow."

He shifted their bodies so that she was beneath him, looking up at him. He had gotten aroused all over again. "All night," he said, a sexy smile forming on his lips as he trailed his fingers down her cheek.

"Yes, all night."

His hand left her face and traveled low, past her stomach to settle firmly between her legs. When his fingers began stroking her, she closed her eyes as sensations began overtaking her.

"Open your eyes and look at me, Patrina."

The moment she did so, he positioned his body over her and slid into her moistness. The connection was absolute, and when he began moving in slow, thorough thrusts, she felt her body give way and began shattering into a hundred thousand pieces. Automatically, she wrapped her legs around him to hold him in.

And when she felt his body begin to shake, she knew that together they were again finding intense pleasure in each other's arms.

* * *

Hours later, the sharp ring of the telephone brought both Cole and Patrina awake. She glanced at the laminated clock on the nightstand before reaching for the phone. It was almost four in the morning. "Yes?"

She pulled herself out of Cole's arms to swing her legs over the side of the bed. "How many minutes are they apart?" Then a few seconds later she said, "I'm on my way."

"A baby decided to come now?"

She glanced over her shoulder at Cole. He had pulled himself up in the bed. "Yes, but this isn't just any baby," she said, standing, about to head to the bathroom to dress.

"Oh? And why is this kid so special?"

She turned and smiled at him. "Because it's your niece or nephew."

At his confused expression, she said, "Veronica is the eighteen-year-old girl who's giving her baby to Casey and McKinnon to adopt. The baby wasn't due for another month or so. While I'm getting dressed, give them a call and ask them to meet me at the hospital."

For as long as he lived, Cole doubted he would ever forget the look of profound happiness on his sister's face as she held her newborn son. He glanced at McKinnon, who was standing beside his wife, gazing down at the blessing they'd both been given, and knew this was a profound moment for him, as well.

"Have the two of you decided on a name?" he decided to ask to break the silence.

Casey glanced at him with tears shimmering in her eyes. "Yes, McKinnon and I wanted to honor our fathers by naming him Corey Martin Quinn."

Cole nodded, thinking the name fitted. According to Patrina, the baby weighed almost six pounds. Cole thought he was a whopper, considering he'd been premature, with a head of curly dark hair.

He switched his gaze from the baby to Patrina when she reentered the room. "The baby will have to remain here at the hospital for another day," she said to Casey and McKinnon. "After that you'll be free to take your son home."

"How is Veronica?" Casey asked.

"She's doing fine, but she hasn't changed her mind about not wanting to see the baby. She says all she wants to do now is get on with her life, move back to Virginia and return to school."

Cole listened. From what Patrina had told him on the drive over to the hospital, the young woman, Veronica Atkins, had been someone who had dropped out of school and taken off with a member of some rock band. After she had gotten pregnant, the guy had dumped her, and with no family to call on for help, she had moved into the local Y and gotten a job at a diner. She had lived in and out of foster homes all her life and wanted something better for her child, a life with a family who would give him stability and love. She had asked Patrina if she knew of a couple who would want her child, and Patrina had immediately thought of McKinnon and Casey.

"But of course as the baby's parents, you're free to visit him as often as you want," Patrina added, smiling.

"Thanks for everything, Trina," McKinnon said, gazing lovingly at his son and his wife.

"You don't have to thank me, McKinnon. You and Casey deserve your son like he deserves the two of you." Patrina then glanced over at Cole, and Cole felt a pull in his gut. Sensations spiraled through him with mesmerizing intensity. He could picture Patrina holding a child the same way Casey was doing now.

He drew in a deep breath and his entire body seemed to tense with an awareness he had not felt until this moment. It was electrifying. It was an eye-opener and it almost made him weak in the knees. He wanted to withdraw but knew he couldn't. He had to face what was so damn clear it was unreal.

He loved her. He had fallen in love with Patrina.

Dear heaven, how did that happen? When did it happen? He knew the answer to the latter. He had fallen in love with her the very first time he had made love to her and she had trusted him enough to give her body to him after holding herself back for so long. And then when her life had been threatened and that lunatic had held a gun on her, a part of the hard casing surrounding his heart had fallen off, as well.

He wanted to cross the room and whisper how he felt and then kiss her the way a man kisses the woman he loves. But he knew he couldn't do that. Casey was already curious about what was going on. She had asked questions after the robbery attempt, but he had refused to give her any answers. She had asked questions again, just seconds before she and McKinnon had been herded off to the birthing room to be part of the delivery as Veronica had requested. She had also requested to be out during the delivery and hadn't wanted to be told anything about the child, not even if it was a boy or girl.

Inhaling deeply, Cole crossed the room to Patrina and lightly stroked a finger down her cheek, not caring if Casey and McKinnon noticed. "Ready to go, Doc?"

She drew in a ragged breath and smiled. "In a second. I just need to clean up first and fill out a few papers."

He nodded and watched as Patrina left the room.

"What's going on, Cole? With you and Patrina?"

He met his sister's gaze. It was filled with accusations and he understood why. She knew his history when it came to women, but he wanted to assure her that this time things were different. "I love her and plan to marry her."

He could tell from the expression on Casey's face that his bold statement had been a shocker. "But how? The two of you barely know each other. You just met last year and haven't spent any time together."

"Yes, we have."

He held his sister's gaze. She seemed more confused than ever, and he knew she intended to get the full story later. She then asked softly. "Does she know how you feel?"

He smiled, tucking a stray strand of hair behind his sister's ear. "If you're asking me if I've told her yet, the answer is no. But trust me, I will."

Chapter 12

When Cole entered the house behind Patina and closed the door behind them, he brushed aside the thought of telling her how he felt while they were making love. He couldn't hold it inside any longer. He wanted to tell her now.

"Patrina?"

She turned from placing her medical bag on the table. "Yes?"

"We need to talk."

Patrina sighed. She had an idea what he wanted to talk about. Being at the hospital around the baby had freaked him out. It had probably hit home more so than ever that she could be pregnant and what that meant, what drastic changes there might be, what demands she might make. She knew she had to assure him that she wouldn't ask anything of him.

"If I am pregnant, you don't have to worry about me asking anything of you, Cole. You've never forced yourself on me. I knew what I was doing each and every time we made love. It was what I wanted."

She turned to walk off, but he grasped her wrist. When she looked up at him, he said in a soft, yet husky voice, "Then maybe you ought to know that I knew exactly what I was doing and it was what I wanted, as well."

Her heart contracted and she couldn't help but wonder what he meant. She didn't want to jump to conclusions, but he was looking at her intensely. "What do you mean?" she asked.

"What I mean is that if you are pregnant, I didn't intentionally set out to get you that way, but *if* you are, then I would be happy about it. I want a baby...with you."

He tightened his hold on her wrist and pulled her closer. "However," he added, "more than anything, I want you. I love you."

She stared at him for a long moment, shook her head and said, "But...but..."

"But nothing. I've never told a woman that I love her before and I don't plan on ever telling another woman again. Just you. And if I need to say it again, then that's fine. I'll say it as many times as it takes for you to believe me. I love you, Patrina. And I want to marry you, regardless of whether or not you're having my baby. It doesn't matter. I want to marry you as soon as humanly possible and live here with you."

"But…but what about Texas? You've never said you wanted to live in Bozeman."

He chuckled. "Baby, I plan to live wherever you are. You know I'm no longer a Texas Ranger. What I didn't tell you is that my uncle left me, Casey and Clint his ranch house and all the acres it sits on. Casey and I retain the rights to the land and, along with Clint, have established a foundation in my uncle's name to protect wild horses and the land is used for that. However, Casey and I sold our share of the ranch to Clint. With the money I got, I invested wisely."

When she nodded, he knew she understood that much of what he was saying. In other words, he was a very wealthy man. "Quade and I, along with Savannah's brother, Rico, are looking into setting up a security firm. Also, Quade and I are talking with Serena Preston about buying her copter service."

Patrina lifted a brow. "What will Serena do without her copter service?"

Cole shrugged. "I don't know. I understand she might be moving away. Why?"

"Curious. She was involved with Dale a year or so ago, and like a lot of other women it didn't take her long to discover that 'Heartbreaker' is his middle name."

Cole nodded and decided to get the conversation back to the two of them. "So now that you know how I feel about you, will you marry me, Patrina? I promise I will do everything within my power to make you fall in love with me, too."

"You'll be wasting your time, Cole."

At his crestfallen look, she smiled and said, "You'll be wasting your time because I'm already in love with you. I couldn't help but admit it to myself that night when I came home totally exhausted and you took such good care of me. I love you, too."

A relieved grin split Cole's face. "And you will marry me?"

She laughed. "Yes."

"As soon as possible?"

She tilted her head. "How soon are we talking?"

"Um, before next weekend. The entire Westmoreland family is coming in for Dad's birthday party and I want to present you to everyone as my wife."

Her heart did a quick flip. "You sure? You don't want to wait until I know for certain if I'm pregnant?"

He shook his head. "Like I said, sweetheart, it doesn't matter. Besides, if you aren't pregnant this month, there's a good chance that you will be next month."

She smiled. "You really want a baby?"

He reached out and placed his hands on her waist. "Yes, I really want a baby. I didn't know how much until I saw McKinnon look down at his son. Then I knew that more than anything I want you pregnant."

Tears filled Patrina's eyes and she knew she'd been given what some people never had, what some never took advantage of. A second go-round at happiness. What she had shared with Perry those five years had been wonderful and he would always hold a special place in her heart. But she loved Cole now and more than anything she would make him a good wife.

She tilted her head up and the moment she did so, his mouth was there, claiming her lips the same way he had claimed her heart. And when she was swept off her feet, she knew exactly where he was taking her. It was just where she wanted to be—for the rest of her life.

A week later

"Wow," Casey said, smiling and looking at the huge diamond ring on Patrina's finger. "My brother evidently isn't as tight with his money as I thought. That ring is simply gorgeous."

Patrina thought so, too. Married four days, she and Cole had decided to wait until later to plan a honeymoon. They'd had a small wedding, with McKinnon's father, Judge Martin Quinn, performing the rites. Immediately afterward, she and Cole, and Clint and Alyssa—the pair had flown in for the ceremony—along with Durango and Savannah, had stood beside McKinnon and Casey, as Corey Martin was christened. Reverend Miller officiated, acknowledging with a smile the three sets of godparents.

"Lucky kid," Clint had muttered after the ceremony. He had then proceeded to announce that he and Alyssa were expecting.

Cole, standing beside Patrina, had touched her arm. They had decided not to share the news just yet that they, too, would be having a baby—close to the New Year.

"I always figured my cousin had good taste," Delaney Westmoreland Yasir said, pulling Patrina from her thoughts.

Patrina glanced up and smiled. "Thanks."

It seemed that all the Westmorelands were here on Corey's Mountain to celebrate her father-in-law's fifty-seventh birthday. And Corey's wife, Abby, along with Casey, had made things extra-special. Patrina glanced across the room. A happy Corey Westmoreland was sitting proudly in his recliner with a grandbaby in each arm. Stone and Madison's three-month-old son, Rock, whom everyone affectionately called Rocky, and Corey's newest grandson, Corey Martin. Before his fifty-eighth birthday rolled around, Corey would have two more grandbabies to add to the mix. Patrina smiled at the thought.

She then glanced over at Alyssa, who was standing near the punch bowl talking to Clint. Whatever he'd said had made his wife smile, and Patrina thought that the two of them looked happy together. She glanced at Alyssa's stomach and thought she looked further along than three months. She wondered if perhaps Alyssa was having twins. She glanced down at her own stomach, suddenly realizing she might be faced with the same fate, since multiple births ran in the Westmoreland family. So far, only Storm's wife, Jayla, had given birth to twins.

"May I borrow my wife for a second?" Cole said, appearing before the group of women and grasping Patrina's wrist.

Without waiting for a response he pulled her away and led her outside. The air was chilly and when he pulled her into his arms, she went willingly into his warm embrace. He then leaned down and gave her a long and thorough kiss.

When he released her mouth, she smiled and looked up at him. "Um, not that I'm complaining, but what was that for?"

He chuckled. "No reason. I just wanted to kiss you."

He then pulled her back into his arms and held her tight before saying, "Spencer and Donnay will be making an announcement in a few minutes. Ian and Brooke will be making the same announcement."

Patrina arched a brow. "About what?"

When he didn't say anything but just chuckled, she pulled back and looked at him. "More Westmoreland babies?"

Cole laughed as he nodded his head. "Yep."

She grinned. "Is that all you male Westmorelands think about? Multiplying and replenishing the earth?"

"Sounds like a good plan to me." He then reached down to tenderly caress her stomach. "How are you and Emilie doing?"

She gave him a teasing frown. "*Emery* and I are doing just fine."

A smile touched the corners of his mouth. "Yeah, whatever."

They had decided to wait until the birth of their child to find out its sex. Cole, however, thought she was having a girl and had decided to name her Emilie after his maternal grandmother. Patrina had insisted she was having a boy and that his name would be Emery.

"I'm not going to argue with you, Patrina," he said, leaning down close to her lips.

"Then don't, Cole."

And then he was kissing her again and for some reason, although she wasn't one hundred percent certain, she had a feeling she would be having an Emilie and an Emery. After all, she had gotten pregnant under a full moon in April, when Cole had planted his seeds of desire.

As far as she was concerned, just about anything was possible when you were dealing with a Westmoreland.

Epilogue

November

Five months later, the Westmorelands gathered again for two special occasions. The first was to be present when Patrina became the recipient of the Eve Award and the second was for a Westmoreland Thanksgiving. It had been decided at Corey's birthday party to return to the mountain for Thanksgiving. They had a lot to give thanks for.

Everyone now knew there would be at least two sets of twins born to Westmoreland women. Brooke would be giving birth in a month to twin boys and Patrina was also having twins. The sex of her babies was still unknown.

Cole smiled when he thought about the ongoing joke

between him and Patrina. He said she was having two girls and wanted them to be named Emilie and Evelyn. She thought that because of all the activity taking place in her stomach, she was having two boys. She wanted to name them Emery and Ervin. Only time would tell and they had only a couple of more months before they found out.

A card game had been going on at his place, but everyone had decided to take a break. Clint, as well as his cousins, Thorn, Jared, Chase and Spencer, had stepped outside, but Quade had stayed in.

Cole glanced across the room to study his cousin. He had noticed lately that Quade seemed restless and wondered if his cousin's decision to retire from his job as one of the president's men had anything to do with it. He of all people knew how it was when you were used to being busy and living on the edge.

"What's this?"

Cole had gotten to his feet and was about to join the others outside when Quade's startled voice caught his attention. "What's what?"

"This."

Cole crossed the room to see what Quade was looking at. It was one of those magazines Patrina had begun subscribing to once she'd discovered she was pregnant. "It's an issue of *Pregnancy*. Patrina gets one each month."

He looked down at the magazine and then back at Quade. His cousin looked like he'd seen a ghost. "It's *her*," Quade said in a trembling voice.

Cole glanced down again at the magazine. A very

beautiful model graced the cover. He raised a brow. A very beautiful and very *pregnant* model. Hell, she looked like she would be having the baby any minute. And Cole quickly canned the thought that the woman would be having one baby. Her stomach was bigger than Patrina's.

His gaze moved from her stomach back to her face. Forget about her being beautiful, she was knockout, drag-down gorgeous. And the outfit she was wearing made her look too stunning to be real. There was no doubt in his mind she was a model and probably married to some movie star.

He cleared his throat and glanced at Quade. "So you think you know her?"

Quade nodded slowly as he continued to stare at the cover of the magazine. "Yes, I know her. I met her earlier this year in Egypt."

It took Cole only a second to put two and two together. "That's her? The woman you met on the beach that night?"

Quade didn't say anything for a minute and then, "Yes, that's her."

Cole stated the obvious. "She's pregnant."

"Yeah."

"And it looks like she's having twins," Cole muttered. Looking at the cover again, he said, "I take that back. Looks like she's having triplets. Or quadruplets. And whatever she's having looks like she's having it any day now."

"What issue is this?" Quade asked, scanning the cover. Moments later he answered his own question.

"It's last month's issue, which means she's probably delivered by now."

Cole nodded. "I would think so." He stared at his cousin. "So, tell me, Quade. You think you're responsible for her condition?"

Quade met his gaze. "Considering everything that happened that night, I would say yes, there's a damn good chance I am."

"Okay. And what are you going to do about it?"

Quade placed the magazine back on the table. "First I'm going to find her. And if I'm the father of her baby… or babies, then a wedding will be in order."

"And if the lady doesn't agree?"

Quade was already moving toward the guest bedroom, no doubt to pack and be on his way. "Doesn't matter. We're getting married."

When he disappeared around the corner, Cole picked up the magazine and studied the picture of the gorgeous, pregnant woman once more and said, "I don't know your name, sweetheart, but I just hope you're ready for the likes of a determined Quade Westmoreland."

* * * * *

HARLEQUIN®
Desire

ALWAYS POWERFUL, PASSIONATE AND PROVOCATIVE.

A brand-new Westmoreland novel
from *New York Times* bestselling author

BRENDA JACKSON

Riley Westmoreland never mixes business with pleasure—until he meets his company's gorgeous new party planner. But when he gets Alpha Blake into bed, he realizes one night will never be enough. That's when her past threatens to end their affair. So Riley does what any Westmoreland male would do…he lets the fun begin.

ONE WINTER'S NIGHT

"Jackson's characters are…hot enough to burn the pages."
—*RT Book Reviews* on *Westmoreland's Way*

Available from Harlequin® Desire December 2012!

HD73210BJ

A Brand-New Madaris Family Novel!

NEW YORK TIMES BESTSELLING AUTHOR

BRENDA JACKSON

COURTING JUSTICE

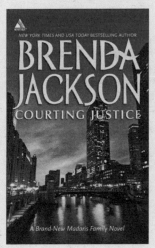

Winning a high-profile case may have helped New York attorney DeAngelo DiMeglio's career, but it hasn't helped him win the woman he loves. Peyton Mahoney doesn't want anything more than a fling with DeAngelo. Until another high-profile case brings them to opposing sides of the courtroom…and then their sizzling attraction can no longer be denied.

"Brenda Jackson is the queen of newly discovered love, especially in her Madaris Family series."
—*BookPage* on *Inseparable*

Available now wherever books are sold.

HARLEQUIN®
www.Harlequin.com

KPBJ4730612R

NEW YORK TIMES AND USA TODAY
BESTSELLING AUTHOR

BRENDA JACKSON

A SILKEN THREAD

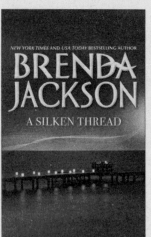

Masterfully told and laced with the sensuality and drama that Brenda Jackson does best, this is an unforgettable story of relationships at their most complex....

Deeply in love and engaged to be married, Brian Lawson and Erica Sanders can't wait to start their life together. But their perfect world is shattered when a family betrayal causes Erica to leave both town and Brian. Yet when a crisis reunites them years later, neither can deny the passion they still feel for each other. Will Erica and Brian fight to save a love that hangs by a silken thread?

On sale now wherever books are sold!

KIMANI PRESS™
www.kimanipress.com

KPBJASTSPR

REQUEST YOUR FREE BOOKS!

2 FREE NOVELS
PLUS 2 FREE GIFTS!

KIMANI™
ROMANCE

Love's ultimate destination!

YES! Please send me 2 FREE Kimani™ Romance novels and my 2 FREE gifts (gifts are worth about $10). After receiving them, if I don't wish to receive any more books, I can return the shipping statement marked "cancel." If I don't cancel, I will receive 4 brand-new novels every month and be billed just $4.94 per book in the U.S. or $5.49 per book in Canada. That's a savings of at least 21% off the cover price. It's quite a bargain! Shipping and handling is just 50¢ per book in the U.S. and 75¢ per book in Canada.* I understand that accepting the 2 free books and gifts places me under no obligation to buy anything. I can always return a shipment and cancel at any time. Even if I never buy another book, the two free books and gifts are mine to keep forever.

168/368 XDN FVUK

Name	(PLEASE PRINT)	
Address		Apt. #
City	State/Prov.	Zip/Postal Code

Signature (if under 18, a parent or guardian must sign)

Mail to the Harlequin® Reader Service:
IN U.S.A.: P.O. Box 1867, Buffalo, NY 14240-1867
IN CANADA: P.O. Box 609, Fort Erie, Ontario L2A 5X3

Want to try two free books from another line?
Call 1-800-873-8635 or visit www.ReaderService.com.

* Terms and prices subject to change without notice. Prices do not include applicable taxes. Sales tax applicable in N.Y. Canadian residents will be charged applicable taxes. Offer not valid in Quebec. This offer is limited to one order per household. Not valid for current subscribers to Kimani Romance books. All orders subject to credit approval. Credit or debit balances in a customer's account(s) may be offset by any other outstanding balance owed by or to the customer. Please allow 4 to 6 weeks for delivery. Offer available while quantities last.

Your Privacy—The Harlequin® Reader Service is committed to protecting your privacy. Our Privacy Policy is available online at www.ReaderService.com or upon request from the Harlequin Reader Service.

We make a portion of our mailing list available to reputable third parties that offer products we believe may interest you. If you prefer that we not exchange your name with third parties, or if you wish to clarify or modify your communication preferences, please visit us at www.ReaderService.com/consumerchoice or write to us at Harlequin Reader Service Preference Service, P.O. Box 9062, Buffalo, NY 14269. Include your complete name and address.

KROM13

New York Times
Bestselling Author

**BRENDA
JACKSON**

**BACHELOR
UNCLAIMED**

Are his playboy days over for good?

In the wake of political defeat, former mayoral candidate Ainsley St. James does something totally out of character—she has a one-night stand with a seductive stranger. Never expecting to see Winston Coltrane again, she accepts a job covering a breaking story…only to discover that the island's most desirable recluse is the lover she has yet to forget.

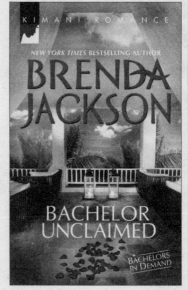

*Pick up your copy January 29, 2013,
wherever books are sold!*

www.Harlequin.com

KPBJ292213SP